THE DEVIL IN AMBER

A "SHOCKER" BY

MARK GATISS

POCKET
BOOKS

LONDON • SYDNEY • NEW YORK • TORONTO

First published in Great Britain by Simon & Schuster UK Ltd, 2006
First published by Pocket Books, 2007
An imprint of Simon & Schuster UK Ltd
A CBS COMPANY

1 3 5 7 9 10 8 6 4 2

Simon & Schuster UK Ltd
Africa House
64–78 Kingsway
London WC2B 6AH

www.simonsays.co.uk

Simon & Schuster Australia
Sydney

A CIP catalogue record for this book is available
from the British Library

ISBN 13: 978-0-7434-8380-3

Typeset in Caslon by M Rules
Printed and bound in Great Britain by
Cox & Wyman Ltd, Reading, Berks

For Winnie – 'Gather the rose of love whilst yet is time'

Acknowledgements

Thanks to Ian Bass, Caroline Chignell, Edward Fitzwilliam Hedley, Jon Plowman, Martin and Tim Stainthorpe, Nigel Stoneman, Rochelle Venables (for devilish editing) and to Ian, as ever, with all my love.

'If you value your souls, don't look in its eyes.'

1

Fallen Idle

He was an American, so it seemed only fair to shoot him.

I'd already winged the beggar once – somewhere in the region of his flabby calves – and was now in hot pursuit with the tenacity for which I'm mildly famous. For reasons too dreary to dwell on, I found myself clinging to the running board of a motor car, wind whipping at my face, positively pelting through the choked streets of Manhattan. Ahead of me loomed the gorgeous elegance of the new Chrysler Building, thrusting like a sword into the cold, brilliant blue sky. Ice and sun glinted off its exterior; sharp as a pin in the eye.

For those of you not in the know (dear me, where have you *been?*), my name is Lucifer Box: painter, occasional memoir-scribbler and agent (most secret) for His Majesty's Government. Sad it is to relate that my artistic career was somewhat in the doldrums. Fashion, that gay but inconstant dog, had moved on and I was regarded with some suspicion by the bright lads of the new school. Passé, old-hat, pre-War (the Great one, you understand: although there'd been nothing particularly great about it from my point of view). Between the Surrealists and the Cubists and the Whatsists, there seemed precious little demand for a spectacularly good portrait painter such as yours truly. Oh, don't protest! Modesty is for *amateurs*.

Even the landed gentry who had once positively drenched me in commissions seemed in thrall to the damned new religion of photography, and were busy cramming the green-damask walls of their country piles with horrid daguerreotypes of their scarcely smiling selves. And so here was I, the gorgeous butterfly of King Bertie's reign: middle-aged and rather neglected, my hair shorter and greying – though my figure still as trim as a boy's, thank you very much.

Crouched low against the cold metal of the motor, I peered at my distorted reflection in the window. Still a head-turner, no doubt about it, and those eyes no less blue, no less cold and clear.

So much for Art! Happily I had other interests and when not exhibiting my daubs to an increasingly bored public, I was engaged, as I've said, doling out death and violence as gleefully as I did Crimson Alizarin or Mars Yellow. Every man should have a hobby.

Trouble was, of late the glee had rather gone out of this too. But I mustn't get ahead of myself.

The chap I'd been assigned to bump off on this charming December day was called Hubbard. Hubbard the Cupboard, don't you know (the Colonials like their schoolyard nick-names), his curious moniker coming not only from his ungainly shape but from his being a dealer in stolen goods. It was said Hubbard's cupboard was never bare.

The fat fool, however, had strayed somewhat from his usual territory of filched diamanté and crudely forged Demuths, being the brains, it was said, behind an influx of cheap cocaine that was currently drowning New York's nightspots. So, before the hooters of all the hoofers were irretrievably rotted, Hubbard was to be removed from the scene forthwith.

I was in town, tying up the loose ends of another job (the startling history of the Sumatran Automata will have to wait for another day), and, at its conclusion, had been hastily shunted off in pursuit of this nefarious drug baron.

I kept my head low as the car slowed down. The fat man's blood was visible in the snow, trailing in neat crimson curlicues as if fallen from a leaking paint tin. If I could finish him off by lunchtime, I knew a place down in the Bowery that did a smashing shad-roe-caviar club sarnie.

Dropping from the running board, I flattened myself against the grimy wall of the nearest brownstone and watched as the flivver chugged off with a backfire like a Lewis gun.

Inclining my trilby at a rakish angle, I paused a moment, knowing I cut quite a dash. I'm afraid I rather fancied myself – but then everyone else did, so why should I be left out of the fun?

The trail led off the pavement – or 'sidewalk' as I suppose I must call it – and I moved off, my breath billowing like exhaust before me. The air was heavy with the stink of Polish cooking and uncollected rubbish.

Hurrying through the churned-up, brown drifts and following the trail as it swung right, I found myself in a light-starved courtyard. At its centre, smothered in snow, stood a quaint little clapboard church, fragile and unremarkable – save for the polka-dot pattern of bright blood on the steps. The door to the church was slightly ajar. I had him.

As quietly as possible, I slipped inside, taking a moment to adjust to the musty darkness with its familiar odour of incense and damp. Rapidly I made out shadowy pews, a pulpit like a ship's fo'c's'le, a narrow spiral stair leading to the bell tower.

My gloved hand closed around my Webley. As I reached the well of the stair, there was movement above and a little rivulet of dust cascaded onto the brim of my hat. Stealing upwards, I emerged into a beam-ceilinged chamber where two great copper-green bells hung in their housings. The hunched figure of a man was silhouetted against the flat light pouring through an arched window. I raised my pistol and he swung towards me, his face a picture of fear. But unless Hubbard had hastily taken holy orders, this was not my quarry.

The priest's face fell as he glanced over my shoulder.

I span on my heel, hearing the scrape of shoe leather on wood and realizing at once that Hubbard was right behind me. Suddenly there was something startlingly cold at my flesh and every instinct thrilled as I felt a coil of piano wire loop about my throat. Without a moment's hesitation, my hand flew to my collar just as the wire tightened, allowing vital room for manoeuvre. I gasped as the deadly lasso bit into the leather of my glove.

Hubbard's sickly breath hissed into my face as he crushed me in a bear-like embrace. I own I was in a pretty blue funk. Trying frantically to turn about and aim the Webley, I felt instead my wrist savagely twisted and the pistol went crashing down the stairwell.

Still the noose tightened. Jerking my elbow repeatedly backwards, I met only empty air as Hubbard the Cupboard swung clear. There was a cold, bright *zing* as the razor wire sliced cleanly through my glove and ripped at the flesh of my hand.

Yelling in agony, I dropped to my knees and reached desperately behind me, clawing at the rotten woodwork of the floor, striving to find purchase on my assailant's ankle. The cold wire sawed into my palm.

'Help me!' I cried to the priest. 'Help me, for Christ's sake!'

But divine intervention came there none, the holy fool merely whimpering and wringing his hands.

Again I cried out in pain but then my fingers closed on the turn-up of Hubbard's trouser leg. It was wet with blood and I realized at once that this was where I'd already wounded the fiend. Frenziedly, I scrabbled at the floorboards till my fingers found the rusty end of a bent nail. Croaking with effort, I prised the nail from the planking and managed to ram it with main force into the wound on my enemy's leg.

Hubbard screamed, stumbled forwards and suddenly the wire noose slackened. I rolled away, nursing my damaged hand, then, leaping to my feet, finally came face to face with him.

He was broad as a meat locker and swaddled in a cheap fur-collared overcoat such as an actor-manager might have left out for the moths. His eyes – buttons in the burst upholstery of his ugly face – glinted black and tiny. I'd never met Hubbard, only shot him, so by way of an introduction I kicked him in his lardy throat, sending the brute flying backwards into the bells. At once, the great shapes rolled in their housing.

He tried desperately to right himself, but the bells moved like quicksand beneath him, clappers ringing off the ancient bronze. He clawed at their surfaces, nails scoring grooves in the thick verdigris; sliding, gasping, out of control.

'This ain't right!' he squawked in a grisly Brooklyn accent, already slipping through the gap between the bells. 'It's a set-up!'

I scowled at him, cradling my wounded hand, totally unmoved by his imminent demise. 'Tell it to the marines.'

Hubbard gasped as he fought to keep from falling, his little feet scrabbling comically at the wooden housing. 'I'm a patsy!' he screeched.

'Cornish?'

'A *patsy!*' he cried. 'Oh, God!'

The corpulent cur knew he was a goner and something nasty flashed in those black eyes. One hand flew to his overcoat, and in an instant a small snub-nosed revolver was in his chubby hand. He wasn't intending to go down alone.

I stood powerless, my heart racing in time with the blood thudding onto the boards from my wet glove. Still the wretched priest did nothing, standing by in saintly inaction.

When the shot rang out I was surprised to feel no pain whatsoever. It took me a while to realize that this was intimately bound up with the fact that Hubbard now boasted a capacious and gory hole in his temple from which startlingly papal white smoke was pouring.

Hubbard gurgled most unpleasantly and then made his final foray between the bells, tumbling to the church floor below and setting the wretched things pealing gaily as though for Christmas Mass.

A cold sweat prickled all over me as I turned to greet my rescuer. He stood at the top of the stairs, still holding the weapon he had used on the ill-famed dealer in stolen goods.

'You're getting slow, old boy,' said the lean, brown newcomer, stepping into the light.

'Hullo, Percy,' I said lightly. '*Thanks.*'

Percy Flarge grinned his infuriating grin, pocketed his pistol and tipped his hat onto the back of his head, setting his blond fringe bouncing. 'Least I can do to help out a chum in his hour of need.' He peered at my hand. 'I say! You *have* been in the wars.'

I stepped away from him. 'I'll take things from here.'

Flarge shook his head. 'Wouldn't dream of letting you, old love. You should really put your feet up! Least I can do, as I say, for the great Lucifer Box.'

The great Lucifer Box suddenly felt a clammy sickness grip him and chose that moment to collapse onto the planking in a dead faint.

I awoke to a biting pain in my hand. I was stretched out on a pew, back in the main body of the church and sat up, blinking for a moment. The light had that strange, vivid quality as before a thunderstorm. The place was abuzz with what I knew to be Domestics – those terribly useful folk who clean up after chaps like me have been splattering haemoglobin all over the furniture – but there was no sign of Flarge.

I shook my head, groggily. My wound had been neatly and expertly stitched and was now being bandaged by a little ferret-faced chap in a short coat and yellow gloves. This was 'Twice' Daley – one of Flarge's favourites. Unlike my own dear Delilah (presently cook, valet, general factotum, bodyguard and thug) back in Blighty, he was a local man of no particular distinction.

'Hi there, Mr Box!' he cried.

I nodded weakly. 'You'll forgive me if I don't shake hands.'

He gave a short, barking laugh and tied off the bandage with his nimble fingers.

I flexed my own digits to assess the damage. 'Thanks for the repair job, Daley. Everything cleared up here?'

He nodded, his rheumy eyes scanning the church. '*Shoo-wer*. We paid off the pastor with enough rubes to make a new roof, and the Cupboard'll soon be doing the breaststroke in the Hudson – face down, if you takes my meaning.'

I did. 'I have orders to bring back everything he had on him. I trust you took care to—'

'Mr Flarge done all that,' he interrupted.

'Did he now?'

'Oh, yeah. Nice and regular. He's very *per-spik-ay-shee-us*, is Mr Flarge. He saved your ass too and no mistake.'

I ignored Daley's taunting and looked towards the back of the church. 'Is the body still here?'

'*Shoo-wer*. You wanna pay your last respects?' He grinned nastily, exposing tiny neat teeth like those of a deep-sea fish.

'Why not?'

Outside, freezing night was creeping on. Daley handed me a pocket torch and led me into the yard, where a tumbledown out-house had been pressed into service as a temporary morgue. Snowflakes as big as chrysanthemums were floating down from the drear sky and I bent down and scooped up a handful to assuage the awful throbbing in my hand.

Daley shuddered open the outhouse door and the body of Hubbard was revealed in the beam of the torch. We went inside.

'What exactly did Mr Flarge take away?' I asked, peering down at the powder-blackened hole in Hubbard's head.

'Whole bunch of stuff,' said Daley, taking the stub of a fat black cigar from his waistcoat pocket. 'Mr Flarge had a big carpet bag on him. Filled it with papers, mostly, and, you know, some merchandise.'

'Cocaine?'

'Uh-huh.'

Well, that seemed to confirm the theories. I nodded absently, and began to search Hubbard's body. Flarge had certainly been thorough. There was nothing in the big man's ghastly suit. No wallet, no identification, no driver's licence.

More than anything, I wanted to spot something that young pup had missed, and Daley knew it. He smoked his spit-wetted cigar and watched my fruitless activity with obvious glee. I'd almost given up when something caught my eye.

It was Hubbard's handkerchief. In sharp contrast to the dead man's vile tailoring, the wipe was made of an exquisite ivory-coloured silk of obvious antiquity. It was folded into three neat triangles, like a miniature mountain range, and there seemed to be some sort of exotic pattern on it. It might be a mere trifle, but trifles ain't to be sniffed at when you've not even been invited to the party . . .

Daley was watching me closely. I cleared my throat and straightened up as though satisfied.

'Very well. There's nothing more to be done here,' I said. 'Thanks for your help.'

Daley gave a little bow. I gasped suddenly, as though in pain, and dropped the torch, which rolled under the table.

'Sorry!' I managed through gritted teeth. 'Damned wound!'

Daley bent down to retrieve the torch and I swiftly whipped the handkerchief from Hubbard's breast pocket, stuffing it into my trousers just as the Domestic bobbed back up.

'You get yourself to bed now, Mr Box, you hear?' he said with a horrible grin. 'Then maybe get on the boat back home to Eng-ur-land, huh? What with Christmas coming and all.'

I smiled tightly and stalked off into the gathering snowstorm, the silken rag tucked firmly into my pocket.

2

You Might As Well Live

Those who have followed these incoherent memoirs may recall that my long and rather lovely hands are not to be trifled with. A youth of my acquaintance once compared them to Our Lord's as depicted in Caravaggio's *Ecce Homo*. I was, naturally, immensely flattered, though my digits had been engaged in singularly un-Christ-like activity at the time.

Now, as blaring taxi cabs crawled around me in the sickly electric-yellow glow of the evening, I feebly raised my injured fingers and hailed one such, muttered the address of my hotel and slid inside the motor, avoiding the driver's invective by studiously pretending sleep. The soft, wet patter of snow against the windows lulled me and I placed my bandaged hand on the wonderfully cold glass. The pain was somewhat tempered.

I've dealt with Art and its shortcomings. Now, as promised, we shall examine the state of my other pursuit, namely espionage. Once again, for the newcomers (Keep up! Keep up!), I must devote a short passage to the Royal Academy of Arts, that bastion of the

Establishment in London's Piccadilly (where *else's* Piccadilly? Must I address you like simpletons?). Fact is, the RA is not what it seems. For strip away the facade of Burlington House – you *can* do that, you know. The whole Palladian front descends into a specially dug trench in case of mortar attack. No, *really* – and you'll uncover a seething hotbed of plotting, counter-plotting and assassination. Of course, that's what you'd expect to find in a building full of artists, but this is a different business altogether. For the RA is the true face of His Majesty's Secret Service. Not that other lot of whom you may have vaguely heard: the blighters who go around destabilizing perfectly friendly democracies in Bolivia or knocking off the Nabob of Whatchamacallit. No, we're the real thing: the ones who oil the wheels of the great machines of state; the ones who make it possible for you to sit down in Lyon's Corner House with a cup of rosie and the 'Thunderer' without some greasy foreigner taking a pop at you with a Walther PP. 7.65.

As I've said, to me it was always the merest hobby of a dilettante, a little like collecting stamps or mounting Red Admirals – but my exploits amongst the Russian navy will have to wait for another day. No, from my youthful adventures at the tail end of the old Queen's reign to my ill-starred work against the Bosch during the last big show, I reckoned myself one of the brightest and best of the Academicians; trotting merrily from continent to continent; cutting, thrusting, derring and doing.

Now, though, the game seemed to be full of arrogant young-bloods like the odious Percy Flarge, an athletic Cambridge Blue of little discernible charm. If there's one thing I cannot abide, it's a smart alec. Unless that smart alec is me. And Percy Flarge was, from the crown of his trilby to the tips of his absurd coffee-and-cream brogues, smart as paint.

At first I'd taken him for one of the legion of doe-eyed admirers who have crossed my path over the years. My *fan-club*, I suppose you would call them. Like so many others, he'd cornered me on the grand staircase of the Academy, brimming with energy and stuffed with tales of my famous cases. The spectacular matter of the Spitzbergen Mammoth! That nasty business with the Italian volcanoes! The explosive urinals of Armitage Shankz and the colourful revenge of the Man with the Wooden Wig! (I've never written that one down, have I?). He was a looker too, which never hurts, forever bobbing aside his silly blond fringe and batting his lashes like a flapper at a Valentino flicker. I was absurdly flattered and rather let down my guard.

Then came a change of regime at the top (more of that later) and Flarge's attitude began, subtly at first, to alter. Sly jibes here, stifled giggles there. Surely old Boxy was past his best? Time for younger talents to take the lead. Of course what really rankled was the fear that the loathsome creature was right. Hubbard the Cupboard, for instance, should have presented scant challenge for the great Lucifer Box but the bounder had almost bested me, had almost *derringered* me into oblivion, and if it hadn't been for that deplorably wiry and sunburnt colleague of mine, he would have succeeded.

I was startled by the blast of the taxi's horn and realized I had indeed flaked out on the cracked leather upholstery. At last we shushed through the filthy drifts and pulled up outside the snow-flecked frontage of my hotel. I felt light-headed still and the darkness, coupled with the ugly illumination of headlamps, conspired to make me giddy. Pressing a couple of dollars into the driver's hairy hand, I clambered out into the cold, rubbing my neck and swiftly making my way into the December-dark lobby. Palm fronds poked out from tobacco-fogged niches where old men, already dressed for dinner, gleefully scanned the obituary columns.

Exhausted, and anxious to take a proper look at the 'handkerchief', I crossed to the lifts and jabbed impatiently at the button. Above my head, a gilded arrow on illumined green glass crawled slowly round. I sank against the wall and sighed heavily. A dull ache was banging behind my eyes and my hand hurt like billy-o. I'd had hell's time that day.

When at last the lift arrived and the heavy lattice screen was dragged back, I stepped inside without looking up. The interior was all walnut.

'Fifteen, ain't it, Mr Box?'

I glanced over, and my scowl melted instantly away. It was a bell-hop I'd noticed only that morning, red-headed and pale as a Tudor portrait, noticing *me* from under long-lashed eyes.

Now he held his head on one side, as though trying to dislodge a marble from his ear, one of those silly round hats at an acute angle on his well-oiled hair. He had huge green eyes and lips as red as raspberries.

'Do we know each other?' I asked at last.

He seemed flustered by this and looked away. 'Um . . . old Van Buren – that is, *Mr* Van Buren, the manager, sir. He told me your name. There's a package come for you and he said, "Rex, you be sure and take that up to Mr Box when he comes back." And I says, "Is Mr Box that tall, refined-looking gentleman—"'

'Yes, all right. Just bring me the parcel, *Rex*.' I stepped out of the lift and looked him directly in his emerald eyes as the grille closed over his face. 'Room Fifteen-o-eight.'

Smiling a little to myself and feeling much better, I let myself into said room. It was large and well appointed, a big white divan cover on the bed, cream-coloured leather armchairs in each corner. The warm aura from discreet lamps prevented the whiteness from appearing too stark and I found it immensely comforting after the privations of the outside world.

Throwing off coat and hat, I reached into my trousers, pulled out Hubbard's silken rag and carefully unfolded it on one of the pillows.

Though roughly handkerchief-shaped, it had clearly been torn from a much larger piece of material. Two of the edges were ragged and bore crabbed text in what looked like some species of Latin.

The bottom corners were highly decorated with coloured emblems, a picture of a mountain and dragon's heads. There was a sort of fiery motif, embroidered rather beautifully, the flames licking over what looked like an animal on a spit.

I examined the thing until my vision swam then decided to abandon it for the night. After all, I was almost certainly clutching at straws. Perhaps Percy Flarge hadn't bothered with it because it was nothing more than a snotty rag.

Pulling off my shoes, I padded to the bathroom and ran a tub. It was a huge relief to strip off the sweat-drenched togs and I stood naked for a moment, letting my bare feet sink into the deep white pile of the carpet, before plunging into the bath. The heat made me feel raw. I closed heavy lids and rested my injured hand on the soap dish.

That I'd failed pretty spectacularly at my mission to rub out Hubbard was scarcely in question. Also, I'd been somewhat humiliated by friend Flarge. But worse things happened at sea, as I knew from that funny old night on the *Lusitania*. And Hubbard was at least dead, so perhaps I was exaggerating the calamity. Come on, old man, I told myself. Chin up. I was sound in wind and limb and, most importantly, *alive*.

Something about this matter, though, didn't add up. Why were my superiors so keen to bump off small fry like Hubbard? The dreary narcotics trade was surely a police matter. What did it have to do with the RA? And why hadn't a local been pressed into service?

Yours not to reason why, Box old chum, you might well say. The doing or dying bit is what counts. But I suddenly didn't feel like doing much doing – and certainly not dying – if I was being kept in the dark by my superiors.

Dimly, through the woodwork of the bathroom, I heard a knock at the main door.

I sighed and ignored it but the caller was insistent.

'Come!' I bellowed, causing a minor avalanche in the foam that covered my naked bod.

A creak from without and then a second knock – this time at the bathroom door.

'Yes, yes,' I barked. 'Why don't you come in?'

A muffled voice: 'Um . . . Mr Box?'

I stood up in the tub, reached across for the handle and wrenched at it. 'Don't stand on ceremony. I've had a bloody day and I'm in no mood for – oh!'

I'd forgotten about the bellhop.

At the sight of him, the venting of my spleen was very much halted. The lovely red-head looked straight down at my pendulous tackle and blushed. Averting his face, he thrust a brown-paper parcel towards me.

I frowned at it, sat back into the water, then pulled at the ribbon that was wrapped like liquorice bootlace around the parcel. Inside was a little purple box and inside that, a block of whitish stuff.

'Soap,' I mused.

'Sir?' The bellhop was still standing there, his pretty face cast into shadow by the opalescent bulb above.

'It's a bar of soap,' I explained. 'Smelling of – yes – violets and bearing the imprinted word "*DISSOLVE*".'

'OK, sir,' said the boy for no apparent reason. He cleared his throat. 'Any answer?'

I looked up, twinkling naughtily. 'What was the question?'

He gulped and looked down at his shiny shoes. He seemed new to this lark but was evidently game and just needed a gentle push in the right direction.

'The question, sir? Um . . .' He lifted his eyes and looked coyly at me from under his lashes. Nice technique. He'd undoubtedly go far. 'Might I come in, sir?' he asked at last.

'The very question I hoped you'd ask. Yes. Come in, won't you? Shut the door. That's it. What did you say your name was?'

'Rex, sir.'

'Well, Rex, what do you make of it?' I said, sliding lower under the foam and noticing how very tight and snug were my new friend's blue trews. 'Ever heard of a brand of soap called "Dissolve"?'

'Can't say that I have, sir,' said Rex, his big Adam's apple bobbing nervously.

'No, no. Most odd. The manufacturers usually favour something more fragrant,' I continued, then looked sharply at him. '*Take off your shoes.*'

The boy licked his lips and slipped off his patent-leathers.

'"Dissolve",' I murmured, then flicked my gaze back to him. 'Trousers – erm – *pants*, if you please. Could it be an instruction to knock about the remainder of our English monasteries? *Shirt.* Seems most unlikely, Rex, don't you think? *Underthings.*'

'I guess,' said the charming youth, slipping out of the last of his clothes until he stood in only his white socks on the wet mat before me. His toes were outlined in black from the new leather like the brass rubbing of a crusader's tomb.

'Happily, I think I know its secret,' I said, dropping the soap into the bathwater. The foam began to bubble and froth and then the whole bar liquefied, spreading a broad purple stain across the water. And lying there on the surface, as though scrawled with a magic wand, was a message.

Rex gawped and read aloud. 'Moscow Tea Rooms. 10 a.m. tomorrow. Joshua Reynolds.'

I wafted my uninjured hand through the water and the message vanished, drifting in inky strands to the enamelled bottom.

'Message from the office,' I said quietly. 'I'd've been happy with a telegram.' I glanced up at Rex. 'Better take your socks off, hmm?'

The youth hopped from one foot to the other as he divested himself of the last of his clobber, then I took his hand and helped him into the hot bath with me.

His long legs slid through the fading violet residue of the secret message. He had a smashing smile and shook his red-head wonderingly. 'Gosh! I ain't seen nothing like that before!'

A moment or two later, I presented him with an even nicer surprise.

3

A Trip to Neverland

At eight the next morning, I left the cosy embrace of young Rex (sucked off and buggered if you must know) to keep my appointment with the boss.

I'd had an uneasy night – once my eyes closed – caught in a nightmarish New York of the future, all sky-scraping apartment blocks and rocket ships, as in those unpleasant German films. The dreamme, wearing only queerly tight underwear with President Coolidge's name embroidered about the waist, sauntered past the Algonquin, the pavement transformed into a howling white tunnel of cocaine. Overhead, Hubbard the Cupboard was performing dazzling aerobatics like Lucky Lindy, but the smoke trailing from his rocket-ship transformed into narcotics too, falling on my shoulders like snow. As his machine roared past, I distinctly saw bright rivulets of blood pouring from the aviator's nostrils and the dead man laughing at me, fit to burst.

Later, out in the real street, I darted between the yellow flashes of the taxi cabs, my brogues tramping through the drifts of mud-coloured slush. Despite the temperature, New York teemed with Christmas activity, the scents of coffee and perfume as vivid as incense. Shopping was approaching fever pitch and I found myself shouldering through crowds like a three-quarter in a greatcoat.

I was mentally preparing myself for the meeting that the soapy message had foisted on me. Joshua Reynolds awaited my pleasure.

He was not, alas, the dwarfish chap whom you may have encountered before: the cheeky fellah with the vivid little eyes who'd steered me through countless adventures too numerous or scandalous to mention.

No, he'd gone the way of all flesh, his titchy heart giving out just one month into the retirement he'd always craved. The name was then passed on like a title – I never did find out the dwarf's real moniker – and a very different personage had ascended to the top of the Royal Academy's secret staff.

We were about of an age but whereas I had taken strenuous efforts to maintain my superlative physique this new J.R. had run to fat. He had the look of a minor bishop – a colonial one, perhaps, always perspiring into his purple and wishing they'd given him the See of Leicester (or something just as dreadful). As I peered in through the window of the tea rooms I could see his rumpled, disappointed face glowing whitely in the gloom like the moon behind clouds in an Atkinson Grimshaw.

I had a hand on the door knob when I caught sight of a chap on the opposite side of the road. Tallish and well built, I noted a suggestion of tousled curls and pocked skin, briefly brightened by the flare of a match. He drew on his cigar and glanced briefly at me. Did I flatter myself that a flash of *something* passed between us?

Then he was gone, swallowed up in the great mass of humanity that surged down the canyon-like roadway.

I stood aside for a plump dowager in silver furs, then slipped inside the tea rooms. The din from outside was immediately replaced by reassuringly elegant chatter and the gentle tinkling of a grand piano. Waiters moved swift and silent as eels through the mahogany dimness.

Joshua Reynolds scarcely looked up as he stirred his coffee, ladling sticky wedges of brown sugar into its creamy depths.

'Morning,' I said brightly, unwinding my scarf. 'I didn't know you made house calls. Or are you here Christmas shopping?'

'Sit down, Box,' he muttered, gesturing towards the plump green velvet.

'I say, public meetings in the Moscow Tea Rooms. Whatever next! Your illustrious predecessor was far fonder of the shadow and the whispered word . . .'

Reynolds's fat face snapped upwards, the flesh wobbling slightly like the skin on cocoa.

'Times have moved on, Box,' he said, the voice oily and self-satisfied. 'You'd do well to remember that. We live in a rapidly changing world. Everything's *faster*. Motor cars, aeroplanes, even the Prince of Wales.'

This might have been a joke. I didn't risk a smile. A waiter brought me a polished silver teapot which tinsel-glinted wonderfully in the dark.

'As it happens,' said Reynolds at last, 'the business of the Academy has brought me this side of the Atlantic. A wretched crossing. I shall do my best never to repeat the experience. How do you find it?'

I allowed a pleasant memory of the bell-hop's bum to surface for the moment. 'Oh tolerable, tolerable.'

'Speaking of speed,' continued Reynolds, returning to his earlier theme, the suggestion of a sneer creeping onto his lips. 'That chap Flarge, he's certainly fast. Particularly when getting up the stairs of belfries, eh?'

'Yes. Very nimble,' I said dryly.

Unconsciously, my hand drifted to my breast pocket, where Hubbard the Cupboard's curious hankie was safely stowed. Flarge wouldn't be getting his mitts on that in a hurry. It might be important or it might be the airiest nothing but it was the only advantage over my rival I currently possessed. I'd hoped to have the thing deciphered and presented like prep to the boss, but the charming Rex had taken up all my spare time.

'Flarge saved your bacon, by all accounts,' continued the fat man. 'Plays a straight game. Best man we have in the show. Clean. Lean. Healthy. Kind of chap the Royal Academy needs more of, eh?'

I took a sip of tea. 'Is that a roundabout way of saying you need *less* of chaps like me?'

Reynolds smiled. 'If you like.'

I shook my head. 'I don't like.'

He took a great slurp of his coffee and set the cup down so heavily that it rang off the saucer. 'Look here, Box. I'll not pussyfoot around. You're getting too old for this game. No doubt you once had some flair for it all—'

'I'm the best,' I said coolly.

Reynolds harrumphed into his fat-knotted tie. 'Not being hidebound by friendship or misplaced loyalty, however, I judge only by results.'

He glanced down at some papers on the table before him. Was this it, then? The great cashiering? I looked about, wanting to fix this moment in my mind's eye, but a big-eared diner's braying laugh cut through the chatter and I roused myself.

Reynolds mouth turned down, as though someone had stuffed a lemon in it. 'Frankly, if it were up to me you'd be back on the boat and daubing your way into your dotage by now but it seems you still have some friends in positions of influence.'

'How reassuring.'

Said friends he dismissed with a casual wave of his flipper-like hand. 'There's a job of sorts come up. Nothing too taxing. Just the thing for you to bow out on.' He smiled and it was like a candle flaring into life behind a Hallowe'en mask.

I sighed. That it should end like this! Trailing a paltry little crook like Hubbard had been demeaning enough. What was this final mission to be? Vetting recruits for evidence of transvestism? Checking the collar studs on King George's shirt-fronts for miniature arsenical capsules?

'F.A.U.S.T.,' said Reynolds at last.

'The opera?'

'The *organization*. Heard of it?'

I brushed biscuit crumbs from my napkin. 'Can't say I have.'

'Out of touch again. Never mind, never mind. F.A.U.S.T. stands for the Fascist Anglo-United States Tribune.'

I laughed. 'An acronym so tortuous it can only be sinister.'

Reynolds looked down at his file. 'That is, I suppose, the thinking of our superiors. This lot want to create closer ties between the fascist movements on both sides of the Atlantic, as the name implies. For myself, I'm not too vexed by these johnnies. Broadly right on the Jews, of course, and you must admit Mussolini's turned Italy round.'

'Always presupposing that it needed turning,' I ventured, smiling. 'Who's in charge?'

Reynolds shifted in his seat, his rump making the leather parp like the horn of a motor. 'Fellah called Olympus Mons. Bit of a swaggerer.'

'Have to be with a name like that. I like him already.'

'Yankee-born, Balliol-educated. Anglophile. Sees himself as the fascist Messiah. His acolytes call themselves amber-shirts.'

'You want me to kill him?'

Reynolds's guffaw almost knocked over his coffee pot. 'I'm afraid such a task will, in future, be left in safer hands. No, you're merely to observe his activities. If you're still capable of doing so.' He shot me a nasty look. 'We've a lead of sorts. One of Mons's amber-shirts seems to have grave doubts about his leader. Wants to tell all.'

'Where do I meet him?'

Reynolds drained the last of his coffee and smacked his lips unpleasantly. 'This is all we have.'

He tossed over a slip of paper. On it was a neatly typed message: 'You: Robespierre. Me: Peter Pan. "99". 8.30'.

Reynolds wiped his hands on the tablecloth. 'No idea what it means. Just that he'll find you there. Tonight. I'm afraid you might have to do a little work, Box, and find out for yourself. Think you can manage that?'

With a flick of the wrist, I was dismissed into the bleak December day.

I looked about, hoping to catch sight of my cigar-smoking friend, but sign of him was there none, so I took a cab back to the hotel and sought out my own couch until lunchtime.

Night-time found me motoring up-state dressed as the renowned French Revolutionary. I was grateful the message hadn't suggested Marat as I wouldn't have been able to fit the bathtub into the Cadillac. As I barrelled along near-deserted roads fringed by pine trees, their boughs weighed down with snow, gas stations and houses loomed out of the darkness, Christmas decorations glittering around their eaves. I swung left down a drift-covered road, passing a pile of the Lloyd-Wright Californian school jutting from a hillside like a great tithe barn, all glass and dressed stone with an imposing tiled roof.

I pulled up at a red light and let the engine chug. Soft, wet snow coated the bonnet. Tugging at my britches (they kept getting caught up in the gear-stick), I mused over my situation. It hadn't taken long to establish the meaning of the message from Olympus Mons's disaffected colleague. A quick word with dear Rex the bellhop (what a useful boy he was) furnished me with all the necessaries and I was now heading towards the mysterious "99" and an encounter, it was to be hoped, with Peter Pan. Odds on that the fellah nursed a grievance against his boss – over lack of advancement, probably – and was now prepared to stick in the knife with gay abandon. With any luck, Mons was involved in some lurid sexual scandal the details of which we at the Royal Academy could store up for future use. Sordid, I know, but it's a living.

The light changed and I threw the Cadillac into first gear. The wipers thrummed back and forth, smearing the snow into bleary triangles. Ahead, projecting from the flat fields, were half a dozen parabolic buildings, pewter-grey and rusty with age. A mesh fence ringed the place, and as I bounced the car along the track, stones spitting up against the wheel rims, a lopsided 'keep out' sign became visible.

A bundled-up figure – all scarf and goggles – stomped towards me and knocked on the jalopy window. With some difficulty, I managed to hinge the glass open. Snow whirled inside, settling on the dark leather.

'Can I help you, bud?' said the newcomer, through his moth-nibbled muffler.

'I have a ticket to Rio,' I said crisply. 'No baggage.' Which is what Rex had told me I must say. Frankly, I've always found passwords and codes a little tiresome. Say what you mean, is my adage. Unless it's 'I love you', of course.

The insulated man gave an affirmative grunt and dragged the protesting gates open. I slid the Cadillac through.

The aerodrome – for such it was – was a sad sight. Through the falling snow, weeds were visible, erupting through the long-disused potholed landing strips. But though the curved buildings were dark and silent, a streak of livid yellow light blazed from under the huge doors of the main hangar.

There were already thirty or so other cars parked up in front of it, and as I clambered out of the motor I saw Genghis Khan and what could have been the Empress Josephine getting better acquainted in the moonlight. Their faces were masked and I slipped on my own, covering me as far as the bridge of my nose. Settling a periwig onto my head, I walked to the hangar and without further challenge, was let inside.

All was light. A wave of warmth hit me like a brick. By way of introduction, I was greeted by the elongated honk of a trombone and the rasped strains of 'I'll Be Glad When You're Dead, You Rascal You!'.

Glancing at once to my right, I saw a septet of jazz musicians attacking their syncopated tune with ferocious relish, limbs blurring in a frenzy of polished brass and banjo, oiled hair falling forward and sticking to their sweating foreheads.

A wonderful room had been constructed within the hangar, a kind of cat's cradle of girders and struts with gantries up a height leading to a series of neat compartments. Great sheets of canvas encompassed the whole like gigantic drapes, surrounding fat sea-shell-shaped easy chairs in exquisitely tooled white leather and a vast glass table.

Dotted about were various items of ephemera: a mirrored cock-tail cabinet, a huge map of the world, a small wood and chrome ship's wheel and a massive Union Flag. It was, do you see, the wreckage of the R-99, the splendid airship that had gone down over Martha's Vineyard some two years previously, happily without loss of life and without exploding in an inferno of hydrogen as they are wont to do.

The fixtures and fittings were so damnably pretty, so the think-ing had gone, that it seemed only right to turn them to good use. Now the "99" was New York's swellest speakeasy and clearly the place to be seen – albeit in fancy dress.

The somewhat arctic style of the ruined airship was currently offset by the astonishing blaze of colour provided by the costumed guests. Coloured streamers poured from the roof girders, mingling giddily with explosions of taffeta, silk and velvet, got up in every form of uniform, toga and frock. It's marvellous how stylish duds can transform even the most commonplace person, and perhaps even more marvellous how a simple half-mask of black or white can render the must lumpen of features strangely romantic.

I swept as gracefully as I could through the carousing throng, passing Cleopatras, Abraham Lincolns and a variety of gorgeously frocked queens (of the divorced, beheaded and died variety, you understand), all gyrating wildly to the strains of the jazz band. There was a frenzied air to their enjoyment and the grins visible under the masks had a fixed, rictus quality that was almost alarming. Perhaps I was just feeling jealous of their youth.

I'm always trying to recapture my youth – but he keeps on *escaping*.

Standing with one bandaged hand on tricoleur-sashed hip, cigarette in the other, I waited until a flunkey in a turban deigned to offer me some pink champagne.

The face of our informant, 'Peter Pan', was unknown but I kept my lovely eyes peeled for such a vision, or even his independent shadow shuffling along the skirting boards. All manner of fairies, nymphets and dryads pirouetted before me, the shimmering of cut-glass chandeliers speckling their lithesome young bodies like sunlight through forest leaves – but there was no sign of any denizen of Neverland.

A giddy couple – Adam and Eve by their state of déshabillé – stumbled past me.

'None of your beeswax!' cried the girl, slurping her cocktail. 'It's just some caper he's got on and – Oh . . . *hi*!'

She laid a friendly hand on my sleeve and giggled. 'Hey. Have you seen Raphael?'

I blew a languid smoke-cloud through my nose. 'The Urbino Master?'

'The *guy*. You *know*. Raphael! Hey, Leonard. Butt me, would ya?'

Her companion leant in and popped a slim cigarillo between her lips. I gave her a light from my own. She clasped my hand as she bent down, glancing up at me with saucy eyes.

'Thanks. Hey, you wanna dance?'

'Aren't you looking for Raphael? And what about Adam?'

But the Biblical first-hubbie was engaged in a frantic Charleston with a dime-store Pola Negri in a bad wig. Eve dismissed him with a curt shake of her lovely head.

She was certainly a stunner in her fleshings, a cleverly embroidered fig leaf covering both her breasts and her unmentionables. Had fate not intervened, I might well have asked her to give me a little tour of the Tree of Knowledge, but just then someone knocked into me, sloshing pop onto my silken sleeve and dragging Eve away. Of course, she forgot me at once and disappeared into the throng.

Tutting, I reached into my pantaloons and pulled out my handkerchief.

'Where'd you get that?'

I glanced up. A small white-blond fellow, togged up as Julius Caesar, was peering at my wipe. Looking down, I realized I'd pulled out Hubbard's curious relic by mistake.

The noblest Roman jabbed out a fat, hairless hand. 'May I see?'

There was a curious timbre to his voice, a kind of faintly hysterical edge as though he was fighting to control his emotions. I waited a moment, not sure how to play the situation, then dropped the ragged silk into his palm. His quick eyes – bespectacled beneath the slits of his half-mask – scanned the relic with hungry eagerness. 'My, my,' he cooed, blinking lashes pale as straw. 'It's *very* old. Medieval, at a guess. Northern European. Quite a miraculous survival.'

He cleared his throat twice and beamed at me. 'Where'd you get it?'

I can recognize affected nonchalance when I see it. For the second time, I ignored the question. 'Do you know what all that writing means?' I asked.

A faint smile broke the small man's impassivity. 'Ah, now.' Cough-cough. 'That's the question.'

I took a sip of champagne. 'You have some . . . expertise?' I ventured.

'A little, yes,' he said mildly. 'Name's Reiss-Mueller. Professor Reiss-Mueller. I work at the Metropolitan Museum. Down in the bowels. Drop by some time. I can give you my honest opinion on it.'

'In return for what?'

The little man hooked a finger over his lower lip, like a child contemplating what it might want for Christmas.

Then, suddenly, there was a low brown Yankee voice in my ear. 'How goes the Revolution?'

It was so close to my flesh and pitched so low that I shivered, then swivelled about on my high-heeled velveteen shoes.

'Not so bad. Are you a friend of Tinkerbell's?' I cried, tucking the handkerchief into my trousers.

Peter Pan was revealed, not the puckish individual I was expecting, but a rather strapping fellow in a challengingly short green tunic and matching tights. A feathered cap looked rather dainty on his expensively cut chestnut hair. Beneath the white half mask, large brown eyes burned intensely.

I turned back to Reiss-Mueller but the little man had melted away into the seething, chattering crowd.

4

I Move In Bad Company

eturning my full attention to the newcomer, I found myself somewhat distracted by the impressive bulk of his thighs. Clearing my throat embarrassedly, I looked Peter Pan full in the face. He had a rather heroic jaw with that indefinably attractive just-shaved glow, only some rather bad pocking spoiling the otherwise flawless effect of his skin. He gripped my arm and pulled me aside. 'Sal Volatile's the name. We gotta talk.'

I took a long drag on my cigarette. 'So I gather. You have some information to impart?'

'Uh-huh.' The brown eyes darted about inside the slitted hollows of the mask. 'Secrets.'

I smiled my wide smile. 'Secrets, eh? Well, you're the boy who never grows old. I beg you to blab.'

His face (or half of it) fell. 'This is serious.'

'I'm sure it is. How much do you want?'

His chin suddenly lunged so close to mine that I recoiled. 'I don't want money!' he hissed. 'Jesus! You think I'd risk it all for . . .'

He glanced away and I followed his gaze. Anne of Cleves and one of the Abraham Lincolns were busily chopping up lines of cocaine with a razor blade. They sat on opposite sides of the glass table, chatting merrily like children divvying up sherbet. The woman inhaled a vast quantity and then shook herself all over like a dog emerging from a pond. Her eyes grew glassy for an instant and then she giggled uncontrollably, her hand flying to her mouth and a little dribble of colourless mucus forming on her upper lip.

'Do you believe in Evil, Mr Box?' said my companion, grinding his jaw and looking at the couple with unfeigned contempt.

'Only on Wednesdays.'

The jest was not appreciated. 'Evil, sir. Old as the Earth. Seductive as a lover's promise. Patient, watchful Evil . . .'

'If you're referring to the narcotics, my boy, then I consider there are greater perils threatening the globe just now.'

'How right you are.'

I sighed. 'Look here, Mr Volatile. I dislike riddles. Has all this cryptic blether got anything to do with F.A.U.S.T.?'

A curiously mad grin suddenly lit up his features. 'Ha! More than you know, sir. More than you know.'

'You're doing it again! Are we going to come to some accommodation or am I wasting my time? These Froggy shoes are awful uncomfortable, don't you know, and I'm hankering for my bed.'

He swung back in my direction and suddenly lifted up his mask.

I took a step backwards. It was the curly-haired chap who'd shadowed me outside the Moscow Tea Rooms! His cheeks looked even more pitted in the curiously lurid light but his whole face blazed with a fierce intelligence. 'If I'm being careful, sir, it's because I'm playing a very dangerous game. I'm going to tell you everything. I swear. About the Lamb. About the Prayer. But first you need to see what you're up against. Come with me.'

'Wait!' I cried. 'What lamb? What prayer?'

For answer, he led me through the thrashing, giddy throng to a little anteroom, much chillier than the main chamber and constructed from corrugated iron.

I hung back, suspecting a trap, but he beckoned urgently to me and something about his manner (or his smashing legs) made me throw caution to the wind and step inside.

He reached across me to close the door and I caught a strong whiff of cologne with an undercurrent of sweat. The racket from the costume party was instantly shut off, lingering only as a throbbing background beat. Without a moment's hesitation, Volatile began to strip, shrugging off his tunic, revealing the curve of muscular shoulders as big as over-ripe oranges. Was this what I was to be, well, *up against*? I felt a lovely rush in my gut as though someone were roasting chestnuts inside me.

Somewhat to my chagrin, he peeled off his tights, bent down into the darkened corner and then threw a bundle of clothes at me. 'Get these on,' he said smoothly, unfolding a silk shirt for himself.

As I changed out of my finery, I thought what a damned shame that matters were clearly too pressing for any extracurricular fun. But was this Lost Boy of my persuasion? Hard to tell. He was so aggressively masculine, though, that I had very grave suspicions.

In a few minutes we were both dressed alike in jodhpur-like black trousers, boots that glistened wetly like chewed liquorice and tailored silk shirts of a rather gorgeous amber hue. I began to get the picture.

'Another costume party?' I said.

'In a manner of speaking,' said my new friend, smiling thinly. 'You got a car?'

The Cadillac roared back towards Manhattan, a freezing wind, peppered with snowflakes, whipping over the bonnet. Sal Volatile was almost completely silent throughout the journey, muttering occasional directions as we crossed silent bridges or swung past another block of looming apartments.

He stiffened as we cruised down a broad avenue somewhere off

Fourteenth Street then nodded almost imperceptibly. 'We're here.'

A spectacular kinema in the Art Deco style blazed, floodlit, from the darkness, a vast votive angel spreading its stony wings over the entranceway. The gangster talkie normally showing five times a day had been temporarily replaced by another spectacle, and as we drove past the entrance we watched hundreds of over-coated figures streaming into the lobby.

Parking around the back of the picture palace, we stepped into a landscape of filthy snow and dustbins, great spouts of steam issuing from the indented drains. Volatile reached into his trouser pocket and produced something that looked like a library card. He handed it to me and I strained to make out the tiny print. 'F.O.I.F.?'

This case was a study in acronyms.

'Friends of International Fascism,' muttered my new ally. 'That's who you represent tonight. We're going to a F.A.U.S.T. rally.'

I shuddered as the wind whistled down the alley, setting the lids of the bins rattling. 'How thrilling. I shall fix a suitably manic gleam into my baby blues.'

Volatile grunted. I didn't honestly anticipate any awkward questions as these rallies, like New Year sales, tend to lean more towards fevered screeching and hysteria than closely reasoned argument.

We joined the crush of delegates streaming into the cinema and divested ourselves of our steaming outdoor wear. The cloakroom attendants were kept as busy as coolies.

Stripped of their fedoras and long coats, I now saw the assembly in all their glory. As a breed they were predominantly men and women of healthy aspect; fine boned and lustrous of hair (scraped back from the forehead for the boys, set in finger waves for the girls). Each and every one of them was dressed as were we in the F.A.U.S.T. uniform.

We queued dutifully and followed the others through into the main auditorium, the smell of damp wool immediately overwhelmed by the charged odour of a thousand light bulbs. The place glowed like a grotto, the interior done out in shades of Italian ice cream, galleries and seats in patterns of repeated ovals. A safety curtain had been drawn down over the kinema screen and an elaborate lectern installed before it. Dominating the whole thing was a vast black flag, draped from ceiling to stage. In its centre, a design in blazing orange showed two flashes of arrow-headed lightning – the symbol of the movement.

We took our seats in a row of excited amber-shirts, faces aglow with anticipation, gossiping as though they'd come to see the hit show of the season.

'All right, Mr Volatile,' I said quietly. 'Now we're snug. What was all that about back at the party? What's the lamb?'

Volatile glanced quickly over his shoulder, then put a finger to his lips.

On cue, a muffled drumbeat began to sound and the audience hissed themselves into silence. The drumbeat slowed into a self-consciously momentous *thrum-thrum-thrum* and unseen cornets shrieked out in fanfare. As one mass, the crowd's heads turned back as dazzling spotlights crackled into life.

'Here he comes,' whispered Volatile.

The spotlights snapped off and then back on again, revealing, with almost magical timing, a phalanx of amber-shirts in a V-formation. The crowd gasped in excitement.

The newcomers were indistinguishable in dress from the rest of the adoring mob but they had the indefinable whiff of glamour about them. They were not the tallest, most muscular, not even the blondest of these Übermenschen but they were the stars of the show and they knew it.

One was a pudgy, balding chap with wispy moustache and horn-rimmed spectacles, another a great horsy woman with her ginger hair in cartoonish Valkyrie braids. I scanned the elite, hoping to catch my first glimpse of Olympus Mons, the great leader. As the spotlights shut off once again, I got a quick impression of a tall, muscular figure with luxuriant black moustaches. Then, as the music rose in a shattering crescendo, the phalanx began to march towards the platform.

Seats banged up like Tommy-gun fire as the assembled crowd rose to its feet, raising their arms in that damn-fool salute we've all seen on the newsreels when the Eyeties slobber over their Duce.

Now more spotlights burst into life as the top dogs of F.A.U.S.T. took their places on the platform and, cheered to the rafters, Olympus Mons made his way to the podium.

Somewhere in the early forties, he was under six feet but carried himself with an athlete's easy grace. There was a great scar running from his broken nose to his chin, so that his lip curled up in a most unpleasant fashion, permanently exposing the right dog tooth. He was handsome – in a thuggish way – but his dark eyes were hooded like those of some reptile. Hooded, that is, until, smoothing back brilliantined hair, Mons smiled his million-watt smile. Then the eyes seemed to grow huge, like ink spreading on a blotter, taking in the whole audience in their hypnotic range. It was as though a powerful searchlight was scanning the auditorium, and each amber-shirt must have felt, as I suddenly did, that the Leader was looking directly at *them*.

Mons stood in silence for a long moment, bathed in white light like a heavenly messenger, the silken folds of his shirt clinging to his impressive physique. Then, with a tiny gesture of his hands, he bade them be seated.

The multitude sat down in a chorus of coughs and whispers as Mons took up his stance before his adoring public, one hand clenched behind his back, the other at his side. The microphone in front of him whistled briefly and then he spoke.

'My friends,' he whispered. 'What a thrill it is for me to stand before you, knowing that, at the close of the year, efforts to strengthen our movement internationally have met with such resounding success.'

The voice was curiously light and had a Yankee twang of no

definable origin. 'For the old order is passing away,' he continued, volume increasing. 'The ancient fault lines of party politics replaced by a new model.' *Louder now.* 'Mankind reborn: vigorous!' *Louder yet.* 'Forward-looking!' *Yelling.* 'In step with a new world order!' *Positively screaming.*

The crowd roared their approval. I shuddered at the ecstatic glitter in their wide eyes.

'The misnamed system known as . . . *democracy*,' continued Mons, his voice dripping with contempt, 'based on antediluvian parliamentary systems, is on its way out! The People want a new system of government. The People have spoken. The People can no longer be IGNORED!'

The People, or the thousand or so amber-shirts buffoons who imagined themselves to be their representatives, set up a deafening cheer that rang back at Volatile and me from the stuccoed roof of the kinema.

For himself, Volatile seemed to shrink from the great man's presence, his face a picture of disgust, as though he'd smelled something that'd been knocked down in the road.

Mons seemed to feed off the throng's energy, his eyes, momentarily closed, now blazing blackly again like the lamp of some mythical lighthouse.

International Jewry, of course, was next on the agenda. 'We in F.A.U.S.T. do not seek to persecute the Jew on account of his religion – for our credo is complete religious toleration. We do not persecute him on account of his race. For do we not seek to conjoin with the British Empire? An empire that counts a dozen races amongst its citizens? No. Our quarrel with the Jews is that they have set themselves up as a nation within our great nations. Now we offer a solution! A final solution. They have always sought a promised land. We shall give it to them. A separate country where they can all live in peace – and cease to bother us!'

This got a shrill, hysterical laugh. The Jew, it seemed, was at the back of almost every bit of mischief from Whitechapel to Wisconsin.

I glanced behind me again, more than a little frightened by the sight of all those flushed faces turned towards their leader like seals awaiting supper.

There was more such simplistic tosh from Mons, laying into the Bolsheviks and the capitalists, larding praise on Mussolini, that Austrian fellah, old Uncle Tom Mosley and all. I found it positively vulgar.

Nevertheless, I yelled appreciation and shouted huzzahs with the rest, marvelling at the strength of Mons's rhetoric. The man was utterly hypnotic, isolated in that burning circle of white light. But was he a real threat, as my superiors at the RA seemed to fear, or simply another third-rate crackpot dreaming of power?

He was speaking now in ever shorter bursts, each ending with a brilliantly judged appeal to the basest instincts of his slavering audience. I was very aware of the throbbing of my injured hand, and its steady beat, along with Mons's voice, the staccato hollering of the crowd, and the stuffy atmosphere of the hall, began to make my head spin. I sought refuge in focusing on the amber-shirted figures in the shadows behind the leader.

Then one face leapt out at me, my head grew suddenly clear and I caught my breath in absolute astonishment.

It was a woman near my own age with neatly bobbed black hair. Despite the fine angularity of her features there was something hatchet-like and cold about them, rather as though a skilled draughtsman, having designed a great beauty, had forgotten to rub out his working.

It was her eyes that drew me, though. Of a peculiar, piercing blue, they were every bit as gorgeous as my own. Not surprising in the least when you consider that the woman sitting there in her neat amber-coloured shirt, gazing up at Mons with unfeigned adoration, was my sister.

5

Sibling Devilry

You may picture me in an ice-shrouded Central Park next morning, lost in remembrance, contemplating sluggish pond water surrounded by wind-ravaged trees that clattered together like sticks of charcoal in a pot.

Pandora! My sister! After all these years.

Fact is, the old sis and I had never got on. Like all the best family spats, its origins were humble enough, stretching back to the dark days when Mama had announced, in solemn yet excited tones, that the three-year-old me was to be blessed with a little friend.

I was a serious child, coddled somewhat by my parents and ever so pale and Victorian, with my neatly brushed cow-lick hair and knickerbocker suit.

I had set my heart on a brother (what boy would not?) and so, when dear Pandora arrived in her swaddling clothes, trailing the scent of my Mama's lavender water, I fixed her with a resentful stare over my wooden fort and made a secret vow. She *had* to go.

All manner of plans were hatched, mostly involving the stoving in of baby's head with an alphabet block or the pitching of baby's perambulator into the Serpentine with Nanny getting the blame. A career in homicide, do you see, was already beckoning.

As time went by, though, and we grew up together within the dreary boundaries of the olive-walled nursery, I got used to the brat. Sadly, as my murderous instincts lessened, Pandora's seemed to grow. Despite also being a looker, she seemed to feel herself to be in my shadow. I couldn't see it myself. As far as I was concerned, my parents meted out their love in equal proportion. That is, they gave us none of it. Each.

For myself I took this as licence to blossom on my own terms, working my way through chemistry sets and the dissection of frogs, learning to scribble, growing faint when glancing at a postcard of the Michelangelo pietà and, later, getting into scandals with the wife of Mr Bleasdale the grocer.

Pandora, by contrast, grew into a very queer fish. Outwardly prim, her hair excessively neat, her dolls stacked in order of height, her bedroom as sterile as a hospital ward; there was always about her something rather frighteningly detached, as though she was waiting, with infinite patience, for the opportunity to strike.

She had remained unmarried and began throwing herself, with bewildering intensity, behind one lunatic cause or another, ranging from the abolition of Christmas to the compulsory introduction of a fruit-only diet.

We had drifted ever further apart as the years rolled by, not helped by my inheriting the family home at Number Nine, Downing Street (one is only disturbed when the hustings are on). There was a brief reunion after a bizarre tragedy engulfed our family (that's another story), but otherwise we remained strangers. These days, I knew little of Pan's life save that she lived by the sea, eking out her meagre inheritance and writing pamphlets on the importance of a thrice-daily bowel movement.

Seeing her again in such unexpected circumstances had left me in a state of shock and I'd half-stumbled from the F.A.U.S.T. rally, numbly arranging to meet Volatile the next evening and, at length, prising my sister's address from a party lackey.

I glanced up now from the bench as over-coated figures slipped by, bent over against the snow that fell as heavy and as thick as blossom onto their bowed shoulders.

And now, suddenly, there was Pandora, looking rather smart in black, her long legs scissoring through the drifts.

I stood, raising a quizzical eyebrow. Pandora stopped dead, and for a long moment there was only the shushing patter of snowflakes.

'Oh, Lord,' came the well-remembered drawl.

'Pan!' I cried heartily. 'You look awfully well, dear heart.' I kissed her twice on the cheeks. 'This fascist brotherhood of yours obviously agrees with you more than a fruitarian diet.'

She seemed astonished at this. 'How do you—?'

'I saw you,' I said. 'At the rally last night. I say, it's freezing out here, fancy a spot of Java?'

'What do you want, Lucifer?' Her accusatory blue eyes – a mite larger than mine – swivelled in my direction over the powdered curve of her cheek.

'Can't I pay a call on my own sister?'

A faint smile puckered her heavily rouged lips. 'No.' She pressed her shiny black shoe into a drift and contemplated the print it left. 'Don't pretend you're getting sentimental.'

'Perhaps a little,' I lied. 'I find myself thinking with some longing about the old days. We were all so happy then . . .'

'I was never happy,' she snapped. 'I had a wretched childhood, as well you know. Principally due to your tormenting.'

'Was I really so rotten? Well, that was ages ago. Listen, since we're both in town, why don't we have some lunch—?'

'Too busy,' she cut across me. 'The business of F.A.U.S.T. occupies me constantly.'

'Yes! I'm sure it does. Rather a surprise, eh, you being interested in the old movement too?'

'I'm party secretary. It's rather more than an interest,' she withered. 'What were you doing at the rally? You want to join?'

'Sympathizer, shall we say? I must say that chap Mons is an interesting cove. I'd love to have a chin-wag with him.'

Pandora looked me directly in the eye. 'Listen. If you're genuinely interested in the Tribune, brother mine, then I may be prepared to forget about the past.' She looked suddenly worried. 'You're not working for a newspaper now or anything like that?'

'The wolves of Fleet Street have never found a welcome at Number Nine.'

She glanced down and gave a little shiver. 'Olympus . . . that is, *Mr Mons* . . . he's, well, he's had some little bother with the press.'

'Poor fellow. I know what they're like. Build you up only to knock you down. I dare say they hate the fact that he's a success.'

'No!' cried Pandora with unsettling ferocity. 'Material wealth doesn't concern *him*! They're frightened because he speaks the truth. He knows that the old order has had its day. All across Europe, capitalism is failing. And the only bulwark we have against the Bolshevik tide is World Fascism!'

'Oh, absolutely,' I said blithely.

'Only by working together can the fascist movements of the world unite to create a better world. An ordered, strong, clean world fit for a better breed of humanity!'

Her breath smoked in the freezing air so that she positively appeared to have steam coming out of her. I gave her an encouraging smile. Lord, but she'd swallowed this stuff hook, line and sinker.

'Any chance of arranging a meeting?'

'Why are you here?' she said suddenly.

'Business,' I lied. 'An art dealer on Fifth Avenue is interested in my work.'

'New work?'

'Not exactly.' I shivered inside my overcoat. 'Apparently there's something of a nostalgia for all things Edwardian just now.'

'Poor Lucy—'

'Don't call me that!' I said through gritted teeth. Then, more mildly: 'Please. You know I hate it when you call me that.'

Pandora's red mouth widened just a fraction. 'A relic of the old days, eh?'

'Seems like it. I must be careful not to be swept aside in this new world order of yours.'

She nodded towards my bandaged hand. 'Had an accident?'

'I picked a fight with an engraving tool. It won.'

Suddenly a smile flickered over her sombre face. Somehow or other I seemed to have touched a soft spot in Pandora's formidable hide. Wrapping her stole tightly about her throat she lit a black cigarillo and was soon wreathed in its smoke. 'Perhaps tomorrow. Mr Mons has some business down by the docks. If you give me your number I'll see what I can do.'

'How splendid! Look, sis, I'm very grateful—'

'I said, I'll see what I can do.'

She took my hastily scribbled number and walked off, her face all but swallowed up by the voluminous collar of her astrakhan coat.

I watched her until she diminished into the whiteness then stamped my frozen feet. What a spot of luck! Pandora was too wily to believe I'd suddenly become a doting brother so I'd been right to appeal to this crazy new fad of hers. And now I had a direct line of contact to Mons!

I began to stomp off through the drifts then gradually slowed to a halt. The wind was getting up again, whipping snow in my face and sending an eerie susurration through the bare branches of the trees. I had the uncanny feeling that something was watching me from the undergrowth.

Sal Volatile's words seemed to echo in my mind. *Evil, Mr Box. Patient, watchful Evil.*

I felt suddenly glad to turn my back upon the park and head for Fifth Avenue.

'A pleasure to see you again,' said Professor Reiss-Mueller. 'I didn't know if you'd come.'

I was deep in the ill-lit basements of the Metropolitan Museum, flanked by shelf upon shelf of labelled cardboard boxes. Behind a desk, illuminated only by a shell-shaded lamp, the white-blond, bespectacled fellow from the "99", was once again examining Hubbard's handkerchief. The desk was covered all over with his scribbled notes.

'You were, I recall,' continued the pallid creature, 'about to promise me something in return for my expert opinion.'

I shrugged. 'What do you want?'

'Absolute frankness.'

'I'm not sure I'm at liberty—'

'You see,' he whined, none too convincingly stifling a yawn, 'it's not much of a life down here. I live amongst the relics of the dead. Dust is my meat and drink, you might say. So it pleases me to hear a little of the life that goes on above me on those crowded sidewalks.'

He coughed twice again, a tic that was already driving me a little crazy. The lamplight flashed off one lens of his spectacles, turning him into a mildly smiling, electric Cyclops.

'You seemed lively enough at the "99",' I countered.

Reiss-Mueller chuckled. 'Mere bread and circuses, my friend. This little beauty,' he cried, waving the hankie, 'promises much more.'

'Does it?'

Again I was conscious that he knew slightly more than he was letting on. Sweat stood out on his chalk-white forehead and yet the gloomy basement was as chill as an ice-house.

'Okey-dokey,' I said, trying to adopt the house style (not without

'The lamplight flashed off one lens of his spectacles.'

discomfort, as I'm sure you can imagine). 'I retrieved that square of silk from the body of a stolen-goods receiver whose brains a colleague of mine had recently blown out. I'm feeling horribly threatened by said colleague – some years younger than me – and am mightily pleased that he managed to miss this piece of evidence. I'd very much like to present it to my superiors so that they'll think me ever so clever and worthy of praise and give the young whippersnapper a ticking off. So, whether it's a clue to the whereabouts of the True Cross or merely Henry of Navarre's laundry list, I'd be most awfully grateful if you'd translate it.'

Reiss-Mueller gave a stuttering laugh. 'How thrilling. All that *violence.*' A little tremor of excitement ran through him. He held the relic close to his face and was silent for some minutes, his breath coming in quick little bursts. 'Trouble is,' he said at last, 'I can't.' Cough-cough. 'In short, though the artefact appears wholly genuine, the language is gibberish. It's *almost* Latin. Then takes another turn to become like Hebrew, then Aramaic. But the words make very little sense.'

'A code?'

'I think not. There's no obvious pattern.'

'Wouldn't be much of a code if there was.'

Another smile, two more coughs. 'Quite. Some of it's a ritual. Other parts . . . how can I put it? *Directions.* See, this part with the picture of the mountain. It's like a map. The ragged edges show it's the bottom corner of a larger piece of material.'

He let the silk droop in his hand. With a disappointed sigh, I reached for it but Reiss-Mueller snatched it back. 'I haven't quite finished.'

He pointed to the images on the ragged edge of the silk. 'These markings. They're Cabbalistic.'

'Black magic?'

'Uh-huh.' He gave an amused smile and coughed twice behind his hand. 'Quite my line of country, don't you know. That little

fellow—' He pointed to a barely discernible goatish-looking creature sitting cross-legged in one embroidered corner. 'That fellow
could be Banebdjed.'

'Bane—?'

'The soul of the god Osiris. His Ba. It's a ram-headed deity.'

'A Ba-lamb?'

Reiss-Mueller chuckled. 'It's all mixed up with the composite
pagan idols worshipped by the Knights Templar,' he said, gleefully
patronizing. 'Speaking of violence. Oh, boy. Those fellows knew
how to party.'

He pointed a milk-white finger at some of the dense text. 'These
could be the names of various demons – Moloch, Belial, Thentus
and so forth – but, like I say, the language is kind of garbled. Still,
if you let me study it for a while, I might make some headway. I
know all about the arts of the left-hand path.'

'Perhaps.'

I watched his plump fingers almost caressing the silk. 'There are
some words here that are very clear, though as to what they
mean. . .'

'What do they say?'

Reiss-Mueller held up the hankie close to his face and read from
it. '"There will come one who is spoken of. All unknowing he will
come. And only he that makes himself alone in the world can defeat
the Beast".'

'Meaning?'

'Don't have a clue!' he chirped.

'What about this?' I continued, indicating the four-legged animal
roasting on a spit in the embroidered flames.

The little man shrugged. 'Some sort of sacrifice? A sheep? A
goat?'

I suddenly remembered Volatile's words. 'Or a *lamb*?' I mused.
'So. An educated guess. Is it a map? A ritual? What?'

He glanced up again and smiled. 'How remiss of me. I'd suggest it's some bastardized version of the Clavicule of Solomon. Or maybe the Grimoire of Pope Honorius. One way or another, it's an invocation.'

'What kind of invocation?'

The light caught his spectacles again so that for an instant he appeared to have huge, blind white eyes. 'Why, for summoning the Devil, of course.'

6

An Attempt On Mount Olympus

Waking to the steady throbbing of my injured hand, I lay for a moment on the cool pillowcase that still bore the imprint of Rex's head. We'd become a bit of an item (I crave diversion constantly) but the boy had risen early to attend to his tedious duties so I was once more alone.

I stretched out my legs under the sheets then reached across to the little bedside table and retrieved my cigarette case from beneath the white Bakelite of the telephone.

Watching the smoke curl lazily to the ceiling, I reached for the handkerchief and, producing a lens, made an effort to peer closer at some of the embroidered pictures – the letters being all Greek (or, in fact, everything but) to me. The mountain, picked out in faded blue and white, was surrounded by dense text that did indeed appear to be some species of directions. There were numbers and repeated symbols and a sort of outlined range of hills that seemed to be an indication of where to find this particular peak.

I suddenly felt a curious prickling at the back of my neck. There was something oddly familiar about that mountain and, for a moment, I almost caught at the remembrance. But it tantalised only briefly and was gone, like the odour of Thomas's *lad's love*, 'leaving only an avenue dark, nameless, without end'.

Further down the relic, towards the embroidered corner bearing dragons' heads and the queer composite demon that my friend in the museum had identified as Banebdjed, was the image of the four-legged animal roasting over flames. Could this be the lamb that Volatile had spoken of? In which case, were the late Hubbard and Olympus Mons somehow connected?

I got up, showered and dressed, then changed the dressing on my wound – it was weeping in rather grisly fashion – and I was slipping into a snug three-piece grey tweed when the telephone rang.

'Yes?' I cradled the tulip-like receiver under my chin as I buttoned my waistcoat.

'Pier Thirty-Nine,' said Pandora's voice curtly. 'Forty-five minutes from now.'

'Pan! Thanks, sis. I'm immensely indebted—'

There was a hiss and a click and the line went dead. Hastily, I finished dressing, folded the silken rag and popped it into my pocket as though it were indeed nothing but a handkerchief, and took the lift down to the lobby.

Another yellow cab took me down to the docks, the outside world only visible through a hastily rubbed circle in the frost-rimed glass. Vignettes of brownstone blocks, diners and spindly towers flashed past.

I realized that in my haste to meet Mons, I didn't actually have a clue what I was going to say to him.

By the time the car drew up at the pier, I'd pretty much resolved to play the silly ass and come across simply as Pandora's mildly famous artist brother, fed up with the way the world was drifting and keen to, *you know*, do my bit.

Peering through the fogged-up window, I saw that a big grey-wheeled Daimler was already parked there, empty save for its peak-capped chauffeur.

I paid off the cabbie and slipped outside onto rotted wooden planks, my freshly shaved face stung at once by the bitter cold. The waters of the great river, visible far beneath me, were frozen hard, several sheets of ice toppling over each other like tectonic plates.

Further from the pier the frozen surface was thinner, and the black waters of the Hudson were lapping and churning around the hull of a disreputable old tub called the *Stiffkey*, its once gay livery faded, rust from its ancient rivets dribbling like old blood and staining the surrounding water.

I spotted Pandora at the far end of the gangway, a cloche hat framing her powdered face. Mons, in greatcoat and trilby, was deep in conversation with a big, disordered sailor with matted white hair and a face blossoming with the signs of heavy drinking. The sailor's clothes were weather-beaten and greasy and a massive ugly watch chain, extending from his top pocket to his hip, seemed to rein him together.

As I approached, Pandora looked up, said something to Mons and the great leader dismissed the sailor with a curt nod, clattering down the gangway towards me, hand extended.

His hooded eyes grew wide again. This close I noticed that they were almost all black pupil, only a narrow halo of white visible, like the corona of the sun during an eclipse.

'Why, Mr Lucifer Box!' he oozed in his oddly light American voice. 'How utterly delightful. I had no idea Pandora here had such an illustrious sibling.'

His hand was warm and dry and he held onto mine just a little too long, fixing me with those extraordinary orbs of his.

'Pleasure to meet you too, sir,' I enthused. 'Dashed impressed by your performance at the rally the other night.'

'Oh, one does one's best.' He looked down, bashfully, and the black suns diminished: the reptile's membranous eyelids, as it were, flicking back into place. Then he smiled and his scarred lip curled up further over the exposed dog tooth. 'Interesting you choose that word. *Performance.* I fear my public expect new tricks of me all the time and I fail to deliver.'

'That's nonsense!' chimed in Pandora. 'You give them everything they want and more—'

Mons held up a black-gloved hand in an impatient silencing gesture.

Pandora's mouth clapped shut as though she'd been struck. A brief flicker of annoyance passed over Mons's face. Then he was all smiles again.

'Your sister has become absolutely indispensable to me, Mr Box.'

'Call me Lucifer, please.'

Mons gave a low chuckle, stroking the end of his thickly waxed moustaches. 'It's a wonderful name. Not much used these days.'

'Lucifer, Jesus, Judas . . .' I cried. 'All the best people have the best names.'

'And Olympus?' speculated the great leader.

'How appropriate for a Greek god!' gushed Pandora, her hand immediately flying to her rouged lips as though to hush them.

Mons smiled patiently, wearily. 'Your sister is very kind but has a somewhat exaggerated view of my talents.'

I shivered within my suit. 'I doubt it, sir. You're the man to get the world out of the fix it's stumbled into. It seems to me, half the population's stuck in the distant past, the other half's too idle to look to the future. They need guidance. They need a man with an iron will. They need *you*.'

Mons flushed with pleasure. He began to walk away slowly from the *Stiffkey*'s gangway, hands clasped behind his back, and I trotted after him, Pandora keeping a safe distance behind.

'I know I have it in me to do great things, *tremendous* things,' he murmured. 'I can mould the people of this world into one wonderful, shining whole. But to achieve great things we must be prepared to take great risks, don't you agree, Lucifer?'

'*Rather*,' I said, grinning like an idiot.

Mons looked me up and down again, perhaps not sure what to make of me. 'You like risk, Lucifer?' His eyes flashed wide again and, with a giggle, he simply stepped over the side of the pier.

Pandora gave a little yelp. 'Olympus! Don't!'

I gasped and leaned over the edge to see what had happened but Mons had landed neatly in a crouching position on the frozen river below. The ice made a weird percussive noise beneath his shoes.

He stared down at the dark water, swirling inches below the ice, then gestured upwards. 'Join me!'

I looked at my sister, shrugged and then jumped lightly over the side. The ice shuddered, took my weight and I walked swiftly and confidently to Mons's side. He rubbed his hands together and began to stride further and further away from the safety of the pier.

'I've always had my own way, you see,' he continued in a low murmur. 'My Pop always said I was born with a silver spoon in my mouth. Silver plated with gold, garnished with platinum.'

'How marvellous for you.' I looked down. The waters of the Hudson pressed and swirled at the ice as though protesting at their imprisonment.

'You think so?' said Mons. 'I'll let you into a secret, Lucifer.'

'Please do.'

'My enemy is not the Bolshevik hordes.'

'No?'

'No. It is ennui. It is the staleness of the commonplace. Life becomes very empty when it's nothing but parties and booze and sex.'

I nodded vigorously. 'Oh, Lord, yes. Couldn't agree more. Though I dare say you'd have a job convincing other people of that!'

Mons put a gloved hand on my shoulder and squeezed it painfully. I think he liked me. 'So I looked for other distractions,' he said cryptically. The inky eyes bored into mine.

'Distractions?' I asked, all innocence.

Mons looked over my shoulder into the middle distance. 'Racing motor cars. Aeroplanes. Eventually I found politics. For a time, the yawning hole within me was filled.'

An expression of utter blankness stole over him now, and for a moment he seemed nothing more than a bored little boy, tired of his toys.

'For a time?' I hazarded.

'Everything becomes flat eventually,' he said bleakly. Then the eyes began to blaze again and a mischievous smile danced around his curled lip. 'Well, *almost* everything.'

Slowly at first, he began to rock on his heels. Again, the strange booming sound of ice under pressure began to reverberate around us. I risked a nervous glance down.

Mons was laughing now, swaying back and forth in his expensive shoes, harder and harder and harder.

Finally, as I knew it would, a narrow fracture opened up in the ice. Black water immediately frothed over the gap, like spittle expelled from a palsied mouth, and the break in the ice grew wider, zig-zagging towards us at worrying speed. Mons looked about, his exposed tooth glittering like a vampire's fang. 'Risk, my dear Lucifer! What's life without it?'

So saying, he pelted back towards the pier, his laughter, picked up by the weird acoustic of the frozen bay, ringing behind him.

The ice began to splinter all around us. I needed no prompting and hared after Mons, feet sinking into the liquefying surface, shoes filling with freezing water, stumbling and unbalancing until we both made the safety of a wooden ladder, its rungs spongy with rot.

Mons pulled up sharp at the bottom so that I actually began to sink into the waters. Trying hard to appear nonchalant, I lurched and bobbed behind him. He flashed a crazed look over his shoulder, teeth flashing like knives, then, in one swift move, pulled himself up to safety.

I followed in an instant, toppling over the bent rungs and affecting a blasé chuckle as though the whole thing had been a childish game.

Mons looked down at me and clapped a hand on my shoulder. 'Let's talk again,' he rapped, then strode towards the Daimler and clambered inside.

Pandora rushed after him, her heels clocking on the sodden planks.

'Happy now?' she called, a faint smile twitching on those very red lips.

She only just managed to haul open the door of the big car and slip inside before it roared off into the traffic.

So much for Olympus Mons! Mad as a March hare, that much was obvious. I squelched back towards the road and hailed a cab.

Rex was waiting for me when I entered the hotel lobby.

'Gentleman to see you,' he cooed, brushing his hand against my thigh in a none-too professional fashion. 'I get off at three.'

'What?' I carefully detached the boy from my side. We were in company, after all.

'Three. I thought maybe we could take in a show and—'

'I mean what gentleman?'

Rex shrugged grumpily. 'Said "Delilah" sent him.'

I frowned, but allowed Rex to show me into the smoking room before dismissing him with a curt nod. He slunk off like a jilted schoolgirl.

Within the warm, panelled room, a big man in flannels was tapping a thick cane against his foot and staring into the fire. Upon sight of him, I immediately relaxed. He had broadened in the waist and his face was ruddy with too much drinking but the handsome features were unmistakeable. A hesitant blond moustache almost covered a ragged scar. He looked up and smiled warmly.

'Hullo, Box, old man,' cried Christopher Miracle.

I gripped my fellow dauber's hand with all the manliness his presence warranted. 'It's been too long, Chris,' I said, with feeling. Sincerity rarely passes these pretty lips of mine so you must get it while you can.

Miracle nodded, laid his stick aside and retrieved a sheaf of papers from inside his jacket.

'Your charming friend Miss Delilah telephoned.'

'Ah.'

'She knew I was here pursuing my usual rootless existence,' continued Miracle. 'Said you wanted all the gossip on one Olympus Mons.'

I nodded. This was a terrific idea of Delilah's. Through family and a wide circle of friends, Miracle had always been the best-connected bloke a fellow could wish to call upon. Though his circumstances had changed greatly since the halcyon days of our friendship, if there was any man who could fill in some background on the shadowy Mons, it was he.

Miracle glanced down at the documents and grunted. 'Interesting blighter. Money to burn, it seems.'

'I don't doubt it. Has all the hallmarks of a spoilt brat who doesn't know what to do with himself.'

Miracle looked up. 'Was like that myself. Once.'

His watery blue eyes grew momentarily dim. He threw a glance towards the crackling fire, then cleared his throat and shrugged as though embarrassed by his admission.

'Olympus Mons. Born in Iowa of wealthy farming stock. Sent to some of the best schools the States can offer – although between you and me that's not saying much – but expelled from the lot.'

'Any particular reason?' I queried, offering Miracle a cigar.

'Refusal to conform. Bully. You know the form. Anyway, he was eventually rusticated so often they packed him off to England where he seems finally to have settled down. Took a fancy to Blighty and the notion of Empire in particular. Inherited pots from his father's death and enjoyed the playboy life until a holiday in Italy got him all steamed up about Mussolini.'

I nodded, blowing smoke rings towards the ceiling. 'So far, so public record. What's the gossip?'

Miracle grunted mischievously, clipped the end of his cigar and popped it into his mouth. 'Well. . .my sources tell me that he created a good deal of resentment when he muscled in on the American fascist movement. Took the whole thing over in six months as though it was his destiny. Usual grumblings from those who'd served their time and done all the foot-soldiering. . .'

This made sense. Sal Volatile, I presumed, was one such. 'Go on,' I urged.

Miracle took a moment to encourage his smoke into life then raised his brows. 'The word is, the true believers reckon this whole F.A.U.S.T. thing is no more than another fad for him. That he'll soon tire of it and move onto some other craze to stave off boredom.'

'Excellent,' I cried. 'Dissension in the ranks. Divide and conquer. Should be a doddle.'

Miracle waved his hand, suggesting more, the tip of his cigar glowing through a veil of bluey smoke. 'The reason they think this, it seems, is that he's been sinking all his moolah into a schloss.'

'A what?'

'A castle. In Switzerland. Despite his Yankee roots and British pretensions, that's apparently where he's happiest.'

'Switzerland, eh?'

'I'm reliably informed there's been a tremendous amount of activity thereabouts for quite a while.'

'What kind of activity?'

'Digging. Under the castle. Apparently he's been pressing the local labour force into service for months.'

I chuckled. 'Is there gold in them thar hills?'

Miracle's mouth turned down. 'Dashed unlikely, I'd say. What there is, is talk.'

'What do you mean?'

'All rot, of course, but those funny Swiss beggars think the place is haunted or something. They reckon Mons is trying to do something unholy.'

My hand stole to my pocket, where Hubbard's silken rag nestled. 'They may not be far wrong.'

I snapped out of my reverie and rose from my chair. 'Thanks for your help, Chris. You want some lunch?'

Miracle held up his hand. 'There's something else, Lucifer, I think you should know before you. . .go any further with this matter.'

I sank back onto the green leather. 'Go on.'

Miracle took a long draw on his cigar and flicked an inch-thick chunk of grey ash into the chromium plate at his side. 'Mons's castle. It's just across the border from France. Little place called Lit-de-Diable.'

Despite the cheery fire crackling in the gate, I grew cold and suddenly knew why the mountain embroidered on the occult relic had looked so familiar.

Miracle's eyes locked with mine for a moment and bleak remembrance was writ large in them.

'Thanks,' I said at last. 'Forewarned is forearmed, eh?'

Miracle stubbed out his cigar and raised himself up with some difficulty. 'I'd better be off.'

I plastered on a cheery smile. 'Busy afternoon?'

Miracle managed the same, his scarred face twisting slightly. 'You know me.'

We shook hands and I had a sudden, vivid impression of him in that gold-leaf summer of '13, arms akimbo, the scents of warm, wind-blown hay in the air, announcing that he was off at once to join up, give Jerry a fat lip and be home for Boxing Day.

The reality of course, had been somewhat different. Every bit as gallant and heroic as one would have expected from such a massive personality, Miracle had sailed through the War unscathed until one night, late in the conflict, when we'd found ourselves working together on a dangerous mission on the Franco-Swiss border. For once, the machinations of the Royal Academy and the more solid business of the British Army had found common purpose: namely the annihilation of Baron Gustavus Feldmann, the most dangerous man in Europe.

Feldmann's deadly plot, centred around the airstrip at Lit-de-Diable, was the Hun's final, desperate gamble and he'd very nearly carried it off. We'd bested him at the last, of course, though at horrific cost to our side. My unit had been utterly smashed and Miracle was found wandering about on the border, whey-faced and talking nonsense, blood pouring from the wounds in his leg and gloriously handsome face.

Once so hale and full of life, poor Chris had never been the same man again.

I saw my old friend to the revolving door and he turned up his collar against the biting wind. With heavy heart, I watched his stooped form until he disappeared amid the cabs and the crowds.

7

I Strike Damned Queer Country

In my experience, if a chap hangs on to secret knowledge he tends to wind up very dead, taking said knowledge with him. I'd fervently hoped, then, that my new contact, Sal Volatile, would spill the beans in the aftermath of the F.A.U.S.T. rally and not delay the final moment.

Volatile was insistent, however. His plans were not yet in place and so, in properly covert style, I was to linger in the bitter weather on the corner of Twenty-third and Fifth. I was there at the appointed time but of my chestnut-haired chum there was no sign.

Sleet slapped against my face as I sheltered in the porchway of the chichi drugstore he'd nominated as our rendezvous, huge display bottles of red and green liquid giving it an unintentionally festive air.

I scanned the street for him, watching umbrella-wielding figures slipping between the motors that crawled alongside.

Suddenly there was a hand on my elbow and I was swung round to find myself looking straight into Volatile's handsome face. His hat was pulled down low but there was no mistaking the fear in his eyes.

'Gotta be careful, pal. Real careful,' he muttered.

'All right.'

He nodded towards the drugstore. 'We can talk in here.'

Despite having chosen the venue, he seemed to reconsider his choice for fully thirty seconds, looking over his shoulder and then peering through the plate glass of the window. The red liquid in the giant bottle gave his pocked face a hellish tint. Finally, he nodded and let go of my arm.

I pushed at the door, setting the 'open' sign swinging, and we swept inside into a mercifully warm interior.

A long bar, studded with stools that had the appearance of uphol-stered mushrooms, took up the whole of one side of the place. On the opposite wall hung a huge rectangular mirror all stuck over with postcards of Florida.

A fat soda-jerk in a white coat and silly white hat beamed at us over his siphons. I ordered two cups of coffee and the fellah set to work, skilfully brewing the java without even glancing up from his sports magazine.

Volatile gulped down his.

'Well,' I said. 'As they say in the flickers: shoot.'

He threw a wary glance outside. 'I'm hoping I can trust you, Mr Box. I *need* to trust you.'

'Go on.'

'Mons is crazy. He's turned the whole organization into his per-sonal fan-club. It wasn't like that before. We had good intentions, I can assure you.'

I nodded encouragingly, though I knew full well the sort of big-oted trash of which his good intentions consisted.

'You contacted us because you have something on Mons,' I queried. 'What is it? You said something about a prayer? And a lamb?'

Volatile leant forward, eyes wide. 'I found the Lamb!' he whispered, as though I should know what he was talking about. 'Right under their noses! Mons is going crazy looking for it. He thinks he's on the right track but he'll find the bird flown!'

A curious, hissing laugh spluttered from between his teeth. I was beginning to worry that everyone around me was a little unbalanced.

Volatile's mood switched back abruptly. He jumped to his feet, crossed swiftly to the door and, shading his eyes, looked out onto the snowy sidewalk. Either he was paranoid to the point of delusion or he was convinced he was being followed.

I glanced across at the soda-jerk but he was absorbed in his baseball literature.

Eventually, Volatile sat down again, rubbing his weary face with long, nervous fingers. 'There's only one place I'll be safe. In a church.'

I almost laughed but managed to disguise my outburst by taking a gulp of coffee. 'Sanctuary?'

Volatile bit his lip and the bristles on his unshaven chin curved upwards. 'Well, not a church, at all really. The Convent of St Bede. It's in England. I've got a passage booked out of here. Got an understanding with the captain. Pier Thirty-Nine. Tonight at midnight. Boat called the *Stiffkey*.'

'The captain being a big, square fellah. Boozy face, long watch chain?'

'That's the guy. Name of Corpusty. Know him?'

'Saw him. He didn't see much of me, though.'

'That's good.'

'Why?'

Volatile leant even closer. 'I want you to go instead of me. The trip's a blind. I've got other means of getting to England. You'll act as a decoy.'

He handed me a sheaf of shipping documents. I looked them over.

'Charming. And what do I get out of all this? Am I to expect company? Company with stout boots and tommy guns?'

'I'll tell you it all!' cried Volatile. 'I've got the inside track on the whole damn thing. How Mons gets his cash. What he's got planned for the Lamb. It's evil, sir! *Diabolical.*'

'So you said.'

'And if I can get safely to the convent—'

'More coffee?' The fat soda-jerk was looming over us, coffee pot in hand, beaming through the steam that poured from its pitted lid.

'No, thanks. Look,' I turned back to Volatile, 'tell me about this "lamb". And what's this alternative escape route of yours? If something goes wrong I'll need to find you—'

'I'll get in touch,' he muttered. 'Soon as we're both in England.'

'No more coffee?' The soda-jerk was grinning stupidly, the steam from the pot fogging his owlish glasses.

'NO! Thank you!' I hissed.

But the fellow pushed back his spectacles from the bridge of his flat nose and shook his head. 'I insist!'

Suddenly he'd upended the pot and scalding black fluid was raining down onto Volatile's hand. Volatile yelled and jumped from his stool. In a flash, the soda-jerk had pulled a snub-nosed revolver from his apron and the dim interior of the drugstore flashed yellow as a bullet spat out. Volatile was hit in the knee and flung backwards into the far wall, shattering the mirror, snapshot images of Key West and Orlando fluttering about him like confetti.

All this I observed as I grabbed Volatile's shipping documents, dropped to the floor, rolled over – my coat skirts dragging in the pool of spilled coffee – and reached for my Webley. It was out of my pocket in an instant and replying to the soda-jerk in kind. Two sang off the counter and the fat man ducked behind a cardboard advertisement for stomach-acid relief.

I looked rapidly about, my bandaged hand throbbing appallingly. There was no way I'd make it into the back room, my only chance was the door to the outside world. Letting fly another bullet, I scuttled over Volatile's prone, groaning form and reached a hand towards the glass door. The big display bottle immediately to my right exploded with a nerve-jangling smash as, once again, the villain blasted at me. Red liquid like diluted blood hung in the air for a moment before splashing down onto the tiled floor and into my eyes.

I let fly another bullet as I rubbed at my lovely face, praying the stuff from the bottle wasn't toxic.

With an ugly grunt such as I imagine water buffaloes give, the soda-jerk heaved his bulk over the counter and landed before me, kicking the gun from my hand as I floundered about.

'Now just stay calm, like a good boy!' he cried, settling himself on the slippery floor and casting a quick glance at the semi-conscious Volatile.

'What do you want?' I moaned miserably, rubbing the red stuff from my dazzling optics.

He dropped to one knee and frisked me very thoroughly, batting my hands apart with the barrel of his revolver and sending my Webley skittering across the tiles with another well-aimed kick. Swinging his pistol towards me again, he aimed it squarely in the centre of my forehead. Naturally, I put up my hands.

'Just tell me what you want!' I cried in a shamefully panicky fashion. 'I can be very accommodating.'

'So I heard,' chuckled the brute in a whiskey-soaked rasp. 'Now get up.'

I sighed, my gaze flicking about for any sign of advantage. 'Who are you? Why did you plug that poor sap?'

He scowled and kicked me hard in the solar plexus. I flopped to the floor, wincing in pain.

'Just keep your mouth shut!'

He lashed out again but this time I twisted onto my side and grabbed hold of his shoe, wrenching his foot over into an unnatural angle. He screeched in pain and tumbled onto me, knocking the breath from my lungs. For a moment, my face was flattened against the cold white tiles, red fluid pooling into my hair, overpowered by the sweaty stink from the barman's grease-splashed crotch. Then I managed to rise to a crouching position, jerking my elbow out and into the rolls of fat that encompassed his gut.

He groaned in pain and fury. I jumped to my feet and slammed the heel of my shoe onto his hand. There was a sound like kindling crackling in a fire and, screaming, he let go of the revolver.

Darting to the floor, I retrieved the weapon and had it levelled at him before he had a chance to recover.

'Now,' I gasped, trying with some difficulty to catch my breath. 'Start talking.'

'Go screw yourself,' he croaked, holding his ruined hand as though it didn't belong to him.

'Not on an empty stomach, thanks.' I sank back onto a bar stool. Volatile was out cold. 'I presume you're working for Mons's lot. You needed to rub out that fellah on the floor there before he told me all about your lord and master, eh?'

He might have talked. We shall never know. Because I was just conscious of a vague movement behind me as someone emerged from the back of the drugstore, a small pinprick of pain on the back of my neck and then a warm, fuzzy, muffled darkness as I crashed to the floor.

My tongue felt like a stick in my mouth. I blinked a couple of times and focused on a tobacco-soiled ceiling and bare bulb hanging from wire that looked like a string of liver. Turning my head slightly, I found that I was resting on a rough candy-striped pillow that had seen infinitely better days. I turned my head the other way and sat up with a yell.

Sal Volatile lay naked in bed next to me, three holes in his chest leaking unhealthy gouts of blood onto the stained mattress.

I blinked and stared at the body, my bare back hitting the cold plaster of the wall behind the bed. The Webley lay on the carpetless floor, and as I moved to get out of bed, I noticed that a man was sitting on a nearby stool, arms folded, smiling over at me with an infuriating insouciance. It was Percy Flarge.

'Oh, Lor,' he said, pulling a face. 'Got ourselves into a bit of a pickle this time, eh, old fruit?'

I didn't move but glanced quickly around the grim, bare room. 'What . . . what the hell's going on, Flarge? Where am I?'

'You tell me. Favourite haunt of yours, by all accounts. We got a tip-off from the owner. You and the stiff came in some time ago, high as kites by his account.'

'He's lying—'

'Checked into your usual room. Started getting up to . . . whatever it is you chaps get up to,' continued Flarge, hatefully. 'Lovers' tiff ensues and . . . well . . .'

He gestured towards the corpse. 'Funny thing,' he grinned suddenly. 'My Pa always said he supposed men like you shot themselves. Turns out, you shoot each other!'

I tried to keep my temper and got to my feet, glancing down at Volatile's stiffening form. 'What the hell are you on about? Listen, Flarge. *Percy.* I was approached by this chap in connection with an assignment for the RA. We arranged to meet earlier this evening. Well, someone must've been onto him, because it was a trap. He was shot – but only wounded – and I was drugged . . .'

Flarge took out a pipe and began to fill it. He looked thoroughly sceptical.

I felt suddenly hot with rage. 'Look here. We can sort all this out. Would you mind awfully if we get out of here and leave the Domestics to clear things up?'

Flarge shook his head. 'No can do.'

The door to the squalid room suddenly flew open and a skinny man in the uniform of a police captain emerged. He looked at my pendulous, swinging tackle, swore under his breath and then, turning back to the open door, beckoned. A chattering flurry of people suddenly piled inside, two of them photographers. Flash bulbs zinged and whined in my face. I threw up my hands to shield myself.

'I suggest we make a move, sir,' said the captain.

'I was just making the same suggestion,' I said, looking about for my clothes. 'Move where?'

'To the station house, sir. Where you'll be charged with murder.'

8

The Buttons Come Off the Foils

This was a new and peculiarly horrid sensation. As long-term readers may recall, I've been in at more kills than the average Scotland Yarder has had bully beef, the victim usually having been knocked off by yours truly. And always – barring the odd assignment well away from civilized society – things have been hushed up nicely by the Royal Academy. True, I had once spent a night in the cells of a filthy Chinese nick when some over-zealous Cantonese mandarin (or a Mandarin Cantonese) threatened me with seven kinds of hell for despatching his Warlord chum with an ornamental tooth-pick. On that occasion, though, the Domestics simply missed their train and glided in smoothly the very next morning, apologizing profusely and leaving the mandarin red-faced and cursing over his stringy moustaches. I was on a fast boat out of there before the sun was over the old clay tiles of the cop-shop.

Now dressed and sitting in the police car this time, I knew I was in real trouble.

Percy Flarge slipped onto the seat next to me, his long blond fringe bouncing into his eyes, a delighted smile on his lips. Both doors of the motor remained open and bitter night air bled over us from the white street.

The police captain – inevitably Irish – was squawking orders to his subordinates, who were pushing back the eager crowd of ghouls that'd appeared around the entrance to the flophouse.

'Look here, Flarge!' I hissed. 'This is insane! What the hell are you up to?'

I flashed a look through the back window of the motor. The captain would return any moment. I didn't have long. 'Come on, man! This isn't how we do things! We look out for each other in the RA. There's a system! Why haven't you called the Domestics? Or Reynolds?'

'I'm merely helping the police arrest the guilty party.'

'There's more to this. You know there is. I've been – what do they say here? – framed up!'

A thought suddenly struck me. Hubbard had said the same thing. That he was a patsy. I decided to risk showing my meagre hand. I was pretty much out of options. 'Listen,' I whispered urgently, 'I've got what you're looking for.'

'What?'

'That "lamb" or whatever the hell it is. I found it on Hubbard's body.'

'You found a lamb on Hubbard's body? Taking it home for Sunday lunch, was he? Hmmph. Nice try, old thing. 'Fraid I searched him thoroughly. No livestock to be seen.'

'You weren't told, were you?' I persisted. 'You weren't told exactly what you were looking for?'

Flarge looked momentarily nonplussed. 'My orders were to bring back everything he had on him—'

'You missed his top pocket, *old boy*,' I mocked. 'A small square of silk like a handkerchief. I know it's important.'

'You're running away with yourself, old sport,' said Flarge smoothly.

I looked wildly about, anticipating with dread the approach of the police captain and the disappearance of all my long-held privileges. I'd be down in the cells with a copper's boot in my guts and that'd be the end of old Lucifer.

'I'll tell you where it is,' I said at last. 'Then you can claim all the credit. Just get me out of this hell.'

Flarge glanced over his shoulder. The captain was still talking, his flashlight bobbing in the darkness.

'All right,' he said. 'I can't promise anything, but . . . Tell me. Quickly.'

He leant forward.

I moved like a panther, jerking back my neck and then ramming my forehead into his nose. There was an awful crack and I felt warm blood jet onto my face. Flarge shrieked in agony but I was already smothering him, muffling his cries with my body as my hands moved expertly over his chest to where I knew he kept his pistol. It was out of its holster and in my hands before Flarge could get his bearings. I swung the butt up against his chin and he grunted into rapid unconsciousness.

Letting him slide sideways onto the sweaty upholstery, I melted out of the motor and onto the road, flattening myself against the freezing tarmacadam and risking a look under the vehicle. I could see the captain's steel-toed boots crunching their way towards me. Scuttling like a cripple, I moved across the roadway and within seconds made the safety of a pitch-dark alley.

Huge black apartment blocks reared up on either side. It was nigh on impossible to make out anything in the darkness but I caught a suggestion of spindly fire escape and reeking bins as I pelted on.

And suddenly there were yells and whistles and I knew they'd found friend Flarge. I ran on – and came crashing to the ground as

I smacked headlong into a mildewed wall. The alley was a dead end!

There wasn't a moment to be lost so I sprang onto the nearest of the metal bins and used it as a vault, finding purchase on the bottom rung of the fire-escape ladder and swinging myself up and onto it.

The metal was wet and cold and smelled rusty. I managed to get some little way up it and onto a kind of gantry before the alley was lit up like a talkie premiere, police flashlights swooping over the black bricks.

The gantry ringed the building, acting as some kind of balcony for the apartment block's residents, and upon it squatted big, ugly plant pots full of withered shrubs.

I looked down at my pursuers. Perished though I was, I knew I had to take a chance, so, shrugging out of my overcoat, I wrapped it around the nearest of the plant pots and hung my trilby onto the drooping remains of a neglected olive tree. I peered at my little decoy, pleased by its resemblance to a crouched man trying to hide himself. Then I jumped back onto the ladder and positively swarmed up it to the roof.

It was flat and asphalt-covered. I heard clanging footsteps, harsh voices challenging the olive tree then I turned on my heel and skittered across the roof towards the far edge of the block.

Glancing across at the neighbouring building gave me pause. My decoy would be discovered at any moment and my only chance lay in a jump across the giddying void.

Queasy street light from far below silhouetted strings of washing that hung between the windows, shirts and trousers made stiff by the frost looking, rather disquietingly, like strung-up felons.

As must now be clear, I was no longer in the first flush of youth but needs must when, appropriately enough, the Devil drives. I shot a last look over my shoulder – flashlights were already bobbing over the edge as the police clambered upwards – then took a running jump and launched myself into space.

I make no claims as to my dignity, scrambling through the smoky night air like a novice swimmer, limbs paddling frantically until, with a winded grunt, I hit solid brick. With one elbow firmly over the lip of the roof, my other hand splayed out in a desperate effort to find purchase, I hauled myself up and heaved my aching chest over the edge, legs dangling below, shoes scraping off the upper edge of a bricked-up window.

My jacket ripped as I kicked upwards and fell, breathless and bruised, onto the roof. I'd made it.

There was little time for celebration, as one look back the way I'd come showed that the roof of the first block was now dotted with pursuing rozzers. If they were bright enough, it would only take one shouted command and they'd have the neighbouring building – upon which I now stood – surrounded and I'd be back in the police motor double-quick.

I could taste iron in my spit and a crippling stitch was already making merry in my gut but I ran on, reached the edge of this new roof, judged the distance – slightly less this time – and once more flung myself across.

This time I only just made it, my chest slamming into the edge of the neighbouring roof. I hooked my hands over the lip and some-how found the strength to haul my exhausted frame to safety, curling into a ball as I struggled to get my breath back.

A huge rectangular area with canvas stretched over it occupied most of the space. The tarpaulin was knotted around a series of stanchions and I realized absently that it must be a swimming pool wearing its winter finery.

I know what you're thinking. Why's old Boxy staying skywards? There's only one way down from there, chum, we've seen it at the pictures. Spreadeagled and strawberry jam-like on the damned pavement. Well, I was thinking along just those lines.

My injured hand was bleeding again – I could feel the bandage growing heavy and wet – but I stumbled forward towards a non-descript hut-like structure. Yanking open the door, I looked down into a cold, dark stairwell. My ears pricked up at once at the muffled yells from below. They were on to me!

Slamming the door shut, I looked wildly around the roof for some hiding place but it was bare and totally exposed. Except for the pool!

Skulking low in the darkness, I raced to the perimeter and searched for an opening in the stretched covering. The tarpaulin, tied off with great knots of nautical rope, was rigid with ice. My hands were already numb and I clawed uselessly at the nearest, mind flashing back briefly to games lessons at school and the almost impossible job of rebuttoning one's shirt after a wretched cross-country run. Still I persevered, fingernails splintering as I worried and tore at the looped rope.

I brought down my shoe onto the stretched canvas, hoping that it might slacken the knot, but the material hardly gave, as unyielding as the dirigible skin I'd seen arching over the dance floor of the "99".

Finally, desperately, I dropped onto my chest and began to pull at the knot with my teeth. And suddenly it began to give!

A rush of hope flooded through me, followed almost immediately by a hollow dread as I heard the sound of footsteps pounding on the stairwell. Grabbing at the rope with useless fingers, I managed to prise the knot apart. The covering slackened, the tarpaulin crumpled and a narrow space opened up, showing up black above the empty pool.

Thanking the stars for my lithe frame, I slid through just as the door to the stairs flew open with a crack like a thunderbolt.

Keeping hold of the loosened rope, I tumbled down the rough render of the wall. I scraped my backside painfully, and was immediately assailed by the foetid atmosphere, somewhere between the grassy pong of a tent and the sickening odour one sometimes finds at the bottom of one's toothbrush mug.

But this was no time to spare my finer feelings. I held onto the rope for grim death, my already-bleeding nails flaking hideously on the frayed end as I tried to make the tarpaulin tauter lest my hiding place be discovered.

From my vantage point beneath the canvas, all I could see were the haloes of my pursuers' flashlights. I held my breath. Through the gap, I saw a familiar pair of two-tone brogues the colour of café-au-lait. Percy Flarge had joined the hunt, no doubt in a perfectly foul mood after my distinctly un-Queensberry dodge.

Flarge's shoes came closer, crunching on the asphalt chippings that covered the roof. I could see tiny droplets of blood from his smashed hooter hitting his creamy leather uppers. He didn't move. A flashlight flared in my eyeline and I looked down at the bottom of the pool. Something I saw there gave me crazy hope.

There was a shout from close by and finally Flarge was on the move. I waited until his shoes were well out of sight and then let myself tumble down the wall, splashing into the inevitable puddle on the pool floor.

What I'd noticed in the momentary gleam of the flashlight was a huge monogram made out in coloured tiles. Some cod coat-of-arms cobbled together by Yanks desperate for historical roots, of course, but, more importantly, the emblem of my own hotel! Somehow or other, after all the shenanigans of the evening, I'd managed to vault onto the roof of my own residence. This had both advantages and disadvantages. In a hotel I could certainly move about less conspicuously, but at the same time they'd be bound to have my room – and probably the whole place – under observation in case I came back.

I scolded myself. It was imperative to keep focused! All that depended upon whether I could get off this damned roof alive. Had Flarge really assumed I'd already made my escape? Or was he lying in wait?

The crunching of boots on the asphalt had died away but there'd been no corresponding sound to indicate the door to the stairwell had been closed behind my pursuers.

I waited a further five minutes and then decided to risk it. Leaping for the trailing end of the rope once more, I hauled myself up and poked my head through the gap in the tarpaulin. Not a soul in sight. With one last effortful grunt, I pulled myself out from under the canvas and lay panting on the poolside, my hand hurting like blazes.

Then, with a great sigh, I jumped up and sprinted back towards the entrance to the stairwell, giving not one thought to the notion that the roof might have been left guarded.

I was down the concrete steps in moments and emerged into the beautifully carpeted uppermost floor of the hotel, a cocoon of mint-green and black elegance after the freezing outdoors. There was no one about so I made straight for the next stairwell, clattering down five floors until I reached my own. Emerging into an almost identical corridor, my heart leapt as I spotted the door to Room fifteen-o-eight. The unguarded door.

It could be a ruse of course but there was also the possibility, the *wonderful* possibility, that Flarge hadn't thought to put a man outside my room. Furthermore, to employ one of the hoariest clichés of cheap thrillers, it might well be the last place they'd think to look for me!

Giving up a silent prayer of thanks to hoary clichés, I padded down the corridor towards my room. My bandaged hand, with newly bloodied fingernails, was almost upon the shiny brass knob when the door began to open.

I spun on my heel, tottering like Chaplin in one of his sentimental two-reelers, and immediately bent low, retrieving the keys from my trouser pocket and scrabbling at the lock of the room opposite.

Now Dame Cecily Midwinter (under whom I'd trained more years ago than I cared to remember) had always advocated hiding in plain sight. Thus, rather than trying to blend into the wallpaper, I began to sing at the top of my voice, feigning a look of pie-eyed incoherence which I hoped might explain away my tattered appearance.

'Come on and hear!' I belted out. 'Come on and hear Alexander's Ragtime Band!'

Out of the corner of my eye I saw the blue of a policeman's uniform as he emerged from my room.

'Come on and hear! Come and . . . hear! It's the best band in the land . . .'

I fumbled with my key and turned to face the copper with a stupid grin on my face. 'Dashed thing won't fit,' I slurred. 'Must've . . . must've picked up the wrong one at recep— reception.'

I threw in a hiccup and a modest belch. The policeman looked mildly disgusted at the sight of this idiotic Britisher three sheets to the wind. He narrowed his eyes and I suddenly remembered that it probably wasn't terribly wise to pretend drunkenness in a city where Prohibition still reigned. 'Sorry,' I stage-whispered. 'I'll get out of your way.'

'I'd advise that, sir,' he said darkly.

I nodded at his sagacity and shuffled towards the elevator. 'Just pop downstairs and get the proper key.'

Jabbing at the brass button I prayed the lift would come with all due dispatch before my law-enforcing friend decided to take a closer look.

The arrow on its luminous dial crawled round to fifteen with wretched tardiness. I gave the officer one last dim grin and then turned back as the lift doors sprang open.

My heart dropped into my boots. Half a dozen uniformed policemen were revealed, crowding the lift. Thankfully I was still wearing my idiot grin otherwise I'm sure my face would have given me away. My luck held and, incredibly, the entire phalanx didn't spare me a second glance, merely peeling out of the lift in two lines, leaving me stranded on the carpet like a gasping salmon.

And then I had an even better piece of luck. For inside the lift, revealed by the exiting coppers, was Rex the bellhop, his hand already on the display of buttons.

'Going down, sir?' he said, automatically.

'Not just now, sugar.'

He turned his big green eyes on me and gawped. 'Mr Box! Jeez! What happened to—'

I stepped across and jabbed at a button. The lift shuddered and began to descend. 'Never mind,' I barked. 'I need your help, Rex.'

He chewed anxiously on his pouting lip. 'Is this something to do with the cops that're here? I heard there's a guy they're looking for. Killed someone and – oh my gosh!'

I clamped a hand over his pretty mouth and nodded. 'Yes. It's me they're after. But I didn't kill anyone, Rex. Not today, anyway. And you're going to help me get out of here, you understand?'

He nodded mutely, his eyes bulging in fright.

I glanced at the floor display glittering prettily like Japanese carp in a pond. 'We'll stop at the second floor. Then you need to find me a cupboard . . . um . . . a closet, all right? And don't do anything silly. It wouldn't be wise.'

He nodded again and I removed my hand. The poor boy looked badly frightened. The lift doors pinged open and we stole out onto the second floor of the hotel, Rex leading the way. His bum looked dashed appealing in those tight blue trousers so I gave it a little pat to show we were still friends. Carnality seemed far from Rex's thoughts, however, as he jangled a bunch of keys from his pocket and unlocked the door to a linen cupboard.

I slipped through, grabbing him by the lapels and pulling him in after me.

'Jeez, Mr Box!' he piped. 'If they find out I been helping you—'

I ignored him and felt for the light cord that was tickling at my face like a cobweb. With a click, a dim, bare bulb struggled into life. I looked about and groaned in dismay.

'What's up?' quizzed Rex.

'Nothing but towels!' I muttered. 'I was hoping for, you know, a waiter's apron. Spare commissionaire's uniform. Anything!'

'You asked for a closet . . .'

I sighed. 'Look, there's no time for this. I have to get out of here.'

I looked Rex up and down. He looked awfully dishy in that nice blue uniform. I gave him an encouraging smile and, not for the first time in twenty-four hours, asked him nicely to take it off.

9

All At Sea

Such promises one makes. I left dear Rex in the linen cupboard, bound and gagged (for verisimilitude, don't you know, nothing deviant), with extravagant assurances ringing in his dainty ears. There was to be dinner at the Twenty-One when all this was over and, as I recall, a cruise to Europe on the *Mauretania*. All eyewash, of course, as I had serious doubts I would ever again set foot in the Land of the Free, always supposing I escaped in the first place.

I emerged into the hotel lobby wearing Rex's uniform and feeling indescribably foolish, my shins showing bare where the lad's not-quite-long-enough trousers exposed my disguise. Pulling the little pillbox hat as far down my forehead as I could without drawing attention, I crossed towards the front doors with the easy swagger I'd seen Rex and his kind adopt on many occasions. I could only pray that as usual the clientele wouldn't spare the staff a second glance, otherwise the sight of a middle-aged man in blue and gold brocade might excite unwanted comment.

Policemen were dotted discreetly around the palm-fringed lobby.

I hovered near the lift for a few moments, patting, for reassurance, my money-belt, where Hubbard's silk relic now reposed. I watched the activity at the front desk with keen interest. A dwarfish fellow in a tailcoat and derby was trying to check in for a night of illicit thrills with a gum-chewing young lady in white furs. The weary-looking concierge looked ill-disposed to help.

Next to them stood a pile of orangey-leather cases, shiny as fresh conkers, awaiting collection. With complete nonchalance, I sailed past the desk, picked up a pair of the cases and glided out through the revolving doors into the street.

More coppers were walking up and down in the brilliantly lit forecourt. Heart pounding and resisting the urge to run for it, I walked as casually as I could around the side of the hotel until the darkness closed about me. Under this blessed cover I took to my heels, gripping the suitcases and emerging onto the neighbouring block, where traffic streamed by in a great blaring confusion.

Stepping boldly into the fray, I hailed a yellow cab and ordered him to take me to Pier Thirty-Nine down by the river, pulling a couple of greenbacks from my money belt to show I was in earnest.

I sank back, utterly spent, and cast an anxious glance through the rear window. All seemed well.

Allowing myself a moment to gloat, I pulled the first of the cases onto my lap and clicked it open. A wave of cheap perfume overwhelmed me. I reached inside and lifted out a negligee decorated with pink Malibu feathers. Not quite the thing for the journey I had in mind. The rest of the case proved equally barren and I moved onto the smaller one, hoping that it belonged to a chap of a similar build to me.

The locks yielded to my thumbs with two satisfying clunks. I stared down at the contents and let out an audible groan.

The driver's inquisitive features appeared in the mirror. 'You OK, bud?'

I sighed. 'Just not my day. Not my day at all.'

I held up several pairs of tiny, gaily checked trousers, garishly coloured waistcoats and bow ties. Tipping back the lid of the case, an old poster that had been pasted into it was exposed.

Adolph the Little Atom, I read. *Mimicry. Minstrel songs. Tumbling.* I recalled with a weary smile the dwarf at the hotel reception. Well, that's where gloating gets you.

The old tub *Stiffkey* lay at her berth at the pier just as I'd seen her only that afternoon, black water lapping at the rusted plates of her creaking hull and looking comprehensively unfit for an Atlantic crossing.

Having paid off the cab, I crept down a set of rotting wooden stairs and hid myself on the jetty behind two great coils of weed-smeared rope. As female drag or midget's stage-wear were unlikely to prove useful to me I was still squeezed into the bellhop's ludicrous get-up, though I threw the pillbox hat into the Hudson where it sank into the freezing water as though swallowed by tar.

Taking Sal Volatile's envelope from my pocket, I took stock of the situation. The dead man's exit strategy was completely open to me and, as my presence on the bitterly cold pier indicated, it was currently my only option. What I wanted very much to avoid, though, was falling into a trap. Did those intent on framing me know about Volatile's plan to substitute me on board the *Stiffkey*? Had I come all this way only to find Flarge's men waiting for me in the rusting old ship?

As far as I could tell, the tub was under no observation save that of an old tramp in a battered pilot's hat, sitting on the edge of the planking and very much at peace with the world. I gave it a few more minutes, eyes keenly scanning the shadowed docks, then, taking a deep breath, I strode swiftly up the rope-banistered gangway and onto the deck.

The pounding of the engines set my already strained nerves on edge.

A woolly-headed sailor in a sweater spat tobacco juice at my feet and eyed me with interest.

'Volatile,' I muttered, handing over my documents.

'Are you now?' he said, smiling in cheeky fashion. 'We shall have to watch you, then, eh?' The accent was thick Norfolk and the sudden sound of home was as comforting as if I was being wrapped in a Union flag.

He nodded towards a stairway and we passed from the darkness into a gloomy corridor, feeble electric bulbs strung down its length. Hooking a thumb over his shoulder, he indicated a battered cabin door. There was a small brass frame inset in it, presumably meant to bear the name of whichever unfortunate soul was travelling on the mangy old ship. I'd taken the *Stiffkey* to be some kind of trawler or merchant vessel with passengers a rare commodity. No doubt Volatile had paid a princely sum for this discreet exit from America, no questions asked.

The sailor flattened himself against the buckled wooden panelling of the corridor so that I could pass. 'When do we cast off?' I said.

'Half hour, ducks,' he replied with a funny little smile.

'Won't the captain want to see me?' I asked, trying not to sound too plaintive.

He let out a gurgling laugh. 'Cor, blast me! Ha! That'd be a turn-up and no mistaking. Ha, ha! Want to see you? Mr Volatile, he don't give a cuss for nothing 'cept getting here to ol' New York and then gettin' home. Now if I were you I'd keep my head down, eat your grub and not go for any long turns on the deck.'

I nodded. 'Very well.'

A slim shape in a white sweater and woollen cap flashed past us – a cabin boy, I supposed – and the sailor caught his arm. ''Ere! Hold you 'ard! You take care of Mr Volatile 'ere!'

The sailor gave me another queer look, tapped his tobacco-yellow fingers to his cap and vanished into the gloom, leaving me alone with the boy, who stooped at once for my cases.

Dog-tired, I ignored the lad and shouldered open the cabin door, revealing a tiny, airless room, very close to the engines judging by the constant drumming that set the brass ring of the porthole rattling. A simple bunk with a grey army blanket slung over it comprised the only furniture.

The boy let the suitcases tumble to the floor and went out. Kneeling on the bunk, I peered through the porthole. Outside the sea stretched like a black sheet towards Manhattan island, the ship's ancient propeller churning the icy water at her stern a startling white as the engines ticked over.

I glanced at my wristwatch. If we could only get going soon, if Volatile's escape route really hadn't been discovered, I might just be in with a chance.

With nothing else to do but wait, I stripped off Rex's jacket and sat there in my under-vest – stained black with grime and perspiration – and opened the two cases again. A more thorough check was in order.

The dwarf's case proved as useless as it had appeared save for some pornographic postcards of dubious titillation and a coral-pink cigar case containing a brace of fine-looking Havanas. I decided to save the smokes until I had something to celebrate.

Turning my attention to the girl's case I was delighted to find not only a roll of ten-dollar bills tucked inside her underwear but (God bless fashion!) a pair of wide-legged culottes that might just about pass muster as a gentleman's trousers. I was just slipping out of Rex's when we suddenly started moving. I moved to the porthole again and watched the blessed sight of the New York skyline begin to slip away into the night.

With a groan of exhaustion, I sank down on the bunk and closed my eyes.

I'd made it.

Poor old Lucifer has always been a rotten sailor, and waking in a fug of engine fumes, I greeted the new day with a dry heave, swung my legs off the bunk and sat up, coughing like a consumptive. I needed some fresh air sharpish.

Tottering into the culottes, I made my way across to the door and stumbled into the corridor beyond but that stank of oil and provided scant relief. As the *Stiffkey* plunged through the sea, I swayed towards the stairwell, only to walk, face-first, into the massive aproned chest of what could only be the ship's cook.

I took an involuntary step backwards and looked up at all six foot six of the brute. Built like the proverbial brick garderobe, this mulatto's ears were bright with silver rings and one hand – in appropriately piratical fashion – was replaced by what looked like a tin-opener.

'So sorry,' I bleated. 'Just . . . just on my way to the deck.'

Sweat rolled in great glistening beads over his bricklike brow. He made no move to stand aside.

'Not feeling too bright,' I managed, putting on my best silly-ass voice again in order to defuse any potentially violent urges he might have. 'So if you'd just let me pass . . .'

A strange guttural croak was his only answer.

Then, rather unexpectedly, he drew out a tin from the ruddily stained pocket of his apron, proceeded to spear it with the end of his harpoon-hand and, with astonishing delicacy, to open it up. Within a very few moments, he was scooping out pinkish meat – corned beef by the look – and stuffing it into his mouth. I shuddered briefly at the sight of his tongue. It had evidently been sliced clean off long ago, and the remains clacked about over the wet meat like some ghastly earthworm.

He croaked again, glared down at me in an openly challenging fashion and held the sharp end of his harpoon close to my perspiring face.

'*Bullfrog!*'

The cry was unexpected as it was welcome. The cabin boy from the previous night came running down the pitching corridor. In the queasy light I could still make out little of his face but I grew suddenly alert at the very noticeable protuberances in the rough fabric of his sweater. The very noticeable and *breast-shaped* protuberances.

'I am Aggie,' said the cabin 'boy', with great gravity. 'Do not mind Bullfrog. He is harmless. Welcome to the *Stiffkey*.'

She was duskily skinned, petite and devilishly exotic, her coal-black hair cut into a manageable crop under the cap. Her eyes were like polished jet and there was the light of another race in their depths. She set up a rather pleasant little fluttering in my churning innards.

'Isn't it meant to be unlucky?' I ventured.

'Sir?'

'Girls on ships?'

'They do not think of me as a girl,' she said, again with a kind of uncalled-for seriousness. 'So I do not either.'

Aggie's voice had a vaguely Indian inflection. Despite feeling as sick as a dog I attempted a ravishing smile. 'What a silly way of thinking. I'm sure if we become acquainted, I should like very much to think of you as a girl. Often.'

Such drawling charm never fails.

Except this time.

She stared at me with what looked very much like concern. 'You are sick. You must get air.'

At an impatient gesture from the girl, the brutish Bullfrog finally stepped aside and clumped off into the innards of the ship. With both hands on the rope banisters I hauled myself on deck, Aggie close behind.

The day was dark and oppressive, the sea like a greasy grey blanket, and I found, much to my distress, that I felt no better. The waves battering at the creaking ship's plates were deafening.

'How do I look?' I cried.

'You are green,' shouted Aggie, with wounding directness.

I swallowed a mouthful of bile and made my way towards the rail, my feet dragging as though they were stuck in glue.

Aggie's hand on my elbow was a great comfort. She narrowed her eyes against the spray. 'I could, if you like, prepare something for your condition. It is not exactly unknown aboard ship.'

I nodded, salty water dribbling down my face. 'You old sea dogs have a dozen tried and tested remedies, eh?'

'Sea dogs?'

I heaved again and put a hand to my clammy forehead. 'I'd be most grateful.'

'Come, then,' she said with impeccable manners. 'It is senseless to linger here when it is doing you no good.'

Aggie began to steer me back towards the stairwell then pulled up so sharply that I almost fell forward. A stout fellow with a liverish countenance had swung into our line of sight. I felt the girl stiffen as he strode with perfect composure over the soaked planks.

'It is the captain,' she hissed in my ear.

So here was Captain Corpusty again, whom I'd glimpsed only briefly when he stood deep in conversation with Mons a mere twenty-four hours before. At close quarters, his face was like a battered sail, strung tight across his bones as though against a force-ten gale. And just as the sailmaker might have patched and worried at the old canvas, so Corpusty's flesh was uneven and terribly scarred. Jaundiced eyes popped out from sweaty, shadowed flesh. He glanced at me for the briefest of moments and was about to resume his patrol of the deck when he suddenly swung back round.

'This our passenger, is it, Aggie?' he rumbled.

'Yes, sir.'

'Sal Volatile,' I croaked, holding out a trembling hand that the captain declined to shake.

'And how are you finding us aboard the *Stiffkey*, Mr Volatile?'

'Well,' I said airily, 'I've only just become acquainted with your friend here, though we did run into a charming one-armed fellow who seemed awful anxious to serve up corned beef for breakfast.'

Corpusty's disastrous face twisted into a semblance of a grin.

'Oh, old Bullfrog's bark is worse than his bite. But then, since I cut his tongue out, he don't have much of a bark.'

'You . . . ?'

'I prize loyalty above all things, sir. Bullfrog got himself soused one night in 'Frisco and fell to telling tales about me. He won't never tell those tales again.'

I swallowed another gobbet of bile. 'Expect not.'

'But he's loyal now,' continued the captain. 'And he keeps a watchful eye on things for me.'

I nodded breezily. 'Right-oh! Well, I must be getting below. Haven't found the old sea legs yet. Good day, Captain.'

Aggie helped me towards the steps. I was aware of Corpusty's eyes on my back the whole time.

10

A Guest Of Captain Corpusty

By the next day, after some food and a modicum of hot water, I was feeling a little better. Aggie and I had become sufficiently pally for me to enquire as to the possibility of getting some togs more suitable for the crossing and I was sitting on the bed that night, the ship pitching horrendously in a gale, grey water slapping at the porthole, when her light knock sounded.

'Yes?'

The girl's head appeared around the jamb. 'I have them,' she said solemnly.

I jumped from the bed and relieved her of a pile of clothes, shaking them out and holding them up to the dim light. A cable-knit sweater, moleskin trousers, thick socks and stout boots comprised my friend's booty yet I fell on them as though they were treasure. I swore a secret vow never again to be so damned fussy about my appearance, knowing that I would recant on such a promise at the first sight of a decent bit of Jermyn Street.

Without a thought to my modesty, I stripped off the wretched vest and culottes and shrugged on the new clothes.

Aggie cast her gaze at the floor, blushing.

'You're a miracle worker, Aggie,' I enthused, pulling the sweater onto my bare torso.

'You must not say such things,' she muttered.

'It's the exact and literal truth.'

'No, no,' she cried, earnestly. 'I am only a foolish girl and miracles are not performed by the likes of me.'

I stopped in the process of putting on my new boots. 'What a queer thing to say. Did someone tell you that?'

Aggie looked at me searchingly for a moment, then cleared her throat. 'It was not too hard to find the clothes. There is much clobber' – she said the word with utmost care – 'aboard the *Stiffkey*. They will not be missed.'

She cleared her throat again, lifted off her woollen cap and scratched her head.

I caught her meaning, nodded and reached into my money belt. As I handed over some dollar bills I saw Aggie's gaze stray to the belt. Hurriedly, I pulled down the jersey. We might be getting on well but I could hardly trust her. I might yet wake in the night to find her pretty face looming over me and a dagger in my ribs.

She put away the money in her back pocket. 'Is there anything else I can do for you, sir?'

'Yes. Why not stay awhile? Have a drink.' I gestured to the small bottle of Scotch I'd liberated from the blonde's suitcase.

She shook her head. 'I must get back. The captain says there is a storm brewing.'

As though to emphasize the point, the vessel gave a great roll and Aggie and I almost toppled to the floor. She fell into my arms and I laughed, but the girl looked confused and hastily got to her feet.

'I can only apologize,' she said quietly.

'For what?' I cried. 'I'm not an ogre, you know, my dear.'

'This I know.'

'Well, then. What say you and I become better acquainted?'

Aggie looked shocked. I had meant what it sounded like I meant, naturally, but I quickly converted my statement into something far more innocuous. 'Tell me your story.'

'No, no. I must go. I shall . . . I shall see you tomorrow.'

She averted her eyes again and slipped out into the corridor, closing the door behind her with a soft click.

I'd discovered from the girl that the *Stiffkey* was heading for Norfolk, swinging round the south coast of England and putting in at one or other of the tiny harbours that pepper that haunted coastline. The thought of home, however straitened my circumstances, was like a balm. Flarge would ensure I was a wanted man but I felt that the reassurance of British soil would do me the power of good.

But what exactly was I to do when I got there? Continue with my mission to investigate Mons? Plead my case with the frankly unsympathetic Joshua Reynolds? Or piece together whatever strange clues linked the silken relic (presumably the 'lamb' of which Volatile had spoken) and the dead man's reference to the Convent of St Bede?

I lay back on the bunk, luxuriating in the relative freshness of my linen. The old divine's name, of course, suggested some northern locale, possibly as far as Northumberland, but I had a vague intuition that the *Stiffkey* had been chosen for a reason. After all, Volatile was desperate to find safety. It wasn't in his interests to go tramping across half of England when he felt sure his life was in peril.

But all that could wait until I was on terra firma. For now, I had the *Stiffkey* to investigate. The ship was apparently carrying dry goods – a description that might cover a multitude of sins. I knew Mons had some interest in the old bucket, but what? He and Corpusty had been thick as thieves when I'd seen them on the quayside what seemed like weeks before. A spot of rooting about was definitely in order.

I waited until the ship had settled down for the night before slipping out of my cabin.

Keeping snug to the stained woodwork of the corridor, I crept into the old tub's bowels, passing the captain's door – no sign of life – and the galley. I peered into the gloom. Bullfrog the cook lay in a stained hammock that creaked back and forth with the motion of the ship. But he wasn't alone. His good arm was draped over, of all things, a salted pig. It nestled alongside him in the hammock, glazed eyes seeming to watch me as I slipped past the door. These voyages do get awful lonely, don't you know?

There was even less light down here but I knew I was getting close to the engine rooms. Sea water sloshed about my ankles and there came the constant tattoo of shifting cargo, banging about in the hold.

I chose the closest door and stole inside. The hold was foetid and in total darkness so I lit a match, trusting that Captain Corpusty's 'dry goods' were not sticks of dynamite. In the brief flare of light, I saw that I was surrounded by about a dozen crates, each branded with what looked like a Maltese cross. I used the remaining light to position myself by the nearest crate and then, as the match spent itself, began to wrench at the lid in the darkness.

The wood protested as I managed to force my ruined fingernails between the slats and then, with an astonishingly loud *crack*, the lid broke open. I felt about inside the crate and was answered by a curious dry, stirring sound. I fumbled in my trouser pocket and drew out the matchbox, lit another lucifer and stared down at the treasure. I laughed lightly. Of the things I thought I might see . . .

The crate was full of Communion wafers.

'*Hosts* of them,' I grunted to myself.

I turned in shock as the door to the hold swung open and a figure was revealed, silhouetted against the dim light from the corridor.

'Mr Volatile?'

It was Aggie. I breathed a sigh of relief, got to my feet and stepped back into the corridor. Taking the girl by the arm, I flashed her my most endearing smile. 'Best not say anything about this, my dear. I lost my way, you see, and was so damned curious about what this old wreck might be carrying—'

But Aggie had a puzzled look on her face as if my sneaking about was of no consequence. 'I beg your pardon, sir,' she said with her accustomed gravitas, 'but the captain asks if you would be so good as to join him for a *nightcap*.'

I straightened up in surprise. 'Eh?'

Aggie nodded. 'You are privileged, Mr Volatile. Captain Corpusty does not usually find time for such pleasantries.'

That was what worried me.

Nevertheless, I closed the door to the hold and dutifully followed Aggie out into the listing corridor. Another set of steps and we were at the captain's door.

A barked '*Come!*' was the response to Aggie's knock and I was ushered in.

The cabin was a riot of disorder; charts and books lay everywhere, drawings and photographs had been tacked to the wooden walls and there were grotesquely carved African masks and a guitar made from alligator-hide slung lazily from the ceiling.

Captain Corpusty was of a piece with his room. He looked up from his contemplation of a book and the lamplight flashed in his yellowish eyes.

'Ah, yes. Mr . . . Volatile.'

I shook his hand. 'At your service, Captain.'

'No, no. No indeed. It is I who should be at yours, sir. I'm heartily sorry not to have properly extended my hospitality earlier in the voyage but I'm a busy man, as you can see.'

He gestured about at the disarray and gave a helpless shrug. His gaze flicked over my shoulder. 'That will be all, Aggie.'

The girl flashed me a worried look and slipped out, the door clicking behind her. Something about the captain's manner and the memory of those eyes boring into my back made me extremely jumpy all of a sudden. Why had the previously unresponsive Corpusty suddenly turned so friendly?

'Drink?'

I accepted gratefully and relished the grog, though the captain knocked back his own measure of brandy in one go. I cradled the chipped custard glass and smiled warmly at him.

'I'm very grateful for your expert seamanship, sir,' I began. 'I know the Atlantic can be treacherous and—'

'Now, then,' he cut across me abruptly, 'let's not waste time.'

'How's that?' I queried.

Corpusty glanced idly down at his book and I caught sight of the lurid, hand-coloured illustrations. 'It's a rum old life out here on the seas,' he grumbled, like some old-world pirate, 'but we're more up to date than you might expect. The *Stiffkey*'s got many of the modern conveniences.'

I found this very hard to believe. 'Really? Don't tell me that cook of yours is a maestro trained at Delmonico's?'

He gave a throaty laugh and his grey skin puckered unpleasantly about the eyes. 'No, sir. But we do have wireless. And we picks up all kinds of chatter on a lonely night. All kinds of chatter . . . *Mr Box*.'

I felt suddenly cold. As cold as though I'd been standing on the prow of the rusty old vessel and Atlantic spray had covered me head to foot. 'Aha,' I said at last.

Corpusty rubbed at his chin and it made a sound like sandpaper. 'Fact is, there's all hell broken loose. The Yanks are after you and have put out a description and a mighty big reward. All I have to do is wire them and the British coppers'll be ready with a nice welcoming party when we pitch up in Norfolk.'

I looked levelly at him. 'So why haven't you?'

'P'raps I've got a natural sympathy for those a little outside the law.'

Oh, Lor, I thought. It can't be my body he's after, can it? Bullfrog's porcine pal showed how lonesome these jack tars could get but surely there were nicer sprats to be landed? And, if like me, he travelled on the number 38 bus as well as the 19 (you get my drift) then a comely little piece like Aggie was surely more in the grizzled old fellow's line? Perhaps it was the novelty he craved. Able to take his pick of the fresh-faced young'uns, Corpusty had long ago tired of feeling the hot, quick breath of the cabin girl as she slipped onto his grimy mattress.

An extremely unpleasant vision leapt into my mind and I hastily banished it. Corpusty seemed to read my thoughts and slammed his meaty fist onto his desk. 'I'm not a savage, sir!' he barked. Then he gestured around the squalid cabin. 'As you can see.'

For the first time, I looked in some detail at the pictures that had been tacked to the walls. To my utter astonishment, I now saw that they were, to a man, photographic representations of Old Masters. Here was Velázquez sharing a warped beam with a Venetian Madonna. An unfinished Romney overlapped the capacious bosom of a flabby Rubens. And dotted between them, Sargents, Whistlers and . . . me! I recognized in quick succession the portrait I'd done of Lloyd George just after the end of the last show that the House of Commons had commissioned, then refused to hang, and an earlier picture of a lovely girl with cornflowers in her hair, which had first brought me to the world's attention.

Captain Corpusty nodded solemnly. 'As I say, Mr Box, I am not a savage. If fate had conspired otherwise, I might have made a living from the canvas and the brush as you have done, but I wasn't so lucky. But I've a brain in my head and a keen eye for beauty. And I should deem it an honour, an *honour*, sir, if you would consent to cast an eye over my humble scribblings.'

I blinked in absolute astonishment.

'Good God,' I breathed at last. 'You're a fan!'

11

A Whiff Of Brimstone

I have known, in my time, many species of praise. The charming art mistress who initiated me into the ways of the world – and of, incidentally, oil pastel – was very fond of the little hollow at the base of my throat just below the Adam's apple. Many a lazy summer afternoon was passed with waxen fruit un-rendered and her pretty, heart-shaped face nestled there, beads of sweat rolling like pearls from her brow.

Then there was the renowned critic with morbidly unruly chest hair who, seeking to make up for his withering of my doodles, chased me around a slipper bath with his tumescent member poking from his pinstripes.

And then there was the boy with the very blue eyes who smelled of honey and stayed by my side for almost ten years until . . . ah, well. *C'est la vie. C'est la guerre.*

Captain Corpusty's effulgent response to my presence, however, counted amongst the best.

'I don't care what you've done or not done, sir,' he announced. 'Far as I'm concerned you're a genius of the first water and that's' – emphasized with slap on corduroyed knee – '*that.*' I had been starved of appreciation for so long I almost wept.

Thus passed the next few days of the voyage, yours truly casting a practised eye over the smelly old pirate's artwork in return for a faithful promise to set me ashore at some unknown spot where the peelers wouldn't find me.

My habit was to rise early and then make my way down to Corpusty's chaotic diggings, where he'd be waiting with a pot of stewed Darjeeling and another of his rather ropey canvases in which the sea, would you credit it, featured heavily. So heavily, in fact, that I began to grow weary of its crudely executed form, ladled onto Norfolk landscapes or Atlantic storm-scapes in thick grey impasto resembling sea-gull excrement.

The routine was enlivened by the captain's occasional foray into portraiture, mostly wretched, though he'd caught something of friend Aggie's impish charm in a pencil sketch that appeared to have been executed during a typhoon.

'Don't spare my blushes, Mr Box,' Corpusty would cackle. 'I can take criticism.'

He couldn't, of course. Who can? So I was extremely careful to lard him with praise for his amateurish efforts lest he think twice and ditch me into the rollers.

Of course, I could see where all this was leading, and the fatal moment arrived one evening after dinner when Corpusty was treating me to a not-indifferent Amontillado. 'I don't suppose,' he said, screwing up one eye as he lit a cigar from the candle, 'you'd ever consent to making a picture . . . of me?'

The old fellow asked it as shyly as a school-girl. Eager to please, I pooh-poohed my talents once more, made a show of resistance but then grudgingly consented. A portrait in oils was completely out of the question given the incessant pitch and roll of the *Stiffkey*, but I would just about be able to manage a creditable pencil sketch.

Mon Capitaine said little during these sittings but simply sat and smoked, occasionally outlining his plans for my disembarkation, which consisted of plonking me in a rowing boat just off the coast whilst the *Stiffkey* herself steamed onwards to Cromer. According to the wireless, all the main ports were being watched, but Corpusty was confident the route he'd dreamt up would put me out of harm's way.

Once or twice I gently probed him as to the nature of his business, hoping that Olympus Mons's name might pop up, but the leathery sailor seemed to be keeping those particular cards very close to his tattooed chest.

As we churned through the leaden Atlantic towards England I actually found a measure of peace in my scribblings. Corpusty's ravaged countenance with its heavy lids and ragged, gin-blossomed nostrils provided real inspiration. Of one thing I was extremely conscious, though: the *Stiffkey* was possessed of a most peculiar atmosphere that hung about it like a noxious cloud. It wasn't just the hissing and chuffing of the ancient engines, nor yet the stifling fug of the airless passageways. There was about the ship a sort of dread, drear gloom, a feeling that something malign lay at its very heart, like the shuttered door to a secret room in some Gothic romance.

I am not a superstitious man. The closest I had ever come to encountering the other side was during the lurid business of the Cardinal's Windpipe. I dare say you read about it in the picture papers. A decrepit Stuart pile (a house, you understand, not a person) was being 'haunted' by a ghastly apparition in a tricorne hat. Turned out to be a doe-eyed youth trying to frighten a hated cousin out of her inheritance. After much kerfuffle, I'd done the decent thing and well, *laid* the ghost.

So, naturally, I shrugged off the curious atmosphere aboard the creaking old tub until an incident occurred that could not be so easily dismissed.

During an afternoon sitting for Corpusty's portrait, I ventured to enquire how he'd managed to come by such a lovely creature as Aggie for a crew member.

He pulled at his pipe and gave a throaty chuckle. 'Wondered when you'd get round to that. Quite the peach, ain't she?'

'Indian?' I asked, coyly, rubbing at the paper with my lead-darkened fingers.

'Yar. With a dash of Swiss, so I'm told.'

'My ears pricked up at this mention of the land of cantons and holed cheese. 'How exotic.'

Corpusty's addled eyes twinkled naughtily. 'You fancying a bit of a Swiss roll, eh, Mr Box?'

I laughed lightly. 'What *can* you mean, Captain?'

Corpusty settled himself more comfortably in his chair. 'Can't say as I blame you. But you'll get nowhere. Aggie Daye's as pure as the driven. On account of her upbringing.'

'Oh yes?'

'Yar. *Nuns,*' he said, pointedly, coughing up a ball of phlegm and spitting it against the cabin wall.

My ears pricked so far they practically grazed the tobacco-glazed ceiling. 'Nuns?' I watched the phlegm roll over the Madonna of the Rocks and Whistler's mother before disappearing behind a cracked lampshade. 'This was in Switzerland, yes?'

Corpusty shook his head, jabbing his pipe in my direction as though scoring a point. 'No! You'd never believe it, but she's local to Norfolk. Settled in my neck of the woods when she weren't no more than a mawther.'

'Hm?'

'A young girl,' he translated.

I affected nonchalance, concentrating on the drawing for a full minute before asking: 'In a convent, you mean?'

Corpusty nodded. 'Funny old place. Out on a causeway.'

My heart thumped in my chest. 'St Bede's?'

Corpusty frowned. 'Dunno. Least ways, don't ring no bells.

Though, if it's a convent, I s'pose it does! Rings bells, that is! Ha ha! *St Bede's.* Suppose it could be. Why? You heard of it?'

'Read about it in some gazetteer or other,' I said with a dismissive shrug.

Corpusty folded his arms and looked up at the low ceiling, where a hurricane lamp swung restlessly to and fro. 'Funny to recall how I first clapped eyes on one of them holy sisters. All black and white like a puffin bird. I wor only a boy and I thought it wor a spook! I says to old Ben – he wor cap'n of this ship afore me – just put that thar crate down, Ben, and lookee yonder, for there's a ghost a-drifting 'cross the pier towards us or I'm a Dutchman.'

I nodded indulgently.

' "Well," says he. "Reckon you'd better break out your clogs, young'un,'cos that's one o' them bloomin' brides of Christ!"'

Corpusty slapped his thigh again, then drifted off into a brown study. 'Poor old Ben. Basking shark took him. Funny, that. I mean, they's harmless creatures and I ain't never heard of no one dying 'cos of 'em, but this shark sort of *sucked* him to death and . . .'

He roused himself. 'Funny buggers, in't they?'

'Basking sharks?'

'Nuns! Fancy wasting their lives on that all that tosh. I ain't never had much truck with Jesus.'

'You do surprise me.' I shaded in the shadows beneath the captain's drooping earlobes. 'So how did Aggie get from being lodged at the convent to sitting below decks on the *Stiffkey* darning your socks?' I continued. 'Ran away to sea, did she?'

Corpusty smiled, relishing the pleasure of slowly unfolding the tale, like a grandfather telling ghost stories round a Christmas fireside.

'Not quite,' he said at last. 'Not quite. I was . . . approached one day. On the quay. The Mother Superior it was, and . . .' He clapped his pipe into his mouth. 'Well, that's another story.'

Feigning indifference, I yawned and stretched. 'I'm done for now, Captain. Might snatch a nap before dinner.'

Corpusty nodded and, with a contented hum, absorbed himself in some chart or other.

I had retreated to my cabin, somewhat fagged out, when Aggie's familiar light knock sounded at the door.

'Come!'

Ribbons of fog drifted inside with the girl, creeping around the jamb like the tentacles of a spectral sea-beast.

'A bad fog is coming up, Mr Volatile,' she said, shaking her head.

'Well,' I said cheerily. 'Don't fret.'

There was no response. Clearly the vernacular hadn't penetrated the walls of the convent. 'You'll be glad to be getting home soon, I expect,' I continued at length.

'Home? Norfolk is not my home,' she replied, mournfully, like something out of Chekhov.

'You favour New York?'

She shook her head, still glum. 'The *Stiffkey* is my only home.'

I sat down on the bunk, gesturing round at the grim interior. 'I can understand that. I mean, why would you want to live anywhere else?'

She looked at me with her huge, tragic eyes. 'Yes. I would miss the bright lights.' Suddenly she grinned and her melancholy beauty was instantly transformed into something altogether delightful. The smile was infectious and I returned it with enthusiasm.

Aggie knew nothing of my planned escape – as far as she was concerned I was simply a fare-paying passenger to be landed at Cromer with the rest of their cargo. Yet at that moment I had a tremendous urge to confide in her. I simply didn't want to say good-bye to this fascinating creature. As I've already indicated, and happily for me, I've always taken whatever's pretty whenever it comes along. Makes life so much more interesting, don't you know?

'Look,' I said gently, 'you've been awfully good to me these last days. Before we part forever, isn't there something I can do to say thanks?'

Her eyes bored into mine, suddenly serious again, then she bounded onto the bunk, knocked me flat on my back and kissed me with somewhat startling fervour.

I hardly had time to respond when she pulled away, licking her lips thoughtfully, and frowning.

'So. This is how it is to kiss a man. I think it is disappointing.'

She began to move off but I grabbed her arm to pull her back. 'Hang on!' I entreated. 'You caught me off guard, my dear. It's really much nicer if we both have a go.'

So saying, I let her crumple into my embrace and planted a long, lingering smacker on her dark lips whilst running my hand over the knotty tufts of her cropped hair. She relaxed a little, then stretched out like a cat, pressing her body tightly to mine.

After the appalling stresses and privations of the past weeks, I felt a kind of fuzzy warmth flood through me like an infusion of sunlight, and my hips moved instinctively forward to grind against the girl's, our belt buckles scraping together. Then Aggie pulled away, giggling.

She flopped back onto the pillow and leant her head on her hand, gazing at me, searchingly. 'I have never in my life thought to do such a thing before.'

Hang on, I thought, there's plenty more still to do! One chaste kiss isn't the bally be-all and end-all.

I stroked the creamy curve of her jaw. 'Aggie Daye,' I murmured. 'Short for Agatha, is it?'

The girl said nothing but languorously closed and re-opened her eyes.

I decided to press my advantage. 'The captain tells me you were raised in a convent—'

She sat up with an angry hiss. 'He had no right to tell you that! No right at all!'

'Hey, hey, hey!' I soothed, slipping an arm round her waist. She resisted and wriggled towards the edge of the bed, trying to plant both feet on the cabin floor. 'It's all right, Aggie,' I cried. 'This isn't an interrogation. I'm just interested, that's all.'

She turned her flushed face towards me, her lip turned down petulantly. 'They did not raise me!' she said proudly, sinking back against the wall, arms folded. 'They imprisoned me!'

'What do you mean?'

Aggie looked glum and her eyes suddenly swam with tears. She let them roll over her cheeks, then impatiently wiped them away. 'All I wanted was to be like them. As good as them. But the sisters told me it was impossible. I was *special*. So special, they kept me locked up!'

Gently, I pulled her back so that her head lay on my chest. She suddenly gave in to racking sobs and I stroked her head, making the soothing sounds one does on these occasions. I said nothing for a long time.

This was all terribly mysterious. Sal Volatile knew of the Convent of St Bede. Indeed it was the only place he said he'd feel safe. But why? And was this beautiful girl somehow caught up in it all?

I was mulling this over when I suddenly became aware that Aggie had stopped crying. At first I assumed she'd drifted into sleep but then I felt a soft fumbling at my fly buttons and an immediate tumescence in my moleskins.

Aggie's neat little hand slipped inside my trousers and I felt a thrill of desire as her cold fingertips connected with my thighs, instantly prickling the skin into goose-flesh.

Lifting her head from my chest, I gazed into her night-black eyes and then leant to kiss her once more, my stubbly chin scratching her soft, downy face. Her lips parted with sudden ferocity, like a snarling lioness, and she bit at my face and tongue. I pushed her down onto the bunk and dragged the sweater from her body, revealing a long, marble-smooth neck and perfect, pert breasts, the nipples huge and brown as toffee.

With practised ease, I slipped out of my trousers and wrenched down Aggie's own till they reached her knees, passion preventing any further undressing.

Must I burden you with the details of that night? Of how we thrashed about in the none-too-clean sheets, plunging towards ecstasy till almost dawn? Of my lean and lithe body (it still was, I swear!) conjoining with hers, our legs intertwining, our mad kisses, locked in a fevered embrace that for a few sweet stolen hours banished all thoughts of Sal Volatile, Percy Flarge, nuns, lambs and mysterious Cabalistic handkerchiefs?

Well, it was shaping up to be a dashed good shag, is all I can tell you, when something rather uncommon occurred.

Quite suddenly, the incessant pounding of the waves against the rusty hull fell quiet, as though I were in a kinema and the sound had suddenly shut off. Even the constant asthmatic grumbling of the ship's engines stilled. I glanced down at Aggie's face but her eyes were screwed tightly shut in pleasure, fully absorbed in the matter in hand. Yet I knew in my very bones that if I opened my mouth to cry out, not a sound would escape me.

And, all at once, the air in the cabin began to thicken. A strange bluey haze, like wood-smoke, began to bleed through it, hanging in trailing threads, one layer overlapping another like a formation of storm clouds. Deep, deep within the smoke there was a noiseless detonation, as though I was looking down the twin barrels of a shotgun, and two points of red light, glowing hellishly like coals, blossomed into life.

I knew even before the smoke that surrounded them began to take on the vague, ectoplasmic structure of some nightmarish face that these ghastly, glowing embers were *eyes*.

I choked in shock and ceased my coupling. Aggie stirred beneath me, and as I felt cold sweat trickle down my neck, the spectre began to take on more solid form, the blood-red eyes leering out from a long, goatish face, crazed with deep lines, black as gunpowder. There was no nose, only a hellish, skeletal hole edged about with scraps of mouldering fur. As for the mouth, it never seemed fully to form. Only a terrible, gaping, indefinite maw occupied the lower half of the face, the bluey smoke drifting in and out of its orbit like rank breath. But in its baleful black emptiness I seemed to see all the dismal, hateful things of the world distilled. I was seized by a sudden, blank terror, rolled off Aggie and curled up into a ball.

I could feel the girl's hands shaking me by the shoulders but still there was no sound.

I glanced fearfully over her shoulder and the goatish face broke into a filthy heathen grin.

Then I screamed.

12

Troubled Waters

The pounding of the waves and the wheezing of the engines crashed back into my consciousness with the force of Dempsey's right hook. I recall opening wide my eyes and calling out, before sinking into the cool embrace of the pillow, where I must have fallen into a deep, deep sleep.

When at last I awoke, there was no sign of Aggie. Lord knows what she must've been thinking, *pauvre petite*, choosing me as her first tumble only for yours truly to screech into her lovely face some little way from any kind of, shall we say, resolution.

My thoughts, though, were somewhat disarranged. I own I was in a total funk, trembling all over and covered in a sheen of cold sweat. What the hell had I seen? Or, indeed, what *from hell* had I seen? It could only have been some fevered hallucination. Perhaps the noxious fumes from the ship's engines had finally taken their toll?

I shuddered at the memory of that dreadful apparition and tried to dismiss it, yet even as my eyes closed the hateful, bestial face sprang back into my mind. Further sleep seemed impossible and I'd pretty much made up my mind to track Aggie down in order to apologize when I heard heavy footsteps in the passage outside.

Staggering unsteadily from the bed and opening the door just a fraction, I caught sight of the woolly-headed sailor who'd taken my papers when first I'd come aboard. He was carrying one of the crates I'd seen in the hold, branded with a Maltese cross, though this one was small and knotted with tarry string.

I let him pass from view, took several deep breaths to right myself, then slipped out of the cabin and followed.

The corridors of the vessel were as stifling as rabbit warrens, swirling with oily vapour and shaking incessantly with the drumming of engines. Passing door after closed door, I suddenly flattened myself against the wall as Woolly-Head gave a stealthy look back and crept into the crew's quarters.

I waited a few moments, then bobbed my head around the jamb.

It was almost completely dark inside but I could make out the sound of stifled giggles and, as my eyes grew accustomed to the murk, the Behemothal form of Bullfrog the cook, squatting on the floor clad only in his shatteringly awful underwear. Above the perished elastic waistline hung ropes of flabby flesh.

Bullfrog was concentrating intently on something at his feet. I strained to see. It was the crate! The string had been sliced off and his meaty hand and rusted hook were busily scrabbling about inside. I could hear vague grinding sounds and for one crazed moment assumed he was preparing supper for his pals.

Woolly-Head was giggling with a kind of manic glee. 'In the name of the father,' he said between hyena laughs. 'And of the son . . .'

'And of the holy ghost!' chorused the others, Bullfrog making a horrible wet response as though swallowing a live eel.

To my astonishment, I saw the mute lift a Communion wafer from the box and break it in two. Then he dropped the two halves into a little pot and began to grind up the stuff with a pestle.

I looked on in fascination as he tipped the powder onto a tin tray and proceeded to divide it into neat lines.

And then I understood. I'd seen Corpusty deep in confab with Olympus Mons and now here was the connection that bound them together! Mons was behind the massive influx of cocaine into Manhattan – smuggled innocuously across the Atlantic in the form of Communion wafers!

And now the *Stiffkey*'s crew were presumably enjoying the leftovers, the last few crates left unsold to Mons's New York supplier. Woolly-Head, Bullfrog and the others bowed their heads as if in prayer and partook of the cocaine in a great snuffling orgy, like sweaty pigs round a truffle-rich tree.

I used the distraction to creep past, but had gone no more than a few yards when a door flew open and Captain Corpusty was revealed, his bulk silhouetted against the glow of the hurricane lamp within.

'Trouble sleeping?' he said, cocking his head to one side.

''Fraid so!' I extemporised. 'Martyr to insomnia, alas. Do you . . . do you mind if I carry on with the picture?'

The old bruiser didn't seem more than faintly surprised and happily consented to this evening shift, busying himself with brewing tea and pouring booze as I sharpened my pencils with a pearl-handled knife.

We sat in silence as I laboured steadily away, my mind racing the whole time, only Corpusty's breathing and the scratch of the lead pencils disturbing the stillness. I had fallen into a kind of trance when there came a light double knock and Aggie's be-capped head appeared around the door.

I flashed her a reassuring look but she completely ignored me, merely announcing we would be in sight of the eastern coast of England that very night. Through busy contractions of my brows, I tried to telegraph my profoundest apologies but the girl didn't even favour me with a glance as she ducked back into the corridor.

Grumpily, I hastened to finish my picture of the captain, ending with a hasty flourish around his wiry eyebrows of which I wasn't particularly proud. I called to the fellow and he craned over my shoulder, nodding appreciatively as I laid down my pencils for the final time.

'Marvellous!' he cried. 'Marvellous, Mr Box! A ruddy triumph. I never dreamed I'd see this day! But there's a little something you've neglected.'

I frowned, looking the portrait over. 'I don't think so.'

Corpusty chuckled. 'Why, your signature, sir! Just scribble it at the bottom there.'

'I thought you a student of my work, Captain,' I said lightly. 'Don't you know I never sign?'

He laughed and rubbed at his chin. 'Of course, of course! I just wondered, perhaps this one time. As a special favour . . .'

'It would be very odd to make an exception, even for you.'

Corpusty nodded, grunted and gestured helplessly with both hands. 'But how else is it to be . . .?' he began. Then, with a sudden burst of energy, he clapped one hand on my shoulder. 'Forgive the hasty words of a mere amateur, Mr Box. For genius is visible in every line, every battered old contour you've rendered of this old mug o' mine! And I shall treasure it, sir. Treasure it as long as I live. These past few days have been a joy to me. Now, let's see about getting you home and safe.'

He gave orders for the rowing boat to be prepared for launch just before dawn, we shook hands and I left him sizing up the sketch, pride lighting up his ravaged features. I made my way back, a mite unsteadily, to my own cabin and began to make ready for disembarkation.

Firstly, I made sure the precious silk relic was still safely stowed within my money belt, then I turned my attention to Percy Flarge's stolen automatic. I was wrapping it in oilskin and secreting it in a pea coat (another treasure the lovely Aggie had procured) when I straightened up, convinced that someone was standing on the other side of the woodwork. Throwing open the door, I revealed Aggie crouched low, her eye level with the keyhole.

She turned at once on her heel but I dashed forward and jerked her back.

'Now you wish to touch me!' she cried. 'Before, I disgust you so much that you flee from my embrace!'

'No, no, no,' I insisted. 'It wasn't like that at all—'

Aggie wriggled about as I tried to restrain her. 'Get off me! I do not wish to see you—'

'Then why were you spying at my door, hm?'

'I was not!'

'Look!' I yelled with finality. 'Just listen for a moment, damn you!'

I dragged her further into the cabin and kicked the door shut. Aggie looked a little shocked and fell silent.

I rubbed my weary face. 'What happened before, it was nothing to do with you. You're divine, my dear, really you are. The cat's pyjamas. But something dashed odd happened. I . . . I saw something. In the air above us. A . . . a sort of face.'

Aggie stiffened in my arms. 'Face?'

I led her back towards the bunk, more or less content that she wouldn't flee. 'It sounds like utter rot, I know. But it was like some demon had appeared. Scared the bloody life out of me.'

Aggie's smooth brown cheeks had drained of colour. 'You have seen it too!'

'You mean—?'

'Yes!' cried the girl. 'Perhaps three or four times since I came to live aboard the *Stiffkey*. At first I thought it was a dream, but . . .'

'No dream,' I insisted. 'But maybe it's some foul concoction Bullfrog puts in the ship's grub? There's narcotics aboard, Aggie. Cocaine. Perhaps there might be other stuff. Heady stuff from Kingston or Shanghai intended to dope us. But why?'

Aggie's countenance resumed its solemn aspect. 'I do not believe this to be true. I have long felt that there is something strange about this ship. The face of the demon – that was just one more part of it. But then I began to feel . . .' She shook her head dismissively.

'No,' I urged. 'Go on.'

'I felt that it was watching over me,' Aggie bit her lip. 'Like . . . like a guardian.'

She turned her fathomless eyes towards me and then, like a child needing reassurance, draped her arms around my neck and we slid back onto the bed.

Though my first instinct was to take advantage, like the good Christian I'm not, I let the girl fall asleep with her head on my chest. With nothing to do until my dawn departure, I attempted to fall into the arms of Morpheus myself.

Yet sleep stubbornly refused to come. I tried to concentrate on the rhythmic motion of the ship and the familiar chug of the engines, yet still I lay awake, my eyes burning.

At first my brain fizzed with chaotic thoughts. Why was I being falsely accused of Volatile's death? He'd been alive, if injured, when last I'd seen him, so what had happened whilst I was drugged? Who had put three bullets in his lungs? Who stood to gain? Was Flarge so ludicrously jealous that he was behind the whole mad scheme?

There was something else, though, something the captain had said, and it kept jabbing at my thoughts like a fat bluebottle banging against a windowpane. That little exchange of ours after I'd completed his drawing. What had he muttered when I'd refused to sign the damned thing?

But how else is it to be . . .?

To be *what*?

I sat up in my bunk, making Aggie stir. How is it to be *identified*?

I knew all at once, with terrible certainty, that I was about to be betrayed. Looking down at my wristwatch I saw that it was twenty minutes to four.

As carefully as I could, I disentangled myself from Aggie's embrace, reached down for my discarded coat and carefully removed Flarge's pistol from its oilskin wrapper.

I glanced quickly towards the bunk – the girl was still sleeping peacefully – then creaked open the cabin door and stole out into the darkness.

The old ship rolled unsteadily beneath my bare feet as I padded through the dinge.

An irregular electronic bleeping told me I was nearing the *Stiffkey*'s radio room. I crouched down in the shadows of the weird greenish aura given off by the dial. Inside the room, Corpusty and Woolly-Head – acting as operator – were conversing in low voices.

'Understood,' said the Captain. I could see his great thick bonce, nodding in silhouette. 'Rendezvous oh-four-thirty hours,' he continued, the sharp, insistent bleep of the Morse telegraph sending out his message into the ether. 'Package to be taken off and . . . disposed of at your discretion.'

Woolly-Head laughed his hissing laugh and Corpusty joined in, throatily.

So there it was! The jolly old smuggler was trying to have his cake and eat it. He meant to turn me in, collect the reward and then, at some later date, flog off the picture I'd done of him. The provenance would be impeccable and my price was bound to rocket once I'd been hanged as a murderer.

I cursed the talentless booby. I'd steal a march on him yet!

There was very little time, though, before the rendezvous. I was supposed to be roused just before dawn for my pretended escape, Corpusty evidently bargaining on catching me asleep.

Feet slapping against the rotten old planking, I dashed back to my cabin. As quietly as I could, I crept back inside – to be met by the blade of a knife jabbing at my cheek.

Aggie sighed with relief and let the weapon drop. 'It is you! I am glad. I woke up and was afraid – what is wrong?'

I stuffed away the pistol. 'Change of plan. Corpusty's trying to double-cross me. I'm off.'

'Double-cross you? But why?'

I decided against putting on my boots. There might be swimming to come and I didn't much fancy being dragged down by the steel toecaps.

'Long story, my pet,' I said with a smile. 'You coming?'

'What?'

'Are you coming with me?' I said, crossing to the cabin door and swinging it open.

Aggie violently shook her head. 'No! I cannot do that!'

'Why ever not, for God's sake? What is there for you here?'

'The *Stiffkey* is my life. I owe everything to the captain.'

'The same captain who's about to give me up for filthy lucre?' I whispered.

She looked pained and confused. 'These people are my comrades. My world.'

I sighed. 'Listen, I need to tell you something. My name's not Volatile, it's Box. Lucifer Box. I'm on the run from America because someone's accused me of murder. Your precious Corpusty is even now arranging for the police to meet this ship and take me away. I'm completely innocent. Well, not completely. There'll come a reckoning outside the Pearly Gates, I shouldn't wonder. But if you like me and you want to help, I'd be most awfully grateful. Are you game?'

Aggie dipped her head, evidently shocked by this revelation. I ruffled her jet-black hair. 'Listen, Ishmael, you can stay. Of course you can. But do you really think your life'll be worth a fig once Corpusty realizes you helped me escape?'

She looked as grave as ever.

'Then there's this convent of yours and the smuggling operation and that devilish face. Don't you want to get to the bottom of it all?'

The girl looked far from certain.

'And then,' I continued. 'There's that private business of ours that was so rudely interrupted—'

Aggie suddenly flashed me a winning smile. 'I shall come!'

'I'm so glad! Now, let's not waste any more time. Come on.'

Tucking in at my elbow, Aggie stepped with me into the corridor. It was ill-lit and suddenly seemed threatening as the pair of us stole quickly along its rocking length, making our way up the rusted stairs to the deck.

At once, I saw that Nature was on my side. The fret that Aggie had earlier complained of had matured into a dense and oily fog, slowing up the *Stiffkey*'s progress and giving us a wondrous cover for our escape.

Aggie and I crept across the deck, treading carefully to avoid the creaking boards, until we reached the rail, the paint all blistered and rusted like that on a seaside pier. The boat, as leaky and unpromising as her parent craft, lay alongside. Corpusty had no doubt ensured it was prepared as planned in case insomniac old me had smelled a rat.

Swiftly, I put a leg over the side of the rail and glanced down at the little boat, swaying in the fog-shrouded swell.

Aggie held back.

'Don't fail me now!' I cried. 'You deserve a better life than this, Aggie! You know you do.'

I put my hand on the rail, preparing to vault over, when there came the harsh clang of metal on metal. Next to my hand had appeared Bullfrog's tin-opener appliance, ringing off the rail by my own vulnerable digits.

My head snapped up and there he was, a great Buddha in his stained underwear, towering over the two of us, his boiled-egg eyes alive with dope-fuelled malice.

13

Flight Across the Marshes

'Hell!' I cried, pulling my leg back over the railing and dodging the mulatto's claw as he swung it towards my head.

It was no good simply trying to make our escape by boat, the cook would raise the alarm and we'd be done for. The only solution was to silence the bugger – if a mute can be silenced – and in as permanent a fashion as possible. Taking advantage of Bullfrog's unwieldy bulk, I put my head down and charged him, connecting with his massive gut and sending him staggering backwards.

Bullfrog let out a guttural rasp, his half-tongue shifting in his mouth like a flayed thumb, then raised his metal claw to strike again.

Aggie was everywhere at once, raining blows onto the side of his head and kicking at his calves until he roared with fury, spit gushing from his lips. He lashed out as though swatting at a bothersome fly and I grabbed one of his massive arms, straining to keep the deadly barb from connecting with anything fleshy of mine.

Jabbing my elbow backwards into his face, I felt his nose break with a satisfying crunch but the beast was so powerful that he scarcely flinched and simply tossed me and Aggie aside like limp dolls.

Skidding over the slippery deck and almost toppling into the freezing sea, I saw Bullfrog stomping towards us again, looming out of the fog like a ghoul from an old sea yarn and waggling his tongue in fury.

Fumbling for the pistol, I tried to take aim but Bullfrog was too swift, smashing me to the deck with one great paw and then raising his harpoon-hand to impale me. The gun went sliding across the decks and vanished over the side.

This pleased Bullfrog, who set up a slobbering chuckle, sweat dribbling from his brick-like forehead and collecting in the pouchy bags beneath those manic, glittering eyes.

Then, all of a sudden, he came crashing down beside me with the force of a felled tree. I slid out of the way just in time. Aggie had clamboured onto the fo'c's'le behind him and swung a fire extinguisher against his temple with every ounce of strength she possessed.

Bullfrog shrieked in pain and put his good hand up to his face. Recognizing that we meant business, he began to stagger back towards the stairs, evidently intent on raising the alarm.

I scrabbled forward on my elbows, grabbed him by the ankles and yanked backwards. It was like trying to topple a block of granite. Aggie appeared at my side with the extinguisher, ready to swing again, but the brute lashed out and speared it with his hook.

At that moment, a terrific wave hit the *Stiffkey* and the vessel bucked violently, knocking the cook off balance.

It was all the chance I needed. Leaping up, I pulled his absurd chef's hat over his eyes and, as he struggled to see, I grabbed him by his filthy neckerchief and wrenched him down onto his knees.

He toppled over and, metal claw rendered useless by the impaled extinguisher, rolled like a carpet towards the railing. For a moment he lay like a crab on its back, flailing and gasping, then I skittered over the saturated boards after him. Planting my feet against his side, I gave a mighty kick and propelled the great monster over the side.

He gave one last strangled cry, there was a brief splash and he was swallowed up by the waves.

A strange quiet fell, disturbed only by the chugging of the engines.

'All right?' I gasped, turning to Aggie.

The girl looked a little dazed but then nodded quickly and jumped to her feet. 'Come!'

Incredibly, our desperate fisticuffs hadn't disturbed a soul. We climbed silently over the rails into the swaying dinghy, slipped from the capstan in seconds and began to row away from the ship for dear life.

The girl stayed at the stern, looking anxiously over her shoulder, expecting, as did I, that we would be discovered at any moment. Yet still I pulled at the oars, with no sign of life from the *Stiffkey*. The old ship gradually vanished into the fog as we struggled towards the mainland.

Aggie wanted to relieve me (from the rowing, you understand) but I demurred, although my arms seemed to have turned to jelly and I could scarcely feel my frozen feet. I prayed we would make landfall with all due despatch.

I rowed until I was sick with fatigue. Then, just as I felt my head nodding on my breast, there was a percussive explosion and the livid glow of a flare overhead. I sat up at once, rubbed my dry, exhausted eyes and looked for Aggie. She was staring upwards at the flare blossoming above us, briefly turning the fog-bank a hellish red.

'They're on to us!' I hissed. Aggie peered into the fog, looking for the first sign of the *Stiffkey* in pursuit. I could only hope we were on the right course. For all I knew I was pulling out to sea, possibly into some hazardous shipping lane where we would be crushed to matchwood.

Fear of capture gave me renewed energy. In my school days, despite my detestation of all forms of exercise, I'd been quite a dab hand at rowing, although I'd only joined the team in order to get closer to a chap called Reggie Side. He was a smasher with a cheeky grin and thighs upon which you could've landed a small aeroplane. Hey ho. Happiest days of your life, what?

Those days were long past, however, and my middle-aged muscles shrieked for release from this unexpected exertion.

Aggie's impish face was suddenly illumined ghoulishly by a yellow glare as she clicked on a flashlight. 'There is a promontory – a kind of spur – hereabouts,' she whispered. 'That is what we are heading for. But the fog . . .'

She trailed off, biting her lip anxiously and staring out into the solid wall of swirling moisture. I strained to hear the noise of the *Stiffkey*'s engines but there was only the steady splash of my oars in the water and the creak of the old boat.

Then, all at once, another sound intruded on my numbed senses: a steady, metrical *thrum*. A ship's engines, no doubt, but not those of the fagged-out old rust-bucket from which we'd escaped.

Suddenly, a big searchlight crackled into life and swung in our direction, throwing out a snow-white beam that bobbed and shifted over the surface of the sea.

'Police launch!' I yelled over the racket of its engines.

Aggie stood up in the boat, taking advantage of the sudden illumination to get her bearings. The craft rocked perilously. As the searchlight struggled towards us, she sat down heavily and pointed starboard. 'There! There!'

I needed no prompting and sculled feverishly in the designated direction. The searchlight, infuriatingly, found the retreating prow and we were suddenly blinded as its glare flooded over the boat.

A voice barked out, muffled by both fog and megaphone, and it was startling in that oppressive murk. 'This is the police! Prepare to be boarded!'

'Not bloody likely!' I muttered, wrenching at the paddles and craning my neck to spy out the elusive spur of land.

Not a moment too soon, the boat bumped against sand and I fell back, the oars skewing crazily and almost catching Aggie on the side of her head. She somersaulted over the side, the water coming to her waist. 'We've done it!' she cried. 'Quick! Ashore!'

I stumbled to my feet, then immediately ducked down as a bullet sang off the boat, sending splinters into the air in a little cloud. They were shooting at us. By James! Was this England?

More bullets hit the water – *ploop – ploop* – as I vaulted into the sea. The cold was intense and took my breath away but I knew we hadn't a moment to spare. Grabbing Aggie's hand, we waded ashore, hopelessly encumbered by our heavy clothes.

I dragged myself onto the shingle, weary to the very bone. Aggie followed suit and stood up, just as the damned searchlight swung round and lit her up, bright as day.

Another shot rang out. She looked briefly astonished, then fell back into my arms.

From somewhere, as though in a dream, I heard more barked commands from the police launch but paid them no heed. Aggie crumpled into my arms and went limp.

The huge dreary sky was beginning to streak with crimson as the dawn took hold, and in the rosy light, I could clearly see the hole in the girl's coat where the bullet had struck her.

'Aggie!' I whispered urgently. 'Are you . . .?'

'I am all right,' she whispered back. 'Please do not concern yourself.' But her eyelids were fluttering weakly and she sagged in my embrace. I yanked the coat from her back. The sweater beneath was darkening with blood. She'd only been struck in the shoulder, I was hugely relieved to see, but it was clear she could go no further.

As if reading my thoughts, she tried to focus on me, her eyes rolling in her head. 'Go! You must go!' she sighed, shakily batting my arm.

She was right, of course, and I had no intention of giving myself up to the bobbies just for her sake, but I nobly shook my head, striking my most heroic pose. 'I'm not leaving you like this,' I breathed, like an overwrought Ivor Novello.

'You must!' she cried. 'I will be all right.' She turned her head towards the sea, where the sound of the approaching police launch was growing louder. 'They are coming! Go, my dear, dark man! We shall meet again soon!'

'Right-oh!' I cried, brightly. Well, chivalry's all well and good but when a chap's liberty is at stake . . .

I laid her gently on the cold sand. Normally, I'd have been confident that, whatever charges were laid against her, we were no longer in America and she would at least be treated well. But the trigger-happy antics of our pursuers gave me pause.

'I'll find you,' I gallantly whispered in her ear. 'I promise.'

She nodded absently, already slipping into unconsciousness.

Taking to my heels, I didn't look back as I hared across the beach, my bare feet sending up sprays of shingle.

It was devilishly hard going. The 'spur' was scarcely more than that, a narrow strip of land with the dark sea on both sides and, as I ran, I willed it to become wider and more solid so as to provide me with at least a scrap of cover.

Perilously exposed, I risked a glance backwards as the sun rose like a dull guinea amidst the cloud. The police launch had beached and I could see a cluster of men around poor Aggie. There was a brief pause and then three of them began to pelt in my direction. I didn't wait for the next bullet but dashed on, clutching my clammy coat around me against the bitter, howling wind.

All at once, the shingle suddenly gave way to marshland but this provided scant relief. Exhaustingly, for every stretch of firm, reed-covered ground there was another of swampy morass. Time and again, I wasted valuable minutes tugging my frozen feet from the ground, the saturated soil gripping leech-like to my shins and only giving them up with a horrible, sucking belch.

I was conscious of little save the huge, cold sky and the smudge of land at the horizon. The bleak landscape was dotted all over with boats, stranded by the low tide, their rudders projecting in ungainly fashion from every limpet-encrusted stern.

Staggering on, I tripped and fell head-first into the reeds, sending a pair of geese clattering and squawking into the air. Lungs aching appallingly and with the familiar taste of iron in my mouth, I lay there for a long moment. I watched the geese flap off into the reddening sky, their path crisscrossed by a ragged 'V' of other birds winging south.

Utterly spent, I could hardly bear to raise my face from the embrace of the soaking soil and took long, laboured breaths, inhaling the scents of the marsh, the musty stink of the reeds, the distant aroma of woodsmoke.

Cracking open an eyelid, I suddenly saw salvation. Lying abandoned and almost completely covered in the long grass was the wreck of a fishing boat. It was upturned so that the peeling planks – Wedgwood blue and positively festive in that desolate landscape – faced the sky. It was exactly what I needed as a hiding place and I crawled towards the wooden shape hoping against hope that the interior was dry.

The knees of my trousers were soaked through to the skin but I inched onwards, pulling myself through a ragged hole in the disintegrating planks and into fusty but wonderful darkness.

I sank down, breath coming in great whooping bursts. It was hardly a permanent solution, but this shattered hull at least gave me room to think.

I could head for the nearest town. Despite my state of déshabillé, I'd pass for a sailor and I still had cash, tucked away in the soaking money-belt. But, of course, the place would be crawling with rozzers. I might as well turn up and bang a gong, announcing the arrival of the celebrated Lucifer Box: artist, bon-viveur, sexual athlete and wanted felon.

An uncontrollable shivering took hold of me and I hugged my knees in a vain effort to keep warm. I knew I should move on, find somewhere genuinely secure to rest, but I felt my head nodding again as the strain of the past few hours began to take its toll.

I snapped suddenly awake at the dreaded sound of baying hounds. With renewed desperation, I felt in my pocket for matches, hoping against hope that they were sufficiently dry to be of use. I stiffened as, below the noise of the pursuing dogs I became aware of another sound. Close to. A sort of *shuffling*.

At once, I tried the matches. Once, twice, three times, I rasped at the sandpaper without result until, suddenly, the little stalk flared into sulphurous life.

I grinned happily at my success until I saw what the match had illumined.

It was as though the whole of the stern of the ruined old boat were encrusted with jewels. Bright, shining shapes glittered at me like rubies in the darkness.

Eyes.

I gawped as the match spent its little life and then an horrendous squealing confirmed what I already knew. The place was alive, was *boiling* with rats.

Scrambling backwards on my rear, I made for the open air just as the mass of rodents exploded outwards and I was over-taken by a torrent of stinking fur. I cried out in sheer horror as they overwhelmed me, their teeth sinking into the fabric of my coat and trousers, their scaly tails, thick as my numbed fingers, thrashing about my face. Gagging with disgust, I tried to scramble under the rotten planks and out into the daylight but the tide of rodents overwhelmed me. I positively *swam* through the onslaught of fur and teeth, my arms flailing as I clawed at the wet ground and dragged myself through into the open air.

Then, all at once, as though obeying some silent command, the rats streamed away into the marshes like a trickle of oil.

Flat on my back, I looked up at the vast expanse of sky, chest heaving.

A strange quiet had descended and I sat up, looking about me. There was absolutely no sign of the pack of rats and not a sound to be heard: no curlew winging through the morning sky, no frog paddling in the soaking ground at my feet. Even the icy wind had dropped completely. I got to my feet and looked about, conscious of the same curious feeling of dread that had come upon me in my cabin on the *Stiffkey*. I felt with absolute certainty that if I stamped my foot it would make no sound whatsoever. It was as though the whole world had been smothered in cotton wool.

And then, as before, the clear air began to blur and change.

I froze in absolute terror as the dreadful, goatish face began to form once more, pitiless eyes shining redder and more lurid than those of the slavering rats. Closer to, the creature's flesh seemed like some horrid mixture of animal remains, squashed together beneath the wheels of a motor car.

As I watched, transfixed in absolute sweating terror, the tendrils of smoke drifted into the marshland and, with a horrible, shrieking peal, the pack of rats appeared once more, spilling out of the grass in three distinct lines, then merging into one. I steeled myself for their attack but the great charcoal-black phalanx took off across the wetland at a rate of knots. My skin crawled at the awful sight of them.

Yet this was nothing compared to the frightful apparition

hovering in the air beside me. I tried to look away but it was as though some queer magnetism were working on my strained frame. My eyelids quivered and my face glowed with cold perspiration as a sense of utter despair took hold of me and I sank to my knees on the spongy ground.

Then, as suddenly as if I'd been slapped across the face, the spell was broken. I cried out in horror, shocked by the sound of my own voice – but of the apparition there was no sign. Instead, I became fully aware of the rumbling bark of the police dogs. Struggling to see into the middle distance, I could make out the bent shapes of men being dragged through the marshland by their excited hounds. They were moving in completely the wrong direction!

I knew at once what had happened. The dogs were in full pursuit of the filthy pack of rats. In which case the hellish ghoul I had seen – had I seen it or was I merely delirious? – *had come to my rescue.*

I thought back to what Aggie had said. That the thing she'd seen was her guardian . . .

*'Yet this was nothing compared to the frightful apparition
hovering in the air beside me.'*

14

Tuppence For A Bloater

Not wanting to waste a moment, I assumed a low crouch and scarpered, keeping out of sight of the men and their dogs, now little more than vague silhouettes on the horizon.

There wasn't time to consider the insane events I had just witnessed. I could only thank my stars that Fate had granted me a chance of escape. Now I had to find proper shelter and food and give some thought to rescuing Aggie.

I rounded a kind of crescent-shaped outcrop that might once have been a harbour, though it was now silted up and choked with marsh grass. Slowing to a brisk walking pace, I almost immediately spied a structure projecting from the landscape like a broken tooth. Tarred and tumbledown, it had evidently been cannibalized from driftwood and resembled nothing so much as the ribcage of some fossilized giant of the Jurassic. In sharp contrast to this, the front door, salvaged, it seemed, from a luxurious Portuguese vessel, was of gorgeous teak and bore the legend *Capitão* in beautiful copperplate script. The door was slightly ajar and the somewhat overwhelming strains of *Don Giovanni* were blasting through it.

Tacked to the outside of the shack and swaying gently in the breeze were dozens of smoked fish glinting like gold leaf, woodsmoke swirling about them. My stomach cramped painfully and I realized, with a jolt, how utterly ravenous I was. Inhaling the bluey smoke until I felt my eyes beginning to sting, I let the music flood over me.

Worn out and ragged since that night in the Manhattan drugstore – how long ago? – it was no wonder I'd started seeing things. What next hove into view seemed merely one more part of my delirium.

There was no sign of life save for the sound of the scratchy gramophone and I was just reaching over for one of the smoked fish when the teak door flew open and an old, old woman came out. With my senses stunned to buggery, I thought she was a witch.

Bent almost double, she leant heavily upon a gnarled stick only a foot or so long, had virtually a full white beard of a rather frightful wispiness and a heavily tanned face resembling a long-perished fig. Her black bonnet, as crow-black as the rest of her apparel, was in the style of forty years back. She fixed me with eyes as moist and clouded as the sky.

'Tuppence,' she cawed, chewing gummily at her lips.

'Pleased to meet you, Tuppence,' I said with more gaiety than I felt. The crone stared at me. I coughed as the woodsmoke caught in my throat.

'Bloaters is tuppence,' insisted the contorted old thing in a strange Australian squawk. 'I'm Mrs Croup,' she said with a laugh. 'Wanna come in?'

'Madam, I could kiss you.'

She looked me up and down and gestured towards the teak door. Introducing myself as Sal Volatile, lately of New York and now tramping about the countryside in search of work, I was ushered into a wonderland of curious relics, mostly, I presumed, reclaimed from the sea. All the furniture was slightly crippled, a missing ball and claw foot here, a patched-together cane bottom there. The tarred walls had patterned fabric pinned to them and, though filthy, the whole place had a sort of weathered charm that well suited its owner.

The principal decoration, however, consisted of newspaper clippings, seemingly hundreds of them, though my exhausted eyes couldn't make out the details.

In one corner, in pristine nick, was the gramophone, with a vast yellow trumpet like a daffodil. Neatly stacked records abutted it, a spidery scrawl identifying them. Mrs Croup plunged me into a disreputable old armchair whose burst cushions sprouted straggly hair as freely as her chin.

'Well!' said the old woman, bending over the dirty old stove and tossing a fish into a pan. 'Mr Volatile of New York, is it? Strewth, you must've seen some of the best'uns out there.'

'Best'uns?'

'Did you see Stanford White shoot Thaw? Or Leopold and Loeb? No, that was out in Illinois, wasn't it? Did you ever go out West? That's where they done for Fatty Arbuckle.'

My face must've been a picture. What the deuce was the old dear banging on about? 'Umm . . .'

'I slipped away from the old man once and caught a peek of Robert Wood. He'd been fingered for the Camden Town business, if you remember. But then the buggers only went and acquitted him!'

My eyes scanned the newsprint-plastered walls and suddenly all became clear. For every yellowing clipping, every carefully scissored paragraph, every damp-mottled photograph related to a notorious murder trial.

'Oh!' I cried, settling back in the chair and anxious to curry favour. 'Oh yes, I've seen some corkers. Both here and in the States.'

Mrs Croup's gums worked feverishly. 'Christ, what I wouldn't give to travel again. The Old Bailey! Manchester Assizes! Too crooked now, though. Almost got to the Bailey when they strung up Thompson and Bywaters, but . . . well, Mr Croup was very strict on these matters.'

I settled my hands on my lap, knowing I could warm to the theme. 'I saw Crippen and Le Neve back in '10—'

'No!'

'. . . and my father knew Dr Neil Cream . . .'

'Never!' she almost screamed. 'Cream? The boss-eyed Canadian strychnine poisoner? I'd have hacked off me arms and legs to have caught the merest glimpse! Strike me down, leave me a limbless torso and stuff me in a trunk at Charing Cross Station if I wouldn't. Cor!'

She gazed at me, from my wet hair to my clammy feet, and blow me if she didn't whistle. 'Strewth. You're a man after me own heart. And a looker too. Just like Mr Croup was. But he wasn't a kind man. No, sir, not kind at all. You can overdose me with hyoscine, steam across the Atlantic and get caught by electric telegraphy but I won't say he was a kind 'un. No I won't.'

What a queer old egg she was. I cleared my throat. 'Any tea on the go?'

Mrs Croup shuffled towards the gramophone, wound it up with great energy, then pulled out a big black disc. 'Murder a cuppa, eh?' she cackled. 'I'll get the kettle on. First though, a bit of "Carmen" Caruso recorded, in San Francisco, night before the'quake. It's a beaut.'

She proceeded to stuff a quantity of woollen knickers into the trumpet of the machine to muffle the sound, then swilled out a cracked Dresden pot. 'You look done in, mate,' she observed. 'Never mind bloaters. I'll fix you some proper breakfast. Agreed?'

'I must bow to your wisdom. You're an angel.'

She cackled and rubbed her chin. 'With these whiskers? Hee-hee! Reckon you've been at sea too long, mate! It's a long time since old missus here turned any feller's head, unless it was to turn away and spew up his dinner! Distil arsenic from me wallpaper and poison me kiddies if I tell a lie.'

I threw myself with gay abandon into a plate of thick gammon, eggs and sausages, washed down with strong tea that ran like quicksilver through my being. I closed my eyes in unadulterated joy.

As I ate, Mrs Croup sang along with Don José in a cracked warble and gave me a neat précis of the illustrious career of the great barrister Marshall Hall. That got us through pudding. I was just belching behind my hand as we reached the Green Bicycle Murder and the old bird paused to smile benevolently at me. 'Enjoy that? Don't you fret about letting your wind out, neither. I hear tell it's a sign of appreciation, somewhere out foreign'

She plonked herself in a shipwrecked deckchair and, rolling a thin cigarette, fixed me with a twinkling stare.

'Still, 'spect you didn't come here just to hear about sundry hangings and gougings and suchlike.'

I returned her frank gaze. 'Then why am I here?'

She shrugged her bony shoulders. 'Reckon you're looking for something. Reckon we're all looking for *something*.'

'I've found everything I could possibly want in your larder, my dear,' I said, folding my arms over my stomach. 'But if you could help me with a little information, I'd be inordinately grateful.'

She spat into the fire. 'I'll help if I can.'

'Is there a convent hereabouts called St Bede's?'

Mrs Croup pulled the fag from her mouth with a pronounced *pop*. 'Like the Venerable?'

I nodded.

'Oh, yeah. There's one. It's out on an island close by, mate. There's a causeway at low tide, otherwise it's a boat trip. You taking holy orders?'

I yawned expansively. 'Not quite.' The cosy room and the crackling fire were beginning to lull me into exquisite slumber.

'You want to get your head down?' she murmured, her hand toying with the ragged hem of her skirt.

I swallowed, nervously. 'Hmm?'

'I can make you up a beautiful little camp bed,' she said, to my relief. 'Then we can head out to the island tonight, if you like. What d'you say?'

I don't think I've ever been so glad to flop my head down onto a pillow. If Percy Flarge and Olympus Mons and the Mongol hordes of Genghis Khan had descended on the old woman's hut I don't think I could've stayed compos.

'That's it, dearie,' cooed Mrs Croup. 'You drift off now. Old Mother here'll look after you. Slice out my guts, throw 'em over my shoulder and leave me in a Whitechapel slum if I don't.'

With which charming send-off, aware only briefly of the rough pillow-ticking in my face and the faded blankets slung about me, I sank into the sleep of the blessed.

When finally I stirred, waking to the muffled strains of 'La Boheme', I felt wonderfully refreshed. Stretching out my long legs under the blankets, I gave a little yelp as my foot hit something cold and hairy.

I cracked open a sleepy eye. A rheumy grey one looked back at me.

Lying on the adjacent pillow in the hastily improvised bed was Mrs Croup!

She was grinning suggestively, a blanket pulled up over her withered – and naked – dugs.

'What . . . what are you doing?' I swallowed.

'Protecting me modesty,' she wheezed. 'What does it look like?'

My toes still lay against her own horribly hairy specimens. I attempted a smile. 'Your . . . um . . . your tiny foot is frozen.'

Mrs Croup seemed pleased with my *bon mot*. 'I can't offer you no artificial flowers, only smoked fish.'

I shuffled backwards on the mattress. Happily I was still fully clothed but my decrepit antipodean Mimi, taking advantage of my exhaustion, had stripped completely. It was rather like waking up next to a quantity of brown tissue paper and it was not a pretty sight.

'Madam,' I said, sounding like an affronted parson, 'I'm very grateful for your charity—'

'Ain't charity,' she grinned, sucking on her lower lip. 'Tuppence for a bloater, as I say. Gammon and eggs, though' – at this she winked suggestively – 'they might be a little more expensive.'

By Jove, this was a pickle! 'What. . .um. . .what would *Mister* Croup say?' I managed at last.

'He's dead,' cried the hag. 'God curse him. Dead as if I'd bashed a chop-axe twenty-three times into his face!'

I went quite cold. 'You didn't, did you?'

'*No!*' she cried, sounding disappointed. 'I only wish I had! The bastard ran off with a winkle-picker from Blakeney! I heard the 'flu took him just after the War. Serves him right. Anyway, I'm alive! I'm here, now! Nice and warm to the touch of your lovely nimble fingers!'

My mind raced. *I'm married, I couldn't possibly, it's against my religion, I'm a Uranian outcast, I'm a eunuch, I prefer goats* (no, that one might not help).

I think I was on the point of smothering her with the pillow when the old girl saved me, creeping out from beneath the covers and pulling on a tattered nightdress that might as well have been a shroud. 'No,' she said, shaking her head. 'I'm moving too quickly for you, ain't I? It's always been my curse. I frighten off the fellers 'cos I'm so eager. There's plenty of time, eh?'

I gawped at her. She'd been an invaluable help and I'd need her to find the causeway so, somehow, I found myself muttering, 'Ye-es. Plenty of time.'

Mrs Croup dragged on the rest of her ancient garments, smiling to herself. 'Jesus, but you're a handsome bastard. Don't get many like you washed up on this old beach.'

I clambered from the bed, stretched, and rubbed my hands together in cheery fashion in an effort to reassert some form of normality.

Night showed through the ragged curtains as an indigo rectangle. I pushed aside the dirty netting and gazed out. The beach was utterly deserted.

'Anyone been . . . hanging around?' I ventured.

Mrs Croup shook her filthy old bonnet and it rustled like newspaper. 'Funny you should say that. It's been quiet as the grave round here for longer than I can recall. Suddenly there's a great hooplah about some escaped convict or other.'

Before I could react, the old woman's leathery face creased into a tortoise-smile. 'We'd best keep an eye out for him, eh?'

I nodded, immensely cheered. Keeping the old bird on a promise might help me out of a multitude of sticky situations.

From somewhere in the recesses of the hovel, Mrs Croup managed to find a pair of boots and some thick socks that I hastened to pull onto my still-frozen feet. I wondered what other relics of male company she kept hidden away. A grisly image of a spider's web dotted with flies' wings sprang to mind.

'Are we ready for the off?' I cried, clapping my hands together enthusiastically and hoping to dissuade her from any more carnal thoughts.

'Almost.' As she rooted out a muffler and gloves, I spotted a stack of cardboard boxes. Noticing my interested expression, the crone smiled slyly and lifted one of the lids. 'What d'you think to these, then?'

I peered down at what at first I took to be cigars. Then the veil lifted. 'Dynamite?'

Mrs Croup gave a chuckle. 'Herring don't catch themselves, you know. Not at my age!'

She carefully replaced the lid, then nodded her bonneted head towards the window and snuffed out the lamps. 'Tide's just about low enough now. We can cross by the causeway.'

Outside it was a startlingly cold, clear, moonless night. The stars shimmered overhead like splinters of exploded champagne bottles. As we made our way across the rocky beach, I cast nervous glances over my shoulder.

'Tide turns about midnight,' croaked Mrs Croup from the recesses of her black bonnet. 'If you're not back by then, you're stuck out there for the night. There'd be no one to save you. Put thirty grains of antimony into me laudanum and leave me to die in shrieking agony if I tell a lie!'

'I'll be fine,' I cried. 'I'm sure the . . . um . . . sisters of St Bede's will give me a bed for the night.'

The causeway was suddenly visible, projecting straight out from the beach and uncomfortably reminiscent of the narrow spur of shingle where I'd first come ashore. Though the tide was low, black water still sloshed over our booted feet.

'On second thoughts, I reckon I'd best come with you all the way,' said my guide. 'Since you keep getting into trouble.'

Fearing the loss of her best chance in years, the old girl clearly didn't want to lose sight of me.

'There's absolutely no need, my dear,' I cooed. 'You get yourself home now.'

At this, she swung sharply in my direction. The starlight glinted off her bloodshot old eyes. 'You want to pack old Mother off to the Land of Nod just when things is getting interesting?' she squawked. 'The bloomin' ingratitude! Youth! I've a good mind to flay you alive and pull off your—'

'Now, now!' I interrupted, hastening to still the cracked voice that was carrying startlingly through the still, freezing night. Taking her by her knobbly elbows, I beamed appreciatively. 'Mrs Croup, I've offended you. I apologize unreservedly. You're clearly made of stern stuff and I absolutely owe you my life. But I have to go alone. I've no idea what I might be facing and I simply won't have you risking yourself for my sake.'

The crone considered this, sucking noisily on wizened gums that pressed together like pencil rubbers. 'I could wait and keep a look-out—'

'These are desperate men—'

'My favourite kind!'

'– who'll stop at nothing. It's too dangerous, my pet. Now I'll be back by midnight, I promise. Have the kettle on ready.'

She sniffed and heaved a sigh. 'All right.'

I turned her about and she began to retrace her steps, though with markedly less enthusiasm.

'Oh, by the way!' I whispered at her retreating back. Mrs Croup turned. 'Thanks for thinking of me as a youth. Does wonders for one's confidence!'

She held up a withered hand and was gone.

What a dear, terrifying thing she was. Still, if I couldn't be considered young next to a witch of eighty-odd then I truly was ready for the knacker's yard.

I put on a real pace now, having had to hang back somewhat to make allowance for Mrs Croup's ancient gait, and sloshed through the water, the insecure causeway shifting beneath my boots.

There was something uncanny about the sight of the wind-chopped sea stretching on either side of me and I hastened to cross, not liking the look of the salty depths and the mysteries they might contain. I was across the causeway in about ten minutes, suddenly finding myself on a soft beach, littered with dark, jagged rocks.

Some way ahead, an imposing Gothic building reared up, utterly black against the starlight save for a single electric light burning in a high window. There was about it the familiar musty smell of a church building; a mixture of damp-foxed books, incense and rotten nosh.

I padded across the sand until my feet hit surer ground. There was a kind of cobbled driveway stretching for about five hundred yards towards the convent's arched porch and I could see at once a canvas-covered lorry – such as the army might use – and a rather smashing silver-coloured motor parked up outside.

Utilizing an old trick, I carefully removed my boots and socks, then put the boots back onto my bare feet and the socks over *them*. I was now free to clump about on the cobbles with impunity.

Obviously in no position to go knocking on the front door posing as an itinerant archbishop, I reasoned my best plan was to try to see what was going on behind that lighted window. Happily, a great verdant bush of waxy ivy was sprouting from beneath the stony crenellations and, grabbing great handfuls of it, I made my way by degrees to a spot just under the windowsill.

I don't know what I expected to find – a studious nun looking like the penitent Magdalen, perhaps, crouched over a sputtering candle and mumbling a catechism. What I certainly didn't expect was to see my sister Pandora, legs neatly crossed ankle over ankle, smoking a cigarillo and pointing a gun at what was evidently the Mother Superior.

15

Whatever Possessed You

The aged nun, her huge white wimple still perfectly ordered like the bowl of an orchid, sat bound to a rickety chair, a desk lamp blazing in her face. Pandora was regarding the woman with detached coolness, her black hair glossy in the reflected light.

I was still hanging there on the ivy. The window under which I perched was old, the lead sealing the diamond panes un-repaired for donkey's years, so I was afforded a pretty good chance to make out what they might say.

Suddenly the door opened and Olympus Mons strode into the room, his face buried in some sort of file. He'd abandoned his absurd uniform for a well-cut dark pinstripe and neatly knotted tie, collar pinched into dimples by a golden pin. He gave the nun a warm smile as though he were a genial solicitor about to tell her she'd come into money, and then fixed Pandora with his penetrating stare.

'Anything?' he said sharply.

My sister shook her head. 'Still refuses to admit there's any such thing.'

Mons put down the file and folded his arms. Again, the dazzling smile flitted across his saturnine features, but this time the scarred lip curled up, exposing the full length of his dog tooth.

'You're not being very bright,' he said directly to the Mother Superior in his light Yankee accent. 'As I've explained, I'll do whatever it takes to get hold of the Lamb. My fellows downstairs will start shooting the first of your order in . . . oh . . . about thirty minutes. So, as the gangsters say in the flickers, "Start talking, sister."'

He giggled at his own witticism and it had the uncomfortably shrill ring of a child's laugh.

The Mother Superior's face was ashen but she raised her chin with dignity. 'I've nothing to say to you. I can only repeat that here at the convent we have little or no interaction with the outside world. Why you think that—'

Mons's hand lashed out with terrible suddenness, catching the poor old girl across the face. His signet ring must have torn her skin because a little teardrop of blood rolled like sap down her withered cheek.

'You're trying to make a monkey out of me,' he said in a low, threatening tone. 'It's awful inadvisable.'

He began pacing the room, arms folded, his chin sunk onto his breast. It put me in mind at once of that strutting popinjay Mussolini and I had a sudden vivid impression of Mons studying hours of newsreel footage in an effort to emulate the Duce.

'We happen to know that the Lamb was bred here,' he went on. 'Was sent out from here. It's a secret your order has been guarding for years.'

'Nonsense!'

Mons swung round to face the nun again, his eyes flashing like beacons. Then his heavy lids closed and he was all sweetness again.

'I'm a reasonable fellow,' he purred. 'I don't expect a Christian lady such as yourself to betray her vows just like *that*.' He snapped his fingers. 'But think of the alternative. All those poor girls downstairs.

They've not done anyone any harm. They're good, studious, pious kids.' As if a switch had been flipped, his face hardened and his voice took on a lethal seriousness. 'And they're all going to die,' he hissed. 'Unless you tell me what I want to know.'

The Mother Superior bowed her head, tears welling in her red-rimmed eyes. Mons approached her and raised her chin. 'Now. Where is she?'

I frowned. What had he said? Where is *she*?

The nun slowly shook her head. 'God forgive me,' she murmured. 'But I must serve a greater good. I will not tell you. I will not!'

Mons's face twisted with rage and his hands flew to the nun's neck. She managed one rasp of shock as his fingers sank into the wrinkled flesh, then only a horrid squawking was audible as she struggled desperately for air.

The American's dark rage grew upon him like a storm, his face growing almost as black as his victim's, oiled hair bouncing forwards into eyes that bulged like pickles.

'You fool!' he hissed. 'You stupid pious fool!'

'*Olympus!*' cried Pandora shrilly.

Still Mons throttled the unfortunate nun, his fingers almost meeting as he grasped at her neck.

'*Olympus, please!*' Pandora raced across the room and tried to prise Mons's hands away. She pawed at him ineffectually and actually hung off his arm but he showed no signs of giving way, standing stock-still like an electrocuted man.

I was about to smash through the window and come to the nun's rescue when my sister saved me the bother, shrieking: 'She's all we've got!'

At this, Mons seemed to come to his senses. He suddenly threw up his hands and stepped back, breathing raggedly.

The Mother Superior slumped forward, gasping for breath, her black-garbed chest heaving, livid red weals already showing up on her throat.

Mons smoothed back his hair, twisting his neck in his tight collar and adjusting his tie. 'You're right. We need this one.'

Then he swivelled sharply round on his heel, his face right by Pandora's, spit flecking his scarred lip. 'But don't ever touch me like that again, do you hear me? *Ever.*'

Pandora positively wilted before his words, her hair falling forwards like curtains over her face.

Mons swung back and addressed the recovering nun. 'I warned you', he said, producing a slim, long-barrelled foreign pistol from inside his jacket. 'I shall shoot the first of your order myself. And you will watch me.'

With that he hauled the unfortunate creature to her feet and began to drag her from the room. She dissolved into bitter tears, her whole frame shrinking, hands wrenching uselessly at the coil of rope that bound her.

Pandora gave the old nun a push in the small of the back, as though blaming her for Mons's response, and then the three of them disappeared into the corridor, slamming the door behind them.

I wasted no more time. Taking the silk 'handkerchief' from my money belt, I wrapped it around my fist and, with a precise punch, knocked out two panes of the diamond-shaped glass, then reached inside to unhook the latch. In seconds I was through and skittering across the stone floor.

The door hadn't been locked and I crept out into a narrow corridor, down which a tomb-cold draught was creeping. Happily there was no guard awaiting me and I was able to move swiftly, keeping close to the scarcely lit walls, until I reached a sort of minstrels' gallery that projected out over a large central hall.

Under a beamed ceiling there was a festive glow of candle sconces: beneath that, a sea of black-and-white-garbed figures. Forty or so nuns had been rounded up into a square formation before a massive fire-blackened stone hearth, penned in like sheep with amber-shirt guards at each corner. Each guard carried a Tommy gun.

There was an air of scarcely suppressed hysteria, although some of the older nuns retained a serene calm, as though above the threat of imminent extinction.

Mons was pacing up and down in front of them, waving his pistol, grinning crazily and seemingly feeding off their distress. Pandora stood to one side, twisting a lock of her hair, a childish gesture I knew very well. She was anxious.

At last, Mons raised the gun and fired into the air. It echoed with a terrific report and splinters tumbled down from the beams.

'Listen to me!'

There was silence, save for the odd whimper of distress. Or the odd wimple, I suppose.

Mons smoothed back his boot-polish-black hair. 'Your illustrious *superior* refuses to tell me what I need to know. So, I shall kill one of you in –' he glanced at his wristwatch – 'two minutes. Unless—'

There was a fresh outbreak of terror amongst the nuns and Mons raised his voice to compensate. Its already high timbre reached a hysterical pitch, the veins on his neck standing out like whipcords. 'UNLESS,' he yelled, 'one of you can help me!'

The Mother Superior, partially recovered from her near throttling, moved swiftly towards Mons, floating like a ghost over the flagstones. 'You silly little man!' she croaked. 'You really think your brutal tactics will—'

Mons blinked, staring down his nose at the woman as though she were an insect who'd suddenly acquired voice. A shot rang out and the nun standing closest to the Mother Superior simply crumpled into her robes as though she'd fallen through a trapdoor.

The still-smoking gun in his outstretched hand, Mons spat on the body. 'You were saying?' he screeched.

The Mother Superior blanched, her hand flying to her mouth.

I looked down grimly from my hiding place. What the deuce could I do? There were too many of them for me to mount any sort of attack. Any advantage I had would be instantly forfeited.

The nuns were positively screaming now and Mons revelled in the sight, darting in amongst them like a fox among sheep, giggling nastily as they veered out of his path, several tripping over their long robes and falling heavily to the flagstones.

'That one,' he yelled, pointing to the dead woman, 'doesn't count. So. Who's going to be next?'

To my horror, the gun spoke again and another nun was sent splaying to the floor.

'Stop this!' screamed the Mother Superior. 'Oh please! Stop this I beg you!'

Suddenly I felt a sharp pain in the ribs and swung round to find a broken-nosed amber-shirt thug jabbing his Tommy gun at me.

'Sir!' he cried and Mons looked up, his face glowing with blood-lust.

Heaving a heavy sigh, I was soon padding down stone steps and across the floor towards the fireplace, hands above my head.

Pandora ceased her hair-twiddling and gasped.

'I say, sis,' I said cheerily, 'I'm not up on the old-time religion and all that but isn't nun-murdering a little. . .beyond the pale?'

Pandora groaned, as though we were children again and I'd kicked over her snowman. 'Olympus, I'm so sorry. I don't know what he's doing here.'

Mons broke into a slightly hysterical laugh. 'But I do, my dear. I do. Would you care to enlighten us, Mr Box?'

I gave a casual shrug. 'I'm on a brass-rubbing holiday, would you believe?'

Mons's face fell. 'I wouldn't.'

'Didn't think so.'

Pandora strode towards me, hands on hips. 'What is this madness? Why the hell have you followed us?'

'I didn't exactly follow *you*, my dear.'

Mons folded his arms and planted a booted foot on the back of one of the dead nuns, like a great white hunter posing for a picture with a recumbent tigress.

'I'm afraid you must prepare yourself for a shock, Pandora,' he oiled. 'You see, my sources have been telling me some interesting things about your dear brother. He isn't quite the gentleman he appears.'

'Oh, I've always known that,' said Pandora with a sour look.

Mons was relishing every moment. 'Whilst presenting the world with the image of a successful artist – well, a *once*-successful artist—'

'That was low,' I said.

' – and fixture of the London demi-monde, your sibling has been, for many years, an employee of His Majesty's Government.'

'A civil servant?' said Pandora, thickly.

Mons shook his head. 'A most uncivil one, I fear. He's an assassin, aren't you, Mr Box?'

'Don't be ridiculous!' chuckled Pandora.

Mons flashed her a dangerous look. 'Be careful what you call me, my dear.'

Pandora flushed anxiously. 'I'm . . . I'm sorry, Olympus. But I simply can't credit it. My brother a . . . a hired killer?'

The Mother Superior was sobbing now and I moved towards her, only to find the Tommy gun rammed sharply in my side. Mons scowled at the old woman. 'Shut up,' he spat.

I plunged my hands into the pockets of my moleskin trousers. 'Your boyfriend does me a disservice, Pan. I do the lot. Sleuthing, derring-do. The assassinating's just part of it.'

Mons clapped his hands together. 'Oh! So your other profession is as workmanlike as your painting. How neat.'

'Now you're just being nasty.'

Still the Mother Superior sobbed, burying her face in her hands. Mons's eyes grew large again, glistening with fury.

'I'm afraid I can't help myself,' he said, between gritted teeth. 'Pandora here will testify to it. I'm a very nasty fellow.'

So saying, he suddenly loosed off a shot and the Mother Superior fell with a sharp cry of surprise, her robes suddenly splashed with scarlet.

As one, the other nuns let out a groan of distress.

'Look here, Mons,' I yelled, 'there's no need for this slaughter!'

'Oh, don't bleat, Mr Box,' he said sourly. 'I'd hate to think that anyone called *Lucifer* could be so feeble.'

Alone and helpless, the poor Mother Superior lay gasping her last on the cold stone floor. She managed to mutter some prayer and then, with a gentle sigh, passed away, a great pool of dark blood expanding like the tide beneath her.

'That was stupid,' I shrugged. 'Now how're you going to find out what you want to know?'

Mons watched the white smoke curling from the end of his pistol, fascinated. 'I have my methods,' he muttered at last. A cracked smile lit up his features, his dog tooth protruding like a glittering fang. 'Yes! After all, why not? I have access to these powers. Why not use them?'

He gestured impatiently to two of his armed thugs and pointed at the corpse of the Mother Superior. 'Pick her up.'

The amber-shirts obliged, dragging the dead woman from the flagged floor and dropping her onto a chair with brutal casualness. Then, stripping the wimple from around her head, Mons pushed back the body so that it sat up straight. The old woman's shorn white hair almost glowed in the crypt-like atmosphere.

Mons stood for a moment, his face raised to the ceiling, swaying slightly on his feet like a dancer picking up a rhythm. He began to mumble in a low, guttural tone. It was impossible to make out his words, but every now and then he would pause, listening, and make some curious sign or other, turning through all points of the compass and raising first his left then his right hand. He crooked his middle fingers so that they dug into his palm, leaving little white half-moon impressions in the flesh.

Then, in one quick movement, he jerked his body round, leant directly over the dead Mother Superior, and pressed his fingers to her temples. The intonation bubbling in his throat grew even deeper and more sonorous.

The effect on all concerned was utterly mesmeric. I, the captured sisters and even the guards had become spellbound. Pandora stared at her leader, twisting her hair with almost feverish eagerness.

Then the atmosphere in the room suddenly changed. The temperature plummeted and I glanced nervously over my shoulder, quite convinced that we were being watched by some new presence. The place was so wreathed in shadow that one might imagine all kinds of terrors lurking there but we could all see that the air was thickening queerly. I found that I was shivering inside my thick coat and sweater.

A kind of miasma began to form on the stone floor of the chamber as though mist were creeping in from the grey sea beyond, and I again had that weird sensation that time had somehow stopped.

At first, I couldn't see what had happened. But then one of the nuns screamed and backed away, revealing the impossible sight of the dead Mother Superior sitting bolt upright, her face tipped up as if staring at the ceiling, her eyes perfectly white and opaque.

And then she spoke.

'*Who has summoned me?*'

The voice was dreadful, low, cracked, flat.

Mons strutted before the woman, his features contorted with hellish triumph. 'I! Olympus Mons! In the name of Asrael, Baralamensis and the Chief Princes of the throne of Apologia! I command you to answer me.'

The late nun twisted in her chair, her chalk-white face screwing up as though in distress. Then some higher authority seemed to overwhelm her and she sagged once more into a waxy death mask. '*As I am commanded, so must I speak.*'

Mons thrust his face towards hers. 'Then tell me! Where is the Lamb?'

A playful half-smile crept onto the nun's face, the weird force within her taking command. '*You parley with dark forces to find the Lamb of God?*'

The corpse's words nudged a fragment of memory somewhere in my overheated brain. The Lamb of God?

'You know why she is important!' thundered Mons. 'I seek to do the Devil's bidding. I command you to aid me!'

The nun's head fell back, a terrible, gargling moan erupting from her throat and she spoke for a moment in her old, gentle tones. 'I cannot tell! I must not tell!'

Mons pointed his bony finger at her. 'I command you! By Him who spoke and it was done! By the most Holy and Glorious names Adonai, El Elohim, Elohe, Zabaoth . . .'

'No . . .'

'Elion, Escherche, Jar and Tetragrammaton . . .'

'*No!*'

Mons wrenched the dead woman by the throat and shook her. 'Tell me! Tell me! I command you!'

Suddenly, as though all resistance had been overcome, the woman went limp in his grip and a torrent of words began to tumble from her slack, dribbling mouth. Mons dashed to her side so as to hear.

'*Bred here. Bred here but sent far away,*' murmured the un-dead nun. '*Far away. She travels by sea. But now she's landlocked again. Haha! They sought to hide her from the likes of you. She is dangerous. A gentle, gentle girl. But so dangerous to the world! To us all! Agnus Dei, qui tollis peccata mundi, miserere nobis! The Lamb. The Lamb of God.*'

I felt cold all over.

An image of the beautiful cabin girl suddenly swam into my mind. Aggie!

Not short for Agatha but Agnes. Agnes Daye!

Agnus Dei: the Lamb of God!

16

Further Adventures Of A
Fallen Angel

I stood in wretched impotence, frozen by the terrible knowledge I possessed. All the attention I'd squandered on that ruddy 'handkerchief'thinking *that* was the elusive Lamb! And it was sweet Aggie they'd been after the whole time!

What part could she possibly play in Mons's nefarious schemes? My mind raced as the garrulous corpse cheerfully spilled the beans.

'Where is she now?' demanded Mons, his hands dancing about the nun's throat as though he were tempted to have at her again. 'Where?'

'*Where the blue lamp glows and the red church looms. And only a friend stands watch over her.*'

'Where is she, damn you!' screamed Mons.

'*Ask him who is fallen,*' smiled the dead Mother Superior. For one last time, her face assumed a look of serenity, then distorted again as though in torment. 'God forgive me!' she shrieked, then slumped to the floor, her dead face smacking on the flagstones. The séance was over.

'Why do they always do that?' raged Mons. 'I hate it when they do that! They talk in damned riddles and I'm left none the—'

'Him who is fallen,' murmured Pandora.

Well, I knew what that meant, all right. Curiously, though, no one seemed to be taking the hint. But what of the blue lamp and the red church? And a friend standing watch?'

Pandora's face creased into a puzzled frown, like a schoolgirl sucking thoughtfully on the end of a pencil. 'Him who is fallen . . . him who is fallen.'

Mons seemed stumped. He gave the Mother Superior's body a swift kick in frustration.

I was finding this difficult to credit. Didn't Mons's mob know their Bible? Particularly the bit about the battle between God and the most comely of his angels? And who had got his comeuppance at the hands of the Almighty?

'Someone who's had a nasty fall recently?' mused Pandora. She snapped her fingers. 'You jumped off that pier, Olympus! Would that count?'

'Unlikely,' mused Mons. 'I'm the one asking the question.' He cracked his knuckles and frowned. 'Perhaps that nun I shot first. She could be said to have fallen—'

'IT'S ME!' I yelled, unable to bear their lack of erudition a moment more. 'For Christ's sake, what did you *do* at school, Pandora?'

My sister swung round. 'You, Lucy?'

Mons brightened up at once. 'Of course! The fallen angel! Lucifer!'

'*Yes*,' I said patiently. 'Really, you're not being awfully bright.'

Mons fixed me with his arc-light stare. 'You know her, then? You know this woman, this Lamb of God?'

I whistled nonchalantly. 'Perhaps. Say I do know her . . . what do you want her for?'

'That doesn't concern a bungling amateur like you!' Mons positively spat. 'Just tell me where she is!'

I folded my arms. 'Or what? I suppose you could shoot me and then try that trick with the hypnosis or whatever but I rather get the feeling it's not something one can just do at the drop of a hat. You do look a mite peaky, if I might say so.'

Mons's hand flew unconsciously to his face. The séance did indeed seem to have taken a great toll on him. His skin had assumed a greyish pallor and his eyes were heavily bloodshot.

He marched right up to me, mouth curling into a snarl. I could smell the tobacco on his breath. 'You'll tell me, Box, or by God—'

'By God?' I queried. 'I rather thought He was out of the picture.'

Mons's reddened eyes bulged beneath his heavy lids and I could see he was building to another of his rages. Thankfully Pandora stepped in.

'Can't do any harm, Olympus,' she drawled, inhaling deeply on a black cheroot. 'After all, he's not leaving any time soon, is he?'

Mons held my stare. 'He's not leaving here at all.'

I gave Pandora my sweetest smile. 'How does the old saying go? One can choose one's friends . . .'

'Don't you dare bring family into this!' she hissed. 'There's nothing left between us! Nothing! What kindness or family loyalty have you ever shown me? You selfish, arrogant whoremonger! For the sake of the Tribune I would cut you down without a second thought.'

She dashed her cheroot to the flagstones and stubbed it into oblivion. A flurry of ash, picked up by the draught, whispered away into the shadows.

I shrugged. 'Well, at least I know where I stand. You were about to outline this great plan of yours.'

Mons clasped his hands behind his back and began his Eyetie strut again. 'Oh, it's nothing much really. I merely wish to summon the Devil himself and use his power to perpetuate my own.'

'Oh, *that* old plan,' I mused, stifling a yawn. 'Well, best of luck, old darling. Where does the girl come into all this?'

'So you do know her!' cried Pandora triumphantly.

I held out my hands, palm upwards, ceding their point.

Mons stroked his waxed moustache. 'There is an invocation. An ancient, ancient thing. It's called the Jerusalem Prayer and it's mentioned in heathen writings and diabolistic tracts going back as far as you can imagine. It shows how not just some minor demon but the Dark One himself, the Goat of Mendez, may be summoned back to hold sway over his earthly kingdom.'

'Rot,' I said simply.

Mons seemed rather pleased by my scepticism. 'Many have doubted as you do, Mr Box, only to find their cherished and simplistic view of the world turned upon its head. But let us return to the Prayer. It describes how, if a chosen one is sacrificed to Satan, he will be released from the supernatural bonds with which he is restrained. That sacrifice is a Perfect Victim, a woman with holy blood running through her veins, descended from an unbroken line of such anointed ones—'

'I've heard of such a legend!' I gasped. 'A child descended from a union between Christ and Mary Magdalene!'

'Don't be so fucking stupid,' snorted Mons. 'There's *hundreds* of those! No, this one is *really* special. In a designated place, at a designated hour, she must become his Bride. It has taken me a long time but finally I tracked her down. To the Convent of St Bede.'

I thought of what Captain Corpusty had said. Aggie had been brought up by the sisters but then placed in his care. But why? Then Sal Volatile's words came back to me. He'd found the Lamb, he said. Hidden under Mons's very nose. The sisters must have seen that Mons was getting close and so secreted the precious girl on the *Stiffkey* as a crew member, never realizing that the ship was already bound up in Mons's drug-smuggling schemes. She'd been hidden in plain sight, indeed.

'Doesn't do you much good without this Jerusalem whatsit of yours, though. Or have your clever boys found that as well?'

Mons nodded excitedly and let out another of his childish

giggles. 'I've spent several fortunes in the hunt but I finally traced it to some filthy little fence back in the good old U.S. of A.'

Hubbard the Cupboard, of course. Pennies, as you can imagine, were now dropping all over the shop. 'But he got greedy, yes?' I speculated. 'Removed part of the Prayer in order to hold out for more money?'

Mons's face darkened. 'To find myself held to ransom by scum like that! After all those years of fruitless searching.'

I grunted unhappily. So Mons had managed to infiltrate the RA and had used his acolyte, the odious Percy Flarge, to rub the fellow out. But Flarge hadn't found the square of silk, the 'handkerchief' that obviously contained some vital missing part of the ritual! The part dealing with the sacrifice of the Lamb of God!

My hand stole to my trouser pocket where the wretched thing now nestled. 'So now you're going to kill this girl – stab her with an ornamental dagger on a stone altar or some such tosh, I'll wager – just to fuel your insane fantasies about black magic?'

Mons seemed surprised. 'You've seen what I can do!' he cried. 'I made the dead speak! I am as one with Banebdjed!'

I glanced down at the motionless form of the Mother Superior. 'A conjuring trick. Some form of deep hypnosis. I wouldn't be at all surprised if she were simply in a deep sleep.'

'She's dead!' he yelled.

'I doubt it.'

'She *is*!' he squealed, like a petulant child, reaching down and grabbing the Mother Superior by the arms.

Suddenly, she let out a dreadful groan. Whether it was the last residue of air in her leathery old lungs or the vestiges of the demonic possession I cannot tell, but Mons stepped back, startled, and the assembled nuns set up a terrible caterwauling. It was all the distraction I needed.

Swinging round, I socked the amber-shirt guard on the jaw and grabbed his Tommy gun, immediately turning it on Mons.

His hands flew up and I yanked him towards me by the lapels of his expensive suit. The other guards rushed forward.

'Not one more step,' I yelled, 'or I'll spray his brains all over the stonework! You understand?'

'Get back!' hissed Mons. 'Get back, you cretins! He means it!'

Pulling Mons to me and wrapping my arm around his neck, I jerked him backwards so he let out a little squawk. Then, pressing the gun to his temple, I looked wildly about for an exit.

Despite the shadows, I could see a huge iron-banded wooden door in the wall behind me and I shuffled slowly towards it, Mons's boots dragging over the flagstones.

'Don't be an idiot, Lucifer!' sneered Pandora. 'You know you haven't a chance. Give up now and we'll be merciful.'

'The quality of your mercy, dear sis, is somewhat strained, I fear,' I cried, eyeing the doorway. 'You!' I jerked my head towards one of the guards. 'Get the door open.'

The pale-faced thug looked to his master, who said nothing. I jabbed the gun into Mons's face to encourage him and he nodded hastily. The guard unlocked the great door and it swung open with a dreadful, protesting shriek of rusted hinges. The outside showed as an arched black silhouette. Freezing air poured inside and over us.

'I could kill you now,' I hissed in Mons's ear. 'Bring this whole thing to an end.'

He swivelled his dark eyes towards me. 'Then why don't you?'

That was obvious. If I cut down Mons, his followers would have no compunction in taking me down with him. He was my guarantee out of there.

Mons laughed mirthlessly. 'And where do you think you're going? We're on an island, Mr Box. There's no hiding place.'

It was true. I hadn't thought much past getting out of the convent in one piece. I glanced feverishly around the chamber. Each of the guards was poised to spring should I put a foot wrong.

I renewed my grip on Mons's throat and hauled him backwards through the doorway and out into the night.

It was good to breathe clean, fresh air after the horrible frowst within. I glanced at the black water lapping close by, whipped up by the breeze.

Right by us was the lorry, and next to it the sleek silver motor that must be Mons's car. The man I was semi-throttling seemed to read my mind and giggled his little boy's giggle. 'High tide, my friend. No one's driving out of here for a while yet.'

I cursed his smug face. The amber-shirts and Pandora had formed a semi-circle just outside the convent doorway.

'Stay back!' I yelled, then aimed the Tommy gun and a spray of bullets ate up the shingle on the threshold.

In answer, a bullet whistled past my cheek – so close I could feel its scorching heat – and I saw that Pandora had let fly with a pistol.

'Don't try that again or I swear I'll cut you down!' I bellowed.

A wonky smile lit up my sister's features and I saw that she was about to take aim, calling my bluff. 'You won't shoot me and you won't shoot him,' she called, calm as a snake.

'Pandora!' hissed Mons. 'Don't risk it.'

'It's no risk,' she said, coolly cocking the gun. 'My brother's a coward. Always has been.'

I chanced a look behind me at the short distance to the sea. The swim back to the mainland seemed to be my only option. My mind was made up, quite suddenly, as Pandora let fly with a couple more shots. I dived to one side, taking Mons with me, then sprayed the whole of the facade of the convent with sub-machine-gun fire. The night lit up like a fireworks display as the bullets sang off the stones.

Mons let out a kind of croak of fear as I dragged him into the shadows. An amber-shirt came pelting towards us and I loosed off a round, smashing his jaw. A spray of blood showed up, black as ink, against the light pouring through the open doorway. The poor fool crashed to the shingle but Mons took advantage of the distraction to twist round and ram his head into my solar plexus. I crumpled backwards, all the air knocked from me, and strained weakly to pull the trigger of the Tommy gun.

Mons scrabbled to his feet, shingle jumping everywhere, and yelled for assistance. I lashed out at his shin and he fell heavily on top of me. I managed a couple of sharp jabs to his face but he was strong and fought back, wrestling with the icy steel of the weapon in my hands. Still winded, I could scarcely retaliate and I felt my grip slackening on the machine-gun. I was done for unless I could pull one last trick. Mons was dragging so desperately at the gun that when I suddenly let go, he toppled over with a cry of surprise.

In the instant before he got up and trained the weapon on me, I scrambled frantically into my pocket and pulled out the silk handkerchief.

Mons loomed over me, outlined against the starlight. 'You'll pay for this little display, my friend,' he raged, spraying my face with his spittle. 'You'll pay right now!'

'Wait, wait, wait!' I gasped, catching my breath at last. 'Recognize this?'

I lifted the square of silk and felt it flapping over my sweat-drenched face. Mons sat back, reached into his suit and flicked open a cigarette lighter. In the long, narrow yellow flame I saw his pitiless eyes widen.

'The missing piece!' he croaked. 'The Jerusalem Prayer!'

With a great cry, I grasped hold of his wrist and pulled it back so that the flame caught him on the cheek. He shrieked with pain and dropped the lighter. I lashed out desperately with my boot, kicked him in the gut, threw off my coat, rammed the silk into my trouser pocket and, without another thought, hurled myself into the icy water.

The waves closed over my head, there was a sharp, piercing pain in my ears and the world vanished into confusion.

I swam downwards with frantic energy, dimly aware of bullets sizzling through the dark water. Weighed down by my heavy clothes, it was a titanic struggle simply not to drown then and there, but I kicked and thrashed at the current, trying desperately to put some distance between myself and the island.

At last, lungs afire, I propelled myself upwards towards the air and emerged, gasping for breath, still perilously close to my tormentors. Amidst the splashing came the sound of yelled orders and a fresh spurt of bullets bit the water. Mons screamed at his men to cease firing. My gamble had paid off. He couldn't risk me dying and taking the fragment of his precious Prayer to the bottom. With the unpredictable current, my body might never be found.

I'd bought myself some time, at least until they managed to launch a boat and come after me. I trod water for a few moments, then began to flog my way through the sea with a steady rhythm. How far was land? It had taken me ten minutes to walk swiftly across the barely exposed causeway. Could I possibly manage to crawl all that way in this bitter weather?

The water slapped and churned about me and I could already feel numbness tingling in my feet and hands. Suddenly I stopped swimming and, chest heaving, trod water again as I became aware of the soft plashing of oars close by. Surely they couldn't be on to me already!

Looking about desperately for the source of the sound, I realized that it came not from the island but from the darkness ahead. And as I paddled, legs heavy as lead, a wonderful sight hove into view. It was a rowing boat and at the oars was a familiar crook-backed personage.

'Didn't I say you'd get yourself into trouble, mate?' said Mrs Croup, reaching out a withered hand for me to grasp. 'Drown me in the bath and claim on me life insurance if I didn't say so!'

I swam with new vigour towards the boat, grinning madly and hauling myself aboard to sprawl like a landed fish onto the weathered planks. They were wonderfully dry and comforting as my cheek pressed against them.

At once, though, the illusion of security was shattered by the roar of an outboard motor. I craned my neck and spotted a sleek wooden shape racing across the waves towards us. Mons had a speedboat on our trail!

17

In Pursuit Of The Lamb

I looked wildly around. Resilient as Mrs Croup seemed, we couldn't possibly out-row our pursuers. To my surprise, though, I found that the old girl seemed remarkably unperturbed. With a heavy clunk, she laid the oars aside and reached between her feet, producing and hastily unwrapping a cloth bundle. Inside were three brownish sticks. Then I remembered my friend's unorthodox method of fishing and let out a peal of laughter. Dynamite!

Mrs Croup's boat began to rock precariously as it was hit by waves from the approaching motor-craft. Calmly, the old woman pulled a quiver of matches from her skirts, lit one on a serrated silver fob at her waist, applied it to the fuse of the first stick and hurled it into the darkness. It span end over end, fizzing like a roman candle and leaving a spiralling pattern on my retina.

I was conscious of the roar of the motor, the lapping of the water and of my own urgent breathing, then the night split apart in searing white flame.

The dynamite had detonated above the sea, and by its sunburst of light we were able to see our pursuers taking desperate evasive manoeuvres.

'I have me target in sight now!' cackled Mrs Croup, lighting the second stick and hurling it towards Mons and his men. There was a desperate scrambling on board the speedboat and the hollering of frightened souls as the dynamite came cartwheeling towards them. There was an immensely satisfying *whoomph!* and the black water erupted, spraying us with foam.

I grabbed at the oars to make for the shore, peered through the smoke to assess the damage to our hunters and let out a spontaneous cheer. The front of the boat was gone, smoke hanging over it like mist, the sea a mass of splintered wood. Coughing amber-shirts were already in the drink, treading water and scrabbling towards the wrecked boat for safety. I couldn't see if Mons was among them but we had bested the swine and I pulled at the oars with a new impetus.

Mrs Croup let out an asthmatic chuckle. 'That should do it. Laws of maritime combat and all.'

I reached down for the last stick of dynamite. 'Bugger that!' I cried. 'Let's finish 'em off!'

With great delight, the old bird lit the fuse and chucked it with main force at the ruined speed-boat. An anguished screech arose from the survivors as it approached but this time the explosive went off early, merely detonating in midair and doing little more than temporarily deafening us both.

My saviour took the oars again as I shrugged a filthy horse-blanket onto my shoulders, willing the elusive shore to come closer.

'I sat there and thought long and hard,' Mrs Croup chuntered, wheezing at each stroke of the oars. 'That young fellow needs me, I thought. Strangle me with a silk stocking and stuff me under the floorboards, he *needs* me and there's an end to it. So I put out my old boat and I come looking for you.'

'You are, quite simply, a life-saver,' I beamed. 'How can I ever thank you?'

She turned a twinkling eye on me and my heart sank. Oh, Lord. I'd forgotten about *that*.

It wasn't long before the old boat bumped into the shingle and I staggered onto terra firma, my exhausted legs quaking like a new-born pup's.

Gripping the blanket tightly about me, I shuddered with cold. 'And now I must be off, my dear,' I chattered. 'I'll make good use of the head start you've given me—'

'But you can't!'

I looked at her with all the earnestness I could muster. 'You know how I long to enfold you in my arms, my sweet. But there isn't a moment to lose!'

She nodded unhappily, seeing the truth of it. 'But you must dry off at least! Some hot tea, eh? And then a steaming pot of my famous porridge! That'll put the bloom back in your—'

'No time,' I protested.

'But you'll catch your death!'

I smiled grimly. 'Save the hangman a job.' Then I glanced down at myself, a shivering ruin, and realized she was talking perfect sense. I'd simply freeze to death out on the open roads in my soaked togs. 'Very well. But I can't linger.'

We crunched swiftly over the shingle towards the rough little cabin. On the higher ground above it was parked a large and rather distressed old motor car, engine ticking over, the beams of its headlights piercing the dark like beacons. Suspicious, I slowed my pace but Mrs Croup merely took my arm and steered me on. 'Midnight fishermen,' she whispered. 'They'll pay us no heed.' As we approached, the door of the motor opened and two bulky silhouetted figures clambered out, rods over their shoulders.

Mrs Croup pushed open the door of her lovely little hovel and I rushed inside to warm myself before the blazing fire.

'Here you are, my pet,' cooed the old woman, handing me a rough towel. I stripped at once, without a blush, though I was conscious of the old girl's eye upon my frankly smashing physique.

Mrs Croup was everywhere at once, brewing tea and rustling up hot porridge whilst simultaneously rooting out a variety of fresh duds for me. I'd been right about the amount of male attire on the premises, though, judging by their age, it was safe to assume she hadn't been 'entertaining' for some years.

Eventually, I found myself in a flannel shirt, plimsolls and a rather nasty late-Victorian tweed suit. But beggars can't be choosers.

I smoothed down the musty-smelling material. 'How do I look?'

Mrs Croup twinkled and looked down shyly. 'Very handsome. I could hide you here, you know. They'd never find you.'

'It's a very tempting offer, but—'

She hushed me, placing a gnarled finger to my lips. 'Tuppence for a bloater, that's all, remember? God speed, now.'

I stooped to kiss her on the cheek but the old minx swivelled round so quickly that I caught her a smacker on her cracked and flaky lips. Then I felt her tongue worm its way around my mouth like a bobbing apple! A little shiver of disgust rippled through me. Well, I *was* grateful, of course, but gratitude has its limits.

Mrs Croup seemed to mistake my revulsion for emotion and turned me towards the door, wiping a tear from her rheumy eye.

I closed the Portuguese cabin door behind me, breathed deeply of the freezing night air and took to my heels. It was perhaps the narrowest escape of my career.

Close by I could make out the silhouetted shapes of those oh-so-keen fishermen as they tramped towards the sea. A sudden inspiration seized me. As quietly I could, I raced across the pebbles, crouched down behind their stately old motor and reached out for the door handle. The metal was freezing to the touch. I clunked it downwards and was thrilled to feel the door swing slowly open.

I slipped inside, conscious at once of the reek of fish and old leather, and felt about the dashboard, praying that the keys had been left in. My fingers found the blessed little piece of metal and I twisted it clockwise.

The engine whirred, turned over and died. At once, I tried again. The headlamps flared into life and I cursed my own stupidity at not deactivating them. There were angry voices coming from the beach and the crunch of feet on the shingle. Still the engine refused to start. I tried once more and, with a bucking, wheezing splutter, the ancient thing roared into life.

In the blaze of the lamps I could see two elderly men, swathed in tweeds, stomping towards me. Abandoning all attempts at concealment, I threw the car into reverse and the still-open door caught one of the poor saps across the legs as he launched himself at the side. The motor chugged backwards, sending a spray of stones into the air. I span the wheel, crunched the squealing gears, slammed my plimsolled foot onto the pedal and roared off.

The beach gave way to a rough road almost at once and the motor bucked as it hit the smoother surface. Peeking into the mirror I saw the unfortunate owners rapidly disappearing behind me.

Gripping the cold Bakelite of the steering wheel, I threw back my head and laughed. By God, I'd see that blessed old woman right when all this was over! Well, I might send her a postal order, at any rate.

Swinging the car from the beach road onto glorious tarmacadam, I found myself tearing through a little village, suggestions of lobster pots and upturned boats all that were readily visible in the white cones of the headlamps. In minutes I was through it and dipping down a steep hill, then up again and onto the first of many twisting country roads. Windmills and pubs flashed by, lying under a countryside hush.

Mons, I knew, would waste little time in procuring transport and would be after me post haste. The question now was, what to do with my head start? Thanks to Captain Corpusty, the British police were already aware of my return. I could head for London, where I was at least assured of help from old friends but the vital thing to me seemed the rescue of Agnes Daye. The nun had spoken of a blue lamp and a red church. It seemed safe to assume the former referred to a police station and the odds were on that my poor wounded Aggie was being held locally, charged with aiding and abetting a wanted felon. I hadn't the faintest idea where this station might be but vaguely planned to find the nearest and bluff my way into discovering the girl's whereabouts. After that, it was simply a question of getting her as far away as possible from these fanatics. In this regard I was definitely ahead. Mons and Pandora knew that *a* girl, originating in the Convent of St Bede, was the Lamb they sought but only I – so far – knew her identity.

I motored at high speed through half a dozen tiny outcrops of houses that hugged the coastline, scarcely passing a single other motor. Just when it looked like I would never hit anything remotely like civilization, another steep dip brought me out into a larger conurbation, dominated by a big ugly church and a rambling inn ablaze with electric light. In the glow from the windows, I could see that the church was clearly built of weathered red sandstone. I could hardly believe my luck.

Slowing down as I drove down the main street, I craned round to look about and gave a grunt of satisfaction at the comforting sight of a blue lamp outside a large, modern-looking police station. So here was the red church and the blue lamp. I glanced at my wristwatch. It was a little after six in the morning.

Parking the car by the edge of the village green, I crept out into the bitter night. There wasn't much of a plan in my exhausted brain. I was conscious that I must look like an escaped lunatic and my description – probably even my photograph – had been circulated to every cop-shop in the land. But the Mother Superior had said Agnes was being watched over by a friend and from this I took comfort. As an innocent man, the police could be said to be my true helpers against the forces of darkness. Nevertheless, I was placing a deal of trust in the dead woman's riddle. Daniel was truly entering the Lions' Den.

I mounted the steps to the station, the facade stained blue by the lamplight as though I was standing in a cathedral transept. Pushing at the frosted-glass door, I was surprised to find it unlocked. But then they were ever so trusting out there in the sticks, I assured myself.

Moving swiftly inside, all seemed absolutely dark but, as my eyes adjusted, I found I could make out the shape of the main desk and a couple of chairs. A door to the side of the desk was ajar. As I'd hoped, barred cells, lit only by starlight, were visible beyond. If the Mother Superior − or whatever possessed her − had been speaking the truth then poor Aggie was inside. And, if my luck held, the foolish local bobbies had left her unguarded!

'Aggie!' I whispered.

No reply. Probably sound asleep, poor thing.

'*Agnes!*'

There came the sound of stirring, the creak of a stool perhaps, and the folding back of blankets.

Then there was movement in the darkness and a flashlight in my eyes. I squinted and held up my hand to shield my eyes.

But it wasn't Aggie who spoke. It was a man's voice, oozing malice. 'Oh, happy day. I knew you'd come.'

The newcomer held the torch under his chin. His nose was almost completely obscured by sticking plaster and both his eyes were black and bruised. It was only the shock of blond hair sticking out like damp straw from beneath the brim of his trilby that told me Percy Flarge was back on the scent.

Even beneath the bruising and the bindings I could see the look of utter hatred he had assumed.

'The fox run to ground at last,' he seethed, brandishing his revolver. 'You've made quite a chase of it, Box, but it's over now.'

Electric lights rattled into life around me and I squinted at the unaccustomed brightness. Uniformed shapes darted from the corners of the room and I found myself suddenly restrained.

Flarge looked at me with utter contempt. Next to him stood an excited-looking local bobby of almost unbearable youth and the weasel-like form of 'Twice' Daley, the American Domestic I'd encountered back in the Manhattan church. He held up a hand and gave me a cheery wave. I felt quite sick.

'We seem to be making a habit of this, old man,' said Flarge, his voice rendered somewhat nasal by the sticking plaster.

'Look, Flarge, I don't give a pin for myself,' I announced heroically. 'But tell me the girl's all right.'

'Formed a little attachment, have we? How sweet. Look behind you.'

I whirled round. We were standing before the cells, and curled in the bunk that lay alongside the wall was Aggie, sound asleep. Her face was pale beneath the crop of dark hair. I moved towards the bars but the policemen held me back.

'She's fine,' cried Flarge. 'Flesh wound in the shoulder. But the charge of aiding and abetting a wanted felon might be more difficult to shrug off.'

'She was coerced,' I lied. 'You can let her go.'

'I might at that. She was useful as bait to trap you. Beyond that . . .'

My spirits rose. Like his odious master, Flarge couldn't know of her importance. Aggie might be freed and could simply vanish, thus depriving Mons of his 'Perfect Victim'.

'Alas,' said Flarge, 'I would be exceeding my powers. She's to be taken back to London to be properly questioned by the RA. You too, of course. Now. We must be off. Daley, get those derbies on nice and snug.'

'Sure thing, Mr Flarge,' said Daley with unpleasant relish. 'Nice to see you again so soon, Mr Box.'

I ignored the tick.

The coppers pinioned my arms roughly behind my back and the little Domestic clapped on handcuffs that pinched pinkly at my wrist. The other end he clapped onto his own arm.

'I believe,' I said at last, 'that I'm entitled to telephone my solicitor.'

'We'll arrange that whilst you're on the train to London,' snapped Flarge.

I shook my head. 'Oh no. There's no telling what you chaps have got cooked up for me. I'd rather do it here, in front of this honest yeoman.' I nodded towards the fresh-faced constable. 'I am only asserting my rights, am I not, officer?'

The constable glanced over at Flarge. 'He is right, sir. I can soon get a call through the exchange—'

'No, that's perfectly all right. No decent solicitor will be up at this hour.'

'Mine will,' I urged. 'He won't mind getting out of bed, at any rate.'

Flarge shook his head. 'Out of the question.'

'It would be the proper procedure, sir,' murmured the boy. 'I shouldn't like to have to face the sergeant when he gets back and—'

'All right, all right!' barked Flarge. 'Just get on with it.'

Daley took me by the elbow towards the desk where, with considerable gentleness, the noble copper asked me to furnish him with the number of my solicitor. I gave it to him and he wrote it down with infinite slowness using a blunt pencil. The figures were rounded and childish. He glanced nervously at me, clearly overwhelmed by the big case that had dropped into his lap, his cheeks flushing in the way only a boy's can.

Flarge threw himself down in a big swivel chair, arms tightly folded, glaring at me until the call was put through.

The constable handed me the cold black receiver. There was a crackle on the other end and then a familiar voice.

'Hullo?'

'Box here,' I said crisply. 'Look here, old thing, I seem to have got myself in a bit of bother. Oh, read about it, have you? Yes, well, all a lot of nonsense of course but I'd be rather glad of your . . . representation. Uh-huh. Somewhere in Norfolk, I think.'

My solicitor's voice sounded as though it were coming from several fathoms beneath the ocean. 'London train,' I said in response to the solicitor's question. 'Well, any minute now.'

I was conscious of my captors listening to every word. I flashed them a pleasant smile. 'Right-oh. Thanks. Yes, thanks awfully. How's Ida? Oh, *really*?'

Flarge rolled his eyes and began to get to his feet.

'Yes, well, I'd bring her, certainly. And try prunes. They always do the trick.'

Flarge's hand came crashing down on the telephone. 'No more chit-chat. You've been indulged long enough, Box. Come along.'

Daley began to drag me towards the doors. The boyish constable moved to the cell door, unlocked it and shook Aggie by the shoulder. She groaned and feebly attempted to push the lad away.

I glared at his back but refrained from speaking. Flarge stood back, made an elaborate bow as Daley yanked at the cuffs, hustled me out of the station and into the bleary dawn.

It was a wonderful sky, black night splashed with pink like an unknown Whistler, and I wished I could have seen it under kinder circumstances. As Daley pushed me down the steps, I spotted the owners of the stolen motor, still brandishing their fishing rods, standing before the rust-coloured church and deep in conversation with another policeman. One of the anglers, a great red-faced walrus of a chap, pointed at me as I emerged onto the steps and there was much swearing and muttering about my 'bloody cheek'.

To my horror, there was also a knot of be-trilbied reporters, and as I was led in cuffs to Flarge's waiting car, a cascade of flashbulbs went off in my face. I held up my free arm to shield myself but the ravening mob got exactly what they wanted: 'noted painter arrested for murder after daring Atlantic flight'. Mrs Croup would be thrilled. I was the new Crippen!

I glanced round and saw the ghastly look of satisfaction on Flarge's bruised face. The door to the station swung open and the policeman emerged, holding by the arm a dazed – and possibly doped – Agnes Daye, her pretty face slack with sleep. Then I felt Daley's gloved hand on my head, the girl and I were pushed into the motor and we were off.

Percy Flarge had got what he wanted. All I had to look forward to was the gallows.

18

Night Train To Death

The railway station we puttered into was large and busy, enveloped in billowing steam from numerous clanking engines, glimpses of gay livery visible between the clouds, pistons flashing like horse-brasses.

With alacrity Flarge and Daley pushed Aggie and me through the crowds. The poor girl didn't seem to know where she was and offered no resistance, shambling along like a zombie, her arm in a neat sling.

If anyone noticed I was cuffed they didn't show it. Scarcely looking up from my shoes, I was only aware of a cloying mass of snow-wetted coats and pale faces beneath dark hats. We passed a couple of steam-shrouded carriages until we reached an old chap, his uniform bright with buttons, his hand on the handle of the train door. Like the constable, he was clearly relishing his moment in the sun helping out what he took to be Scotland Yard.

'Mr Flarge, sir?' he cried, touching his cap. 'All's prepared, sir, as per your instructions.'

'Thanks,' grunted Flarge. 'Let's get them in.'

Flarge stood guard as the door to the carriage was hauled open and Daley stepped inside, pulling me up after him. I made no attempt to resist, merely glancing around at the bustling station. This was the rummest set-out imaginable. It was all so impossibly normal! How could these people be going about their daily business whilst I was being led away to face arrest and probable execution for a murder I had not committed? Even more startling had been those snatches I'd seen of another world, a shadow world of spirits and such that I could scarcely conceive as possible in the twentieth century. And yet here were these worthies, these bankers and clerks and type-writers boarding the same train that would lead them to mundane routine.

The compartment was dark and stank like damp dogs. There were six seats and Daley and I took up one pair, the short chain between the cuffs that bound us catching tight over the armrest. Flarge and Aggie settled into the green upholstery opposite, the girl drifting immediately into unconsciousness. She was very pale and there were unhealthy dark rings under her eyes.

The railway official shot me once last look, a queer mixture of awe and disgust, then slid the glass door to.

Flarge crossed his feet one over the other and opened a news-paper. 'Well, isn't this nice?'

I heaved a deep sigh. 'Why are we taking the train, Flarge?'

'Speed is of the essence, old thing,' he said, snapping the paper outwards so that it billowed like a sail. 'I say, you're all over *The Times*. Would you care to see?'

'No, thanks. Any chance of a cigarette?'

He smiled nastily from beneath his bindings. 'If you're very good.'

All four of us lurched forward slightly as the train began to pull away from the station. Aggie stirred and groaned. Flarge looked her up and down.

'Quite a dish, old man,' he said, hatefully. 'Dear me, I wish you'd make up your mind which way you incline. A chap struggles to keep up.'

'Story of your life, Percy,' I retorted.

He grunted mirthlessly.

Putting my free hand to the window, I rubbed at the steamed-up glass, the condensation squeaking beneath my fingers. The terminus – and freedom – slipped away as we steamed out, melting into a blur of colour then a monotonous succession of telegraph poles.

I pretty soon fell into a reverie, rocking from side to side as the train crawled south.

Aggie, looking very beautiful and vulnerable, curled into a tight ball on the fusty upholstery, a little pulse beating in her slender throat. I'd promised her a better life away from the *Stiffkey* yet all I'd succeeded in doing was thrusting her into the hands of her enemies.

'Twice' Daley fell into a doze, his yellow-gloved hands folded over his belly, his ferrety face occasionally enlivened with little twitches like that of a sleeping puppy.

After a few hours, Flarge relented and allowed me a smoke. I inhaled deeply on one of his expensive Turkish numbers and felt heaps better, though it made me slightly dizzy after so long without. The short winter day faded with miserable rapidity and electric light suddenly sprang into life above our heads.

Daley's eyes flickered open and he looked about as though unsure of his surroundings. I gave him a cheery wave with my free hand and he shot me back a look of undiluted East-Coast venom.

'Don't suppose you'd care to chat?' I opined to Flarge, picking shreds of tobacco from my teeth.

My nemesis was invisible behind the paper. He seemed engrossed in the football scores. 'What about?' he said at last.

'About this trumped-up bloody charge, of course,' I cried. 'And why you seem so keen to believe in it.'

Flarge collapsed the paper onto his lap and I saw fragments of lurid headline. Humming a little tune – he seemed in a very gay mood – he began filling his pipe. In a short while, a haze of cherry-smelling tobacco smoke conjoined with the harsher stuff from my fag, hovering over us all like ectoplasm.

'I just do as I'm told, old boy,' said Flarge blandly, jamming the pipe into the corner of his mouth. 'Something you should have considered doing a long time ago. It was inevitable you'd get tripped up.'

'I had nothing to do with Sal Volatile's death!' I insisted.

'That's not what the evidence says, old dear. Wouldn't be the first time a chap from the RA has abused his privileges, of course, but I think it's the only time anyone's tried to cover up a domestic murder as being all in the line of duty.'

'Must we play these games?' I sighed. 'I'm not really in the mood, to be honest. I could pretend I don't know what you're up to, we could exchange quips and *bons mots* till the cows come home, but we both know what's going on over on that island.'

Flarge's brow wrinkled. 'What?'

'Don't let him bamboozle you, sir,' muttered the Domestic.

'Shut up, Daley.' Flarge looked irritated from beneath his sticking plaster. 'What're you talking about? What island?'

I sighed wearily. 'The convent! Your chum Mons and his fascist goons. I didn't realize you'd added Satanism to your list of hobbies.'

Flarge bit on the pipe with an unpleasant clack. 'You really are raving. Perhaps the papers have it right. Balance of the mind disturbed, and so forth.'

Daley liked the sound of that and chuckled, raising a gloved hand to his tiny teeth.

I suddenly remembered the fragment of the Jerusalem Prayer and my hand flew to my trouser pocket. Daley twisted in his seat to stop me but Flarge didn't flinch. 'It's all right,' he said mildly. 'It isn't there.'

'What isn't?' I said.

'The relic, of course! Worth a king's ransom, so I'm told. Ah!' He snapped his fingers. 'Got it! You were in league with that fellow

178

Volatile. You both conspired to get the silk whatsit off that Hubbard chap and divide the spoils. He tried to double-cross you so you shot him. Good job we searched you thoroughly or we'd have missed the damn thing.'

'As you did last time.'

Flarge dipped his head. 'As you say. The first and only time you will best me, Box, old chum.'

I dragged on the stub of my cigarette. 'That blasted hankie's only part of the puzzle, Flarge, and you know it!'

'Charmin' little thing, don't you think?' continued the blond nit. 'All those doodles embroidered on. Like that ruddy Frog tapestry. What's the one? With poor old King Harold gettin' his daylights poked out.'

I looked hard at Flarge. Did he really know nothing about the truth behind this? Could he possibly be as silly an ass as he appeared?

'So where is it now?' I asked.

Flarge sucked on his pipe and let his gaze drift to the ceiling of the compartment. The tobacco smoke was shifting restlessly above the luggage rack like a restless spirit. 'Mr Daley here has it nice and safe. Until it can be returned to its rightful owner.'

'Mons?'

'Now there you go again. You're quite fixated on that fellah. What on earth makes you think it belongs to *him*?'

I had no chance to enquire further. There was a terrible, tortured screech of metal on metal and I pitched forward, my face almost burying itself in Flarge's lap. Daley fell forward, his knees thumping against the uncarpeted floor of the carriage, and he uttered an unmentionable Yankee oath.

The screaming of the brakes continued for a full minute as the train ground to a shuddering halt. Aggie didn't even stir. The lights flickered, then died.

Flarge pushed me off him and leapt to his feet, cocking a pistol.

Daley got up and twisted the handcuff chain painfully as he forced me back into my seat.

'You all right, Daley?' said Flarge, outlined starkly against the bluey light coming through the fogged-up window.

The flunkey nodded. 'Shoo-er, Mr Flarge.'

With a stuttering crackle, the lights came back on. Flarge looked about, weapon raised. 'I don't like this. Wait here.'

Great plumes of steam were hissing past the window as the stalled train marked time. Flarge slid back the compartment door, stepped out into the corridor, glanced quickly up and down it, then pointed the gun at my face. 'If you try anything,' he warned, 'anything at all, Daley will you shoot you down, you understand?'

'You make yourself abundantly clear, Perce,' I cried.

The door crashed shut over Flarge's scowling face.

I glanced over at poor Aggie, still curled up in her seat, then shrugged and smiled cheerily at my guard. 'Well, Mr Daley. It's just the three of us now—'

'Shut up, you lousy faggot,' he began – then his head snapped round at the unmistakeable sound of gunshots from outside the train. 'You heard what Mr Flarge said. I'll blow you away if you get clever.'

'Charmin',' I retorted. 'But I can't *get* clever, Mr Daley. I *am* clever.'

And the lights winked out again.

In the sudden darkness, I was instantly all over the little creature, battering the heel of my hand against what I took to be the fleshier parts of his face as he struggled to aim his Colt.

We toppled over Aggie – she merely grunted – and onto the floor. I fell awkwardly and Daley's whole weight hit me square in the chest, the dusty carpet scraping at my cheek as I struggled to get back my wind. Daley succeeded in raining several solid punches into my gut, whilst my fists met merely empty air.

Scrabbling desperately at the upholstery, I failed to raise myself up and was beginning to funk when, remarkably, I found salvation. I spotted a little red glow and my splayed finger-ends touched Flarge's pipe, forgotten in the crisis, the bowl still warm and smouldering with tobacco.

More shots rang outside. Daley's knee found my crotch and he leant heavily forward. It was agonizing.

'Now I got you, Mr Box,' he spat.

I could smell the sharp metallic tang of his Colt as he jabbed it into my face. I tugged at the old upholstery, sending up clouds of dust as I struggled desperately to roll the pipe towards me. At last I gained purchase and grasped the blasted thing. I settled the bowl in my palm and then lashed out with main force towards my assailant.

My weapon met almost no resistance and I would've assumed I'd missed had it not been for Daley's sharp, surprised cry. I moved the pipe a little and there was a dreadful soft, wet sound.

He fell forward and, in the pitch blackness, I touched his face. The still-warm bowl of the pipe was projecting from his left eye socket. I'd driven the stem of the pipe right into his brain.

Oh, Christ, I thought. That's torn it.

There was no time to hang about. Reaching out towards Aggie, I felt for her face and slapped at her cheeks.

'Aggie!' I urged. 'Aggie, my dear. Wake up!'

There was no response. I tapped her face again, gently at first then gave her a good crack across the chops. She moaned and stirred, but clearly whatever Flarge had doped her with was infuriatingly efficacious.

What the hell to do?

With athleticism born of desperation I dashed to the exterior carriage door, dragging Daley's dead weight still chained to my wrist. More cries and whistles and gunshots sounded from outside. I pushed down the window, leant out, grasped hold of the handle and swung open the door.

Clambering down into the freezing night, my boots crunched on

the chippings of a parallel rail line. The handcuff chain was
stretched taut over the threshold of the doorway, Daley's corpse
still slumped on the carpet within. I knew I couldn't linger – Flarge
might be back any moment – but I obviously wouldn't get far with
this great lump attached to me.

First of all, I leant back in and scrabbled in the dead man's pockets in search of the key. But trace of it there was none. Instead, I
found the silken relic – even in the dark I could feel the familiar
ragged edges – and stuffed it into my trousers before grabbing
Daley's gun. Could I blast off the chain, freeing myself? Hardly. In
the pitch blackness I would be more likely to shoot Aggie or myself
in the foot. If a train came along, the perfect solution would present
itself, the lumbering rolling stock making short work of the chain.
But I could hardly hang around all night waiting for the blasted
eight thirty-eight to Cromer to flash past and, besides, my own
wrist would have to be uncommonly close to the rail.

No, there was only one thing for it. In my adventures I've had to
do a lot of unpleasant things – in amongst the fun and frolics – but
this one is up there with the grimmest.

The night was briefly lit up by more gunfire.

Panting hard, I hefted Daley's body forward until only his hand
projected. Carefully, I let the carriage door creak closed, the cuff and
chain that connected him to me glinting in the starlight. I took a
deep breath, grabbed hold of the brass door handle and slammed
the door with all my strength. It met the dead man's wrist with a
sickening splinter.

I couldn't see anything much so I traced the chain from my own
handcuff to Daley's. My fingers came away warm with blood. I'd felt
tendons and smashed bone but it hadn't been quite enough. I repo-
sitioned Daley's wrist as best I could and swung the door shut again.
There was a softer percussion, as though I were chopping on damp
green wood. I tried to open the door again but it had fully closed.
Pulling backwards, I felt the last sinews snap and suddenly I was

free, the corpse's hand – still firmly gripped by the cuff – dangling and dripping in ghastly fashion from the chain at my wrist.

There was no time to think about this latest act of carnage. With tremendous effort, I managed to lug open the carriage door once more and pull myself back inside. In once swift movement, I picked up Aggie and threw her over my shoulder then, knees almost buckling, jumped back out onto the tracks and slammed the carriage door closed.

Aggie was light but in my exhausted state I could hardly manage to carry her. Just as I was about to set off away from the stalled train, I almost leapt out of my skin as the carriage door flew open and a shot rang out. In the brief, flaring illumination I saw Percy Flarge framed there, his face contorted with fury. I reached for Daley's gun to reply in kind but Flarge gave a startled cry and I heard him pitch forward out of the carriage. Evidently he'd tripped over the late Domestic's prone form.

Taking to my heels, I lumbered as swiftly as possible alongside the train, expecting a bullet in my back at any moment, the still-unconscious girl draped over my shoulder.

Suddenly, I was clear of the train and crunching over the exposed tracks. A flashlight snapped into life and I was momentarily dazzled.

'Mr Box, sir?'

I staggered towards the figure, shielding my eyes with the back of my hand.

'Turn that ruddy thing off, Delilah,' I commanded. 'What kept you?'

The massive, squarish form of my devoted servant loomed up at me, swaddled in greatcoat and balaclava.

'Motor's just halong 'ere, sah,' she said efficiently. 'Sorry to take so long but you didn't give much notice to get the obstruction set hup.'

'Not to worry. Would you be a dear?'

I set Aggie gently down on the ground and Delilah scooped her up as though she was a child. We ran swiftly towards a waiting car, engine turning over, its headlights masked by slitted baffles.

Delilah threw open the door and settled Aggie inside. I slumped in gratefully after her, the severed hand flapping horribly against my leg.

'Let's go!' I yelled.

But Delilah merely peeled off the balaclava, revealing a blotchy, weathered face like Christmas-turkey giblets left to linger until New Year.

She sniffed, miserably. 'Begging your pardon, sah, but there's ha gentleman 'ere what wants to see you.'

'Gentleman? What gentleman?'

As you can imagine, I'd had quite enough surprises for a while.

Delilah shook her head, as though saddened.

I heard two delicate coughs and a figure leant forward out of the shadows of the car's interior.

'So sorry, Mr Box,' said the figure. 'But there's no time to explain.' He seemed to be holding something in his hand. Darting forward, he pressed it to my face. I was very much surprised to find it was chloroform . . .

19

Eastwards By Monoplane

To long-time readers, this will come as a blow to make their whole fabric shiver. Has the faithful Delilah, stout companion of the Adventure of the Palsied Alienist, the Wakefield Thumb Murders et al, turned her outsize coat? Was the ugly old thing in the pay of Mr Percy Flarge?

By that stage in my career, my pleb of a factotum was retired from the Royal Academy's Domestic staff and employed full time as cook, butler, valet and bottle-washer to yours truly. She had never let me down in all the years I'd known her and she wasn't about to start doing so now.

We'd executed an existing plan (all that blether about 'bringing Ida' and the 'prunes', you understand, being code for the stopping of the train and my rescue), and as I emerged from my drugged state, I was confident she'd have an explanation for this latest turn of events.

Awaking from fevered dreams of goatish pandemonia, I found myself looking out through a little squarish window, a bar of brilliant sunlight across my face. I was airborne, don't you know, and could see the fuselage of the monoplane glinting like tin.

Far, far below, snow-capped mountains glittered in the rarefied atmosphere, looking for all the world like a three-dimensional map rolled out for my benefit. I craned forward and a beautiful landscape of lush green firs sprang up, dusted magically with snow that draped every branch and trunk. I was at once overwhelmed by an odd sensation. I knew with absolute certainty that I'd seen such a landscape before.

Before I could contemplate further, a shadow fell across me and Delilah's ugly mug loomed into view. She gave me the dubious benefit of her smashed-tooth smile. 'Morning, sah.'

'What the hell's going on?'

Sinking to her knees – they cracked like pistol shots – my menial began to fiddle at my wrist with a hairpin. Glancing down, I shuddered as I realized I still had 'Twice' Daley's severed hand flapping from the chain. It gave off a queer smell like a butcher's shop at closing time.

'Ave that hoff in a jiffy, sah.'

I looked behind Delilah at the length of the cabin. 'Where's the girl?'

Delilah sighed. 'She's hall right.' With a cry of satisfaction, she un-clicked the handcuff and tossed the grisly relic of my railway adventure onto the seat across the way. 'We his honly minutes hoff hour destination,' she concluded.

'And where's that?' I steadied myself in my seat as the aeroplane gave a lurch.

'Switzerland,' said a new voice. I turned my head.

Sitting behind me was a small man in a serge suit. He was as pale as his own hair and, rising, he gave a couple of tiny coughs behind his gloved hand. 'It's good to see you again, Mr Box. We have much to discuss, you and I.'

So this was Delilah's mysterious 'gentleman': Professor Reiss-

Mueller of the Metropolitan Museum, the curious fellow who'd given his expert opinion on the hankie back in New York. He sat down opposite me, a chrome-bordered, blond-wood table between us.

'I'm sure we do,' I rejoined. 'Care to start with why you've kidnapped me?'

The aspirin-white expert gave a helpless shrug. 'Time was of the essence, friend. Once I'd contacted Delilah here and came in on the plan to liberate you, it was essential we get on our way forthwith.'

I threw an unimpressed look at Delilah. 'Hi didn't know what to do, Mr Box, sah!' she shrugged helplessly. Her face brightened. 'Hi saw your picture hin the paper!' she cried happily, rather as though I'd been snapped opening the Chelsea Flower Show rather than caught in a flophouse bed with Sal Volatile's naked corpse.

'Hi knew something must be a bit rum,' she continued, chewing her lip. 'What the 'ell's the hacademy hup to, I thinks, letting Mr Box take the drop for this? Hand then the Prof 'ere got in touch and it all started to make sense.'

I scratched at my unshaven chin. 'And what's your story?' I said to Reiss-Mueller. 'You got in touch? How? And why drug me?'

The Professor put his hand to his pursed lips like a coy child. 'I had to do that! We'd only have wasted time on tedious explanations in the back of a freezing English automobile! Whereas now we have the luxury of our Armstrong Whitworth Argosy –' he patted the sleek upholstery of his seat – 'and can chat at our leisure.'

'I happen to like tedious explanations,' I protested. 'What the deuce is going on? Where's Aggie?'

Reiss-Mueller gestured towards a royal-blue curtain that divided the cabin. 'Through there, enjoying two boiled eggs. Three and one-quarter minutes. Just the way she likes them, apparently. She'll join us presently.'

'All right,' I said with an exhausted sigh. 'Explain.'

Reiss-Mueller gave a funny little laugh that dissolved into a double cough. 'I'm afraid I haven't been fully frank with you, Mr Box. Or, rather, my government hasn't.'

'Meaning?'

The little man balanced his homburg on the table and moved it round in a clockwise direction, contemplating it like an indecisive shopper. 'Well, let's just say that the Metropolitan Museum and the Royal Academy have more in common than you might think.'

I frowned. 'You're not . . .?'

'Agents of a secretive bent, yes!' he giggled. 'Nothing for the FBI to get their pretty little heads worried over. But like you at the RA, we like to think we keep a more watchful eye on things than the headline-grabbers.'

'But that's impossible. We'd know!' I felt a sudden lack of confidence in my country's intelligence network. 'Wouldn't we?'

'We're *very* discreet, is all I can say. I'm afraid I wasn't at that party at the "99" by coincidence. I was tailing you.'

I raised an eyebrow.

'Just routine, you understand,' he continued. 'And then I saw the relic and couldn't help asking. It's not just a pose, you see. I really am an expert.'

'But not enough of one to recognize the Jerusalem Prayer?'

He sat up at that. 'You know what it is?'

I waved an idle hand. 'Oh, just the most powerful occult object of all time, or some such.'

'Quite.' Reiss-Mueller took off his glasses and polished them with his colourless tie. 'Things have changed so much since we last met. I didn't realize the importance of it at the time. I've seen a lot of fakes and what-have-you so I've learned not to get too excited. But then I did some more research. Talked to other experts. When I realised the fragment must be genuine, I nearly had a fit.'

He cast a glance towards the window. As the 'plane banked to the right, a little patch of sunlight climbed the curved wall of the cabin and ignited the lenses of his spectacles. 'The prayer's been lost for so many centuries,' continued Reiss-Mueller, 'that many believe it to be mere myth. I never dreamed' – cough, cough – 'I'd get to touch it . . .'

His watery gaze settled on me. 'The most powerful occult artefact in history,' he repeated.

The curtain was suddenly thrown back and Agnes Daye raced through. She was flanked by two well-built men in pork-pie hats who, although not laying a finger on her person, were clearly guards of some species. Each was glowingly tanned and white of teeth as though they'd stepped from the pages of a Sears-Roebuck catalogue. They didn't try to prevent her from throwing her uninjured arm about me.

'You are awake!' Her lovely face lit up but there was real worry and exhaustion behind her eyes and egg yolk on her neat little chin.

'Hello, there,' I said chirpily. 'You all right?'

'It is not for me that you must be concerned,' she cried, with her customary gravity, stroking my cheek. 'My poor Lucifer. You have been through so much. When the police took me, I thought I would never see you again. And then that terrible man put me to sleep. Now there is this fellow with the spectacles. What is happening? Will you tell me what is to become of me?'

'I think that rather depends on the Professor here,' I mused, turning to the little fellow. 'Perhaps you could explain more fully to Aggie and me – any Scotch on the go? – why this Prayer thing's so powerful?'

Reiss-Mueller nodded vaguely to one of his pork-pie hatted chaps, who scurried off behind the curtain, reappearing moments later with a decanter. Delilah, whose department this was, gave a low growl and took it off him. The fella didn't argue.

The Professor took off his glasses and rubbed at heavily bagged eyes.

'There's a legend,' he began at last, leaning forward, 'old as Mankind but long forgotten. In the time after the Flood, Satan's power on Earth grew so strong that God was forced to rejoin battle. The Devil was eventually defeated and God imprisoned him in a kind of living death, trapped like a fly in amber . . .'

Delilah handed Reiss-Mueller a tumbler and I mixed one for myself and Aggie.

The little man downed his in one. 'Such was Satan's malign power that not even this could keep Evil from the world, but so long as the Dark One himself remains thus bound, Mankind is safe from ultimate destruction.'

'I have heard this story,' Aggie piped up, wincing a little as she moved her shoulder. 'The sisters taught it to me when I was small.'

I sipped my Scotch. 'And the Jerusalem Prayer . . .?'

Reiss-Mueller shrugged. 'Is the key to unlocking the enchantment that chains the Devil. Almighty God, it is said, granted us free will and so the means of releasing this horror have always been available. The Prayer was separated into fragments and hidden around the world. That square of silk is one of the fragments.'

I turned to the window and allowed myself a moment to contemplate the beautiful and serene landscape below. 'And it could really happen? It's not just all purple robes, black candles and how-d'you-do?'

'I know it might be hard to believe—'

'Not so hard as you might think, my friend,' I sighed, thinking back to the horrible visions I'd endured on the *Stiffkey* and the Norfolk marsh. 'You don't know what I'd give to believe Mons was using it all as an excuse to seduce a lot of nubile Swiss serving girls. But I've seen things in the past few days that make me doubt every one of those cosy little certainties that make life tolerable.'

Reiss-Mueller nodded slowly, then brightened. 'Luckily Mons had only the fragment. And he doesn't even have that any more. My orders are to take him . . . um . . . out of the picture, as it were, and return the relic to the US.'

I thought for a moment. I knew a few things that the Professor evidently did not.

'And you've not involved the Royal Academy? They don't know anything about this?'

Delilah shook her head determinedly. 'The Prof 'ere don't want 'em to know. 'E don't trust 'em. That's why I took 'im in on hour little scheme.'

Reiss-Mueller picked a thread from his sleeve. 'This is an entirely independent operation. You've nothing to fear.'

'So why all the hoo-hah? Why not just take the relic off me?'

Reiss-Mueller looked hurt. 'Take it off you? We're not thieves, Mr Box. You and I are partners. Once we're safe, you can fully debrief me.'

I grimaced inwardly, a horrible picture of a naked Reiss-Mueller popping into my overheated brain. I'd much rather de-brief Aggie. 'Where exactly are we heading, by the way?'

'One of the Met's safe houses. On the Franco-Swiss border. We'll hole up there and keep an eye on Mons's activities.'

'Is he in Switzerland?'

'Oh, yes. Our sources tell us he's returned to his schloss within the last day or so.' Reiss-Mueller's mouth turned down. 'I suspect he thinks he's found the Tomb of Satan but the exact location is contained in your fragment so he's digging in the dark, as it were.'

I took out the silken object and smoothed it over the arm of my chair. 'I think I have a surprise for you too, Professor Reiss-Mueller,' I said, choosing my words with care for maximum dramatic impact. 'You see, it's not just a question of arresting a deluded fascist bully and hiding away this little rag in our communal attic. Olympus Mons has the rest of the prayer. Every last fragment. And he intends to use it.'

Reiss-Mueller's milk-white face turned paler still. He leant across the table and pawed at my sleeve. 'You've got to be kidding me?'

'I rarely kid. Brings me out in hives.'

His plump hand shot to his mouth. 'But do you know . . . do *they* know . . . what power the prayer possesses?'

'I think I have some notion.'

Reiss-Mueller straightened up in his seat. 'If the Prayer is performed, the Dark Powers invoked and the Horned One released from his bonds, then chaos will engulf us all as surely as night follows day.'

With perfect timing, the 'plane suddenly began to descend. It was as though the bottom had fallen out of the world.

20

Memento Mori

We dropped in wide, looping arcs, the plane's engines groaning, and I gripped the arms of the seat to steady myself. As the craft finally thumped down, my stomach gave a great lurch and only settled itself as, with a last shudder, we slowed to a halt.

I sank back as the machine taxied along, sun-glinted snow already settling wetly on the glass of the portholes, the flickering shadows of the slowing propellers crisscrossing my face.

Aggie was gazing thoughtfully at the relic, her dark brows drawn tightly together. 'Why do we not just destroy it?'

'Hmm?'

'Destroy this thing, then the Prayer can never be complete and the . . . evil . . . will never be released!'

Reiss-Mueller shook his head. 'It's not so simple.'

'Why not?' I cried.

'No, no.'

'Look—'

I lifted up the Prayer fragment and, producing my cigarette lighter, struck my thumb off its stiff wheel. A neat yellow flame jumped into life only inches from the ragged cloth.

'No!' cried Reiss-Mueller. 'It's priceless!' His hands danced about in the air in agitation.

I waved the flame closer. 'Wouldn't you destroy the *Mona Lisa* if it meant saving the world?'

'No! I mean, of course, yes, but there's no need. Mr Box, please! There's another way!'

'Sure?'

'Yes!'

Relenting, I let the silk flop back onto the arm of the chair.

The Professor sighed with relief and ran his palm over his suddenly sweaty brow. 'What you've told me changes things somewhat. I'm minded to follow the course of one of your illustrious predecessors. That hunchbacked fellow who gave the Gunpowder plotters enough rope to hang themselves? Or so they say. Why don't we let Mons's plans mature then grab him red-handed? If he's taken *in flagrante* trying to summon the Devil then we'll get him and all his crazy followers at the same time. We can pump him for everything he's got on the Anglo-American fascist network, and with the world situation brewing up the way it is, that'll be pretty hot information. After that, we'll nail him with something commonplace. The IRS are trying a similar dodge with Capone. Tax evasion, would you believe?'

Armed with one of my few scoops, I decided to show off a bit. 'You could try this. Mons makes his moolah from smuggling cocaine into New York.'

Reiss-Mueller gave a low whistle. 'You don't say?'

'In the form of Communion wafers.'

'How very enterprising. That's sure good to know. You see, my dear sir, this partnership's going to go splendidly! Now, tell me what you've learned about Mons's plans—'

I yawned expansively. 'Details later. Are we to be fed and watered?'

'So Hi am hassured, sah,' put in Delilah, pushing aside the two pork-pie-hatted chaps and stooping to open the door. Cold, crisp air and sunshine immediately flooded the cabin.

I got up, hooked my arm through Aggie's and popped my head through the hatch.

We'd landed on a private airstrip, bordered on all sides by dense green forest with snow-bright peaks bobbing above the treeline. I froze on the steps, not because of the temperature but because, as I'd suspected from the view above, I *had* been there before.

I recalled Christopher Miracle's warning and a kind of numb misery washed over me. 'What did you say this place was called?'

'I didn't,' said Reiss-Mueller, appearing behind us and popping his homburg onto his neatly parted hair. 'Little village called—'

'Lit-de-Diable?'

Reiss-Mueller looked surprised. 'How did you know that?'

I gazed around at the airstrip. It was much changed but I knew every inch of the wretched place. 'I've been here once before. A long time ago. Lit-de-Diable.' I laughed mirthlessly. '"The Devil's Bed". Never realized its significance at the time.'

'When was that?' asked Aggie, gently.

I closed my eyes as though against the glare of the sun but, for a moment, that still and beautiful morning dissolved into a shrieking nightmare of remembrance, the air red as Hell, rain pounding like a hail of bullets in the mud, dying men strewn over the barbed wire, screaming and screaming . . .

I snapped open my eyes, shook my head. 'It's not important.'

Looking above the tree-line, I oriented myself. 'Mons has taken over the castle, then?' I said at length.

'See for yourself,' said Reiss-Mueller, producing a pair of brass binoculars and pointing towards the snowy peaks.

Above the forest loomed a familiar mountain, its surface dotted all over with searchlight housings. It was, of course, identical to the image sewn into the silken fragment of the Jerusalem Prayer.

At the mountain's peak, like something from Hans Andersen, stood a huge fortress, two of its smooth-faced stone walls towards us, a massive tiled keep projecting from the centre.

I'd known it under different circumstances and, clapping the binoculars to my eyes, strained to make out a new addition. For a moment, the view swam about, like trying to focus on a distant star through a cheap telescope. Then I caught one of the castle's absurdly spindly turrets and suddenly made out the strong lines of steel cables heading from it towards the ground. Seconds later, the gondola of a cable car trundled into view. I watched its progress downwards with keen attention, noting that, at several points, the vehicle came close to touching the rock face.

'Suits his dreams of grandeur, I guess,' said Reiss-Mueller, giving a short wave to the pilot, who was just a blur of goggles and flying coat behind the glass of the cockpit. 'Pilot'll stay ready till we need him again. Now, if you and the young lady are okay, Mr Box, it's only a short walk.'

I shrugged, knocked somewhat for six by the strange co-incidence of finding myself once more in the quaint Franco-Swiss town of infamous memory. For the moment I was content to give myself over to the Yank's plans, and draped an arm around Aggie's waist, taking care to avoid her be-slinged arm, as the four of us walked slowly off the airstrip towards the woodland.

I tried to banish the memories and enjoy the sunshine on my face. After a time, I began to feel a little more chipper. Reiss-Mueller's chloroform may have been an unorthodox sleeping draught, but at least I'd had some rest.

A short walk off the tarmacadam over snow peppered with pine needles and Reiss-Mueller came to a halt. Delilah, Aggie and I pulled up too, gazing in unconcealed delight at the sight before us. It was a cottage so idyllic that it could have been the castle's fairy-tale twin. Its weathered blue door was bordered by hoar-bush, berries sparkling as the frost that rimed them melted in the sun. Mullioned windows were set deep in the thick old stonework and the high, tiled roof could have been made of gingerbread and icing.

Fiddling with a key, Reiss-Mueller swung open the door and ushered us over a doorstep worn with a deep groove by the passage of centuries.

Inside, it was every bit as cosy and delightful as we could've wished for. I received a hurried impression of pale yellow walls, flag-stones and rustic furnishings. A huge stove dominated one corner. Hugging herself with happiness, Aggie scurried over to a plump armchair and threw herself into its downy embrace.

'Hi shall hattend to lunch at once, sir,' said Delilah, clicking her heels together like a maître d'. 'There'll shortly be 'ot water and food has well.'

As the Professor and I seated ourselves, Delilah got the stove blazing and soon after began filling the tub upstairs with buckets of steaming water. There were plenty of togs in storage and, after a brief, heavenly soak, I changed into canvas trousers, soft-collared shirt and pullover. Immensely comforted, I settled down for Reiss-Mueller's questioning. Aggie, meanwhile, prepared herself for the next bath.

The Professor steepled his fingers as he relaxed into the chair. 'So Mons has the rest of the prayer,' he mused. 'How'd he come to lose the most important piece?'

'Mustn't ever have had it, surely? Otherwise he'd know the loca-tion of the . . . um . . . Devil's tomb and wouldn't be digging up half his estate.' I smoothed back my still-damp hair. 'No, it seems a chap called Hubbard was trying to extort millions from Mons for that last piece. He must've known how much it was worth, but Hubbard reckoned without an agent called Flarge.'

'Flarge?'

'Percy Flarge. A swine of the first order of merit. He's the one out to frame me up. Whether it's just him or the whole of the Royal Academy, I simply don't know. All that's clear is that I got the drop on the brute. Found the one thing they'd been searching for just tucked into Hubbard's breast pocket.'

Reiss-Mueller contemplated his nails and gave his double cough. 'But all this is academic, anyway, unless Mons has found the Perfect Victim.'

'Well, she was hiding in plain sight just like the relic. That cocaine-smuggling business I told you about? Leaky old crate called the *Stiffkey*, operating out of Norfolk. Among its crew members was a girl brought up in the Convent of St Bede. A girl descended from an unbroken line of such victims, all waiting for the appointed hour.'

Reiss-Mueller looked at me steadily over the top of his spectacles. 'You know where she is?'

'She's taking a tub upstairs right at this moment.'

At this, the little chap positively exploded in staccato coughing. I told him everything about Aggie's identity, how Sal Volatile had discovered her location and then attempted to prise himself away from Mons's clutches and frustrate his schemes.

Finally, after Delilah had served us with a deliciously simple lunch of hot rolls and ham, we fell to examining the Prayer again. I peered at the embroidered mountain and at the lamb burning on the spit. Then I remembered our previous conversation and turned my attention to the dense, crabbed text.

'These other specialists,' I said to Reiss-Mueller. 'Did they have any clue about the words? How did they go again?'

The Professor tilted back his head and contemplated the low ceiling. 'That there will come one who is spoken of. All unknowing will he come. And only he who makes himself alone in the world can defeat the Beast.'

My eyebrows rose interrogatively.

'Not a clue, I'm afraid,' sighed the Professor.

I straightened up, stretched and popped the relic into the pocket of my new trousers. 'Well, Devil or no Devil, I need a kip. If you'd excuse me.'

Reiss-Mueller bobbed his head. 'Of course. I'll leave my boys on guard so you've no need to worry. Get some shut-eye and I'll join you later. I need to speak to the Met as to how to proceed.'

We rose to our feet simultaneously and briefly banged into one another, the Professor's glasses dislodging. He mumbled apologies and went out. Once upstairs, I looked in on Aggie and found her sound asleep, still wrapped in a huge rough towel. I carefully unwound it from her and she murmured something, one slender coffee-coloured arm flopping carelessly behind her head. The other was still in its sling, the bandage wet from the tub.

Then, languorously, Aggie opened one eye. 'Can I help you?'

I gazed down at her frankly wonderful form and smiled as a droplet of water slid from my hair and splashed onto her exposed tummy.

'I'd better dry that off,' I murmured. 'You'll catch your death.'

Pressing my fingers to her smooth skin, I wiped away the moisture. Aggie reached out and gently grasped my hand, moving it to touch her lips, her throat and then to cup her breast. Her wet hair was plastered to her forehead and, for once, her curiously serious expression was mingled with something altogether more naughty.

I slunk in beside her, the rough towel strangely comforting as I stripped off my clothes and nuzzled my freshly shaven face over her firm nipples. She clasped her free hand behind my head and pulled me closer, tighter as I thrust forward, the terrors and privations of the last weeks melting away into a glow of pleasure.

She fell to biting my ears and murmuring in a low, low fashion that prickled the hairs on my neck.

'Keep me safe,' she sighed. 'Promise me you'll keep me safe.'

I promised. I promised many things as we plunged wonderfully on. It seemed of suddenly vital import that I celebrate my existence, my life force, there in Lit-de-Diable, that place of dead and dread remembrance. And, as the girl and I conjoined in bliss, I decided there was some unfinished business I had to attend to.

Afterwards came the glorious lull of lovers' sleep until, with the winter day fast waning, I crept from Aggie's room and sought out my own. I was just lacing up my boots when the door opened and Delilah entered.

'The Prof's not back yet, sir,' she announced. 'So hi was wondering, hif we is not likely to storm Mr Mons's barricades any time soon, sah, what you and the young lady might want for your tea, sah.'

'Miss Daye is sleeping,' I said. 'And I have to go out.'

'Go out, sah?'

I nodded. 'There's something I have to do, Delilah. I'll be back before nightfall.'

The drudge looked worried. 'You sure, sir?'

'Absolutely.' I gave her a warm smile. 'Don't fret, I know this place like the back of my hand. Look after the girl, won't you?'

I found a long leather flying coat hanging on the back of the door, slipped it on and headed out of the cottage, straight into the path of one of the Professor's horribly healthy, pork-pie hatted friends.

He seemed in no mood to let me pass.

'Just going for a stroll,' I said airily.

The po-faced fellow shook his head. 'I don't think the Professor would like that, sir.' His accent was as regulation as his regulation American suit. 'We have your welfare at heart.'

'My welfare? Look here, you're supposed to be our guards not our gaolers.'

'Of course, sir. And that's why it wouldn't be wise to let you go wandering off. Surely you see that?' He flashed me his dazzling pearly whites.

I looked him up and down. Definitely not the type to be won over by friendly persuasion, I decided. Instead I nipped back through the doorway. 'My dear chap, of course! Quite understand. Night night.'

Closing the door behind me, I leaned back against the woodwork and frowned. No doubt Reiss-Mueller had the best of intentions but I've never liked being fenced in, as you may have noticed, and instantly made the decision to break free of my friendly confinement. Unfinished business, as I said.

Creeping softly back up the stairs I emerged onto the landing and made my way to a small sash window. Peering out, I saw Delilah in the snow-blanketed garden, chopping wood for the stove. A short distance away, arms neatly folded, sat the second of the Professor's Metropolitan Museum pals, his hat pulled down over his no doubt frost-nipped ears. I moved swiftly to the other end of the landing, where there was an identical window. This one looked out onto a neglected-looking roadway, and scrambling at the insecure lock, I heaved it open and slipped through onto the slippery drainpipe.

In moments, I had shinned down and landed with a crump in a thick drift. Keeping low, I crept along a hedgerow bordering that side of the cottage and was soon out onto the roadway and free.

The village of Lit-de-Diable was only marginally Swiss – as I knew to my cost – and had been fought over by various factions for centuries. It was little more than a couple of streets of quaintly cramped houses, inns and a pretty, onion-spired church. As a result, it took me only minutes to move through it towards the airstrip and across the un-patrolled border into France. I could have walked the way blindfolded.

Just past the airstrip where our plane was still parked, an area of woodland turned into a neat avenue of poplars. This in turn led, after some five hundred yards, to a small stone memorial that was quite lovely and glowing like coral in the pinkish light of evening.

My boots crunched through the drifts as I made my way towards it, then I paused, gaze averted, letting the memories wash over me.

I circled the memorial, the names standing out clearly.

PTE JOHN ROPER (small, keen, delightful), PTE SAMUEL FORTUNE (gloomy, Welsh, loyal to a fault), SGT JEREMIAH FORRESTER (good man in a tight spot), PTE INNES COPELY (no, didn't remember him) . . .

The next face of the stonework ran on in the same fashion, the inscribed names picked out by the fading light of the setting sun. CAPTAIN WILLIAM BUNSEN . . . PTE DAVID HENDRIX

In all those years, I'd somehow never managed to make the short journey. I could have come at any time but now, in the teeth of this strange adventure, fate had conspired to return me to that little place on the Franco-Swiss border.

LT HAROLD LATIMER (ill-tempered, drank), SGT GABRIEL BOOTHE (Yorkshireman, prim, humourless), PTE PETER HOLLIS (a real smasher. Made good grub) . . .

The names began to blur as I moved round the snow-covered stone. And then I saw it. The last simple inscription amongst all the others.

PTE CHARLES JACKPOT

I plunged my hands into the deep pockets of the flying coat and wished I had a cigarette. Charlie was always good for a gasper. I would've liked to have smoked one for him at that moment.

There was no body under the French turf, of course. Like so many others, the young man's corpse had never been recovered. He was listed as missing. Forever. And we'd been so close to the Swiss border and freedom . . .

There'd been many an adventure since we'd first met in that bizarre brothel in old Naples but, perhaps, none so bold and terrifying as the mission in '17 that finally parted us.

'A neat avenue of poplars led to a small stone memorial.'

I briefly touched my fingers to the cold stone, then turned on my heel.

Plunging my numbed hands into my trouser pockets, I suddenly panicked. The Prayer was gone! Oh Lor!

Taking to my heels, I pelted towards the airstrip. As Reiss-Mueller had promised, the pilot of our 'plane was sitting on a low wall, awaiting our instruction. He held up a hand in greeting, then slid the same hand into his jacket and pulled out a pistol.

I stopped dead.

The pilot reached up and hauled off his goggles and flying helmet in one smooth movement, revealing a shock of blond hair and a very bruised and broken nose.

'Don't say a word,' said Percy Flarge, between gritted teeth. 'Just come with me.'

21

Devil's Bargain

I followed meekly but my mind was afire. It was imperative I get away from Flarge and retrieve the fragment of the Jerusalem Prayer! Everything else – my life, Aggie's safety – was mere beer and skittles in comparison. And I would destroy the cursed thing if it meant saving the world from eternal darkness.

I crossed without fuss towards the aeroplane, which was now shining like a toy in the last beams of the purple sun. The cabin door was open and Flarge prodded at my side until I clambered inside.

'Don't gloat,' I muttered. 'I can bear anything if you don't gloat.'

'Shut up,' snapped Flarge.

I flopped down into my old seat, gaze flickering towards the door. Could I overcome him and get back to the cottage? 'Neat trick, that,' I murmured with faux nonchalance. 'Substituting yourself for the pilot. How did you cotton on to us?'

Flarge seemed anxious, his usual smug smile replaced by a sort of blankness. 'You're joking, aren't you?' he scoffed. 'The Metropolitan

Museum is wide open. We know about almost everything they do. Standing joke at the RA.'

I refrained from mentioning that I didn't even know of the Metropolitan Museum's espionage credentials. Dear me, I *was* getting too old for this lark.

Flarge waved the gun about. 'What we've certainly known for a long time is that chap Reiss-Mueller's as leaky as a sieve. Whatever discretion he once possessed has flown out of the window. He asks questions a bit too loudly these days and people listen. Didn't take too much to penetrate his plans. I reckon the Met want the Jerusalem Prayer for themselves.'

Something about Flarge's tone disquieted me and thoughts of immediate flight subsided. 'There's something wrong, isn't there, Percy?'

Flarge scowled. 'Yes, there's something wrong! There's something bloody wrong! You smash my face in, escape capture, escape again, kill my Domestic and then slice his blasted hand off!'

I shook my head. 'No. Something else. By now you should be thumping me and swearing seven kinds of vengeance for all I've put you through.'

'I should!' he rasped. 'I know I want to. Ever since I joined the RA I've had your ruddy name and reputation rubbed in my face. I thought I'd never get one up on you. But then I saw a little chink. Just whispers from on high. Scribbled notes from no one in particular telling me to shadow you because you weren't up to it any more.'

I would normally have bristled at this but bristling didn't seem called for. Something interesting was up. Instead I shrugged. 'You saved my life back in that church tower. I'm very grateful. But why the hell are you persecuting me? Because I found that blasted silk rag and you didn't?'

'I knew it was there!' protested Flarge. 'I saw it. But my orders . . . my orders didn't mention it. I was to keep an eye on you and on no account let you get hurt.'

'What?'

Flarge put his foot up on the chair in front and chewed his lip. 'Look here, Box. I was thrilled when I got the tip-off to come to that flea-bitten hotel and I found you in bed with the corpse. I was even more thrilled when the Academy told me that normal rules didn't apply. That the Domestics would not be called, and that you would have to face the full rigour of the law. It was perfect. Lucifer Box reduced to this! Caught with his trousers down in a sodomitic bloodbath. In *America*! As I say, perfect.' He heaved a sigh and let the barrel of the pistol droop slightly. 'Too perfect.'

Flarge cleared his throat and stared into space. 'I know what you think of me and I dare say you're right. I've admired you, resented you, wanted to see you utterly smashed so that I might advance but one thing I'll never do. I'll never see you go down for something you didn't do. I may be a swine but I'm not a traitor.'

With which remarkable statement, he took out a small and ancient-looking book and tipped out a folded piece of foolscap that lay within.

I read it over and then read it again. My skin grew clammy and I felt sick to my stomach. 'Where did you get this?' I managed at last, my voice reduced to a croaking whisper.

'It was inside Daley's coat,' said Flarge. 'Inside this book. I found it when you escaped from the train. Looks like the draft of a cryptogram. Makes things pretty clear, what?'

That it did. The thing, scrawled in Daley's untidy hand and annotated with various jottings showing where words would be substituted in a cryptogram, ran this way:

'Planted the rag, as requested. Box took the bait. Took him down in the drugstore and interrogated Volatile re: Lamb. Subject died during process. What should I do?'

I looked up. 'Daley set up that little charade in the hotel so that I'd carry the can?'

Flarge nodded. 'There's more. A reply.'

He tossed over an actual cryptogram on thin yellow paper with Daley's patient decoding in pencil beneath.

'Box will find the Lamb for us. He's still the best we have. He must have the Prayer. And Banebdjed shall rise! . . .'

Clearly, then, 'Twice' Daley and not Flarge was in league with Mons – but who else had betrayed us and fallen in with the fascist's diabolical schemes?

One thing I still failed to understand. The cryptogram reply had said 'Box must have the Prayer'. But didn't they already know that, having given Daley orders to plant it on Hubbard's body?

'And all this time I thought it was you,' I muttered.

'What?'

'This will sound crazy—' I began carefully, but Flarge held up his hand and contemplated his pistol.

'I know,' he said flatly.

'Hmm?'

Flarge scratched at his flaxen hair. 'All the Satanism stuff. Efforts were made to initiate me. All dark rooms and hooded robes. Never found out who was at the root of it. They were very subtle at first. Told me there were ways a chap like me might gain advancement, not just in the Royal Academy but in life. There's a route to true power, they said. Power over the wills of others.'

'What did you have to do?'

'The whole caboodle. Bell, book and candle. I mean, at first I took it for first-class tosh, but. . .whatever it might take to get on, you know? Then it got more serious and I . . . I saw things. Terrible things. And I wanted out. They seemed disappointed but agreed. I'd thought I was clear of the wretched business. Now I know I've been their damned pawn all this time! The question is, now we're on the same team, what're we going to do?'

I nodded towards his gun. 'We *are* on the same team, then?' I said.

Flarge stood up and his face was grim from beneath his sticking plaster. 'We might never be best pals, Box, but we can rub along for as long as it takes to sort out this mess, can't we?'

I looked the fella over. I'd loathed his very guts for so long it was going to take an effort of will not to knock him down where he stood. At last I got to my feet, put out my hand and Percy Flarge gripped it, firm and almost painfully.

'Chums?'

'All right, *old boy*,' I said. 'Chums. Now let's get the hell back to the cottage.'

As we opened the plane door, it was clear the weather was worsening. The day had faded in a riot of crimson and purple but there were huge, fat storm clouds lowering on the horizon. Snow was already falling thickly. We raced from the airstrip and onto the practically deserted streets of Lit-de-Diable as though afraid of the creeping dark.

The wind was roaring down the narrow streets and I'd stopped to catch my breath by a charmingly tumbledown inn when the brick just by my face shattered into fragments. Whirling round, I'd hardly managed to register the shot when another rang out, slicing into the ground at my feet and sending up a great plume of snow.

Flarge – slightly ahead of me – span on his heel and replied in kind over my shoulder. I had a brief flash of receding pork-pie hat in the fading light. Snow was pelting down in a great rushing fall.

'It's Reiss-Mueller's men!' I hissed.

One of the beggars was right behind me, concealed behind a pale yellow cottage. The location of the other was confirmed at once as his pistol rang out, shattering the window of the inn. Weaponless, I was helpless to respond, but my new ally Flarge was on blistering form, sending round after round our enemies' way.

We took immediate shelter behind the old market cross but we were hopelessly pinned down. The snow screamed in our faces.

'What the hell are they playing at?' snapped Flarge.

'Damned if I know,' I shouted. 'But the world's gone so corkscrew I half expect to be double-crossed every minute of the day!'

Flarge fired off three shots in rapid succession and was answered by two single bullets from opposite directions. 'Why would the Met want you dead?'

My mind raced. 'They could've killed me any time. Instead they brought me all the way over here. Why?'

Flarge pulled the trigger again but nothing happened. He slammed the weapon against his palm.

'Damn it all! Jammed!' He shot me a defeated look.

'All out for a duck, old boy?' I cried.

A bullet whined past, a great splinter of stone erupted from the market cross and the fragments caught me in the eyes. I threw myself to the ground, getting a mouthful of snow and lay there, utterly helpless. Then I lifted my head, eyes stinging and quite unable to get my bearings.

'Look out!' cried Flarge.

I tried to clear the snow from my eyes but was only blurrily aware of a figure stepping into my line of sight, the yellow flash of his revolver and a deafening percussion. This was it.

I waited for the bullet to hit me but something very queer happened. I was vaguely aware that the freezing night air had turned yet colder but the wind dropped suddenly and then that awful low depression gripped my guts like a cramp. There was a strange choking gasp from Flarge kneeling at my side.

'My God, Box,' he cried. 'Look!'

Great dusty tears were welling in my eyes, and as I rubbed desperately at them I saw the bullet hovering in the air right by my face.

As I watched incredulously, the damned thing simply faded away. Blinking stupidly, I looked up to see Reiss Mueller's men gazing down on us in unfeigned shock. Then, as if on cue, Flarge's pistol made a little clicking sound. He looked at it, raised it and, in one swift movement, put two bullets into our enemies' regulation suits.

The Men from the Met crumpled into the snow, wearing looks of complete bewilderment in addition to the new blood-blossom buttonholes in their lapels.

The wind suddenly rose up again like an unstoppered genie.

'What the deuce happened there?' squeaked Flarge above the din.

I shook my head. Once again, it seemed some supernatural power had come to my aid. And I didn't want to dwell on it. 'Don't ask,' I yelled, 'let's go!'

We were back at the cottage in minutes but, as soon as I saw the half-open door, I knew something was horribly amiss. Keeping close to the wall, Flarge moved to the worn step and kicked the door fully open. There was no one inside.

Flarge and I exchanged glances and I crossed swiftly to the back door. There was no sign of Delilah.

With a horribly heavy heart, I began to mount the stairs, Flarge following closely behind, revolver cocked. I moved swiftly across the landing and threw open the door to Aggie's room. Expecting to find her dead, it came as something of a relief to find the bed merely empty, the blanket I'd so carefully pulled over her gently sleeping body wrenched back like the snarling lip of Olympus Mons himself.

Sinking down on the bedspread, the full horror of the situation dawned on me. And I'd promised to keep her safe.

'What now?' said Flarge glumly.

'They've got Agnes and they've got the Prayer,' I sighed. 'What else can we do? We've got to get into that castle.'

Outside, the weather had closed in, transforming the night into a howling maelstrom. The sleet-choked wind shrieked through the bare trees and I clutched my leather coat about me as we set off towards the mountain. The cold was simply appalling, snow lashing at our exposed faces like a shower of needles.

Keeping to the Swiss side of the border, we soon cleared the tiny airstrip and found ourselves enveloped by dense forest, trees looming up like soldiers in our flickering flashlight beams. It was fearfully hard going, the drifts underfoot had refrozen and were treacherous, the snow that fell thickly onto our shoulders only added to the slog.

Pretty soon I was spent. Merely keeping from falling on my arse was hard enough, but the trudge upwards soon began to tell on my protesting leg muscles. Neck and face swamped by the upturned sheepskin of the flying-coat's collar, I strained to see the mountain through the black curtain of the forest. For a very long time, though, there was only the dreary regularity of the snow and the trees.

Then, all at once, a small, rectangular building seemed to spring up out of nowhere and we emerged into a clearing to find ourselves facing the departure point of the cable-car. Flarge and I exchanged glances and then trudged swiftly and noiselessly towards it.

Closer to, I could see that the terminus was divided into two so that, as one carriage arrived another set off upwards in the opposite direction. To my delight, I saw that a car was rapidly approaching.

Crouching in the snow just outside of the pool of electric light thrown from the station, Flarge and I watched as the vehicle clunked downwards. A shadow flickered in the window and I breathed a sigh of relief. The car sliding down the wire towards us was empty and there seemed only to be a single fellah on guard in the station itself. Flarge and I hastily devised a plan and then waited for the cable-car to come to a halt.

I signalled to my new ally, who nodded and covered me with his pistol as I crept forward, boots crumping through the impacted snow. Marching boldly to the steamed-up glass door of the terminus, I knocked and plastered a pleasant smile onto my face. Through the fog of condensation, I watched the guard frown, unshoulder his Tommy gun and slide back the door.

'*Pardon,*' I cried. '*Je suis un peu perdu.*'

Like a flash, Flarge leapt from his hiding place, reared up and plunged a knife into the guard's sternum. The unfortunate chap slid noiselessly to the floor.

Flarge dashed inside, studied the controls for a moment and then set the opposite lift moving. Without hesitation, the pair of us ran across and piled inside.

The car rocked and then began to lurch upwards and I let my gaze drink in the huge spotlit carpet of snow that illumined both the mountainside and castle with a bone-white glow.

Within the car, the atmosphere was pretty stifling: melted snow puddling on the wooden floor and rising off our clothes in great steaming clouds. Flarge was watchful as a hawk, gazing down at the glittering landscape below as we shuddered heavenwards on the narrow steel cable.

I was silent and anxious. The situation could hardly be more grim. Mons had both his Perfect Victim and the completed Jerusalem Prayer. My only hope lay in his not knowing the exact location of the 'Tomb' – the place where Aggie's sacrifice was destined to occur. That at least might buy us some time. I caught sight of myself in the glass, reflection distorted and ghastly-looking, my face clammy and beaded with sweat that stood out on my forehead like diamonds on cloth.

Still the lift clanked onwards, a persistent squeal coming from the steel wheels as they trundled over the cable. I watched as the ground disappeared into the inky darkness below and the jagged, snow-streaked rocks of the mountain reared up before us.

'All right,' said Flarge at last. 'Any bright ideas? We'll be arriving at Mons's castle in a few minutes and there may well be a welcoming committee—'

'Look!' I cried suddenly. 'There! Down there. Do you see them?'

'What?'

I dashed across the cabin and hauled open the sliding door. A wild and chilling wind immediately whipped at our hair and clothes. 'Come on!' I called.

'Don't play games, Box!' cried Flarge. 'What did you see?'

I glanced outside and saw that the trajectory of the cable had brought us within six feet or so of the mountain's jagged surface. Clambering over the lip of the car, I swung like an ape, jumped into space and landed softly in the snow. I beckoned urgently to Flarge, who calmly dropped onto his rear, pushed himself off and fell into the powdery drift.

The now-empty cable-car continued at once on its upward ascent, but I was already striding forward towards the two shapes I'd espied from the cabin, screwing up my eyes against the snow that lashed at my face. From the deeply drifted ravine on which we'd landed, I led the way towards a track that wound around the mountain.

And suddenly, there they were. Two huddled human shapes, snow already piling over their prone forms.

'Who is it?' cried Flarge, racing to my side.

I turned over the first: a massive, familiar bulk, still breathing – thank the Lord Harry. Delilah!

'Out cold,' I muttered, examining her pallid features. Reaching inside my coat, I pulled out a hip flask and managed to get some whisky past my old friend's frozen lips.

Flarge had bent to uncover the second body but suddenly cried out, stumbled onto his rear and, with a guttural retch, vomited copiously into the drift.

I trudged towards him and knelt before the second body, knowing from its size and clothing that it was Professor Reiss-Mueller. In all honesty, I was grateful for these clues, as what lay before me was scarcely recognizable as human.

Reiss-Mueller's skin was shiny and black as rotten fruit, his eyes – fixed in an expression of absolute terror – rolled up horribly into the very limits of their sockets. His nose and mouth, merely flayed holes now, ran with a dreadful green pus that steamed in the frozen air.

And, tucked neatly into his breast pocket, was the silken fragment of the Jerusalem Prayer.

22

The Tomb Of Satan

I whipped the relic from the corpse and plunged it into my coat pocket. The unfortunate Reiss-Mueller must have swiped the wretched thing back in the cottage when he'd 'stumbled' against me. Well, much good had it done him.

Flarge staggered to his feet, wiping the bile from his chin and studiously avoiding the dreadful sight before us. 'What the deuce happened to him?' he croaked.

There was a low groan from Delilah's prone form and I hastened to her side. Despite the thudding snowfall, I could see from the tracks that surrounded her that she and Reiss-Mueller hadn't been alone. There'd been a third party – Aggie, of course – but from the agitated state of the snow, clearly others had arrived.

Delilah suddenly sat up and yelled in absolute terror.

'No! Ho Gawd!' she cried. 'Ho my ruddy Gawd! No! No!'

I tried to push her back down with a soothing hand. 'It's all right, Delilah. It's me. It's Mr Box. You're safe now.'

She looked wildly about then grasped my wrist, her ravaged

countenance streaming with sweat. 'Mr Box, sah!' she rasped, swallowing repeatedly. 'Hif you'd honly seen it!'

I detached myself from her grasp with some difficulty. 'Now just take it easy. Tell us what happened.'

Delilah collapsed onto her back, breathing stertorously and shaking her massive head in disbelief. 'The Professor,' she gasped. ''E come back, hout of the blue. 'Ad words wiv 'is boys and sent 'em horf. Then 'e pulls a pistol on me and says, "Get the girl."' Delilah flashed me a look of desperate appeal. ''E'd've shot me down then hand there, sah, Hi swear it!'

'It's all right,' I soothed. 'I understand. What happened then?'

'Well, Hi 'ad to drag Miss Haggie downstairs, sah, and we set horf for the castle. Hi thought we'd perish out 'ere, sah, but the Professor – blast 'is heyes – 'e says 'e 'ad heverything 'e needed now hand we must get to the tomb come 'ell hor 'igh water.'

She grabbed the hip flask from me and drained it dry. Whisky bubbled over her cracked lips. '"Hit's my time," his what 'e said. "I shall be the one the Prince of Darkness favours."'

I nodded slowly to myself. Flarge crouched down and tried to get his arm around Delilah's waist in order to help him up. To my astonishment, the old girl lashed out and clocked him on the side of the head.

'What the hell!' he ejaculated.

Delilah rolled over and began to box poor Percy about the ears until I dragged her off by the shoulders. 'No, no! He's with us now. It's all right, believe me!'

'But you said 'e was trying to—'

'I know, I know! But things have changed, Delilah. Please. Let go of Mr Flarge's head!'

With great reluctance, my wonderfully brutish slavey did as she was bidden and Flarge flopped into the snow, spluttering and heaving up a little more of his lunch. Delilah shook herself all over and then continued her tale. 'We got up 'ere, hand then . . . then . . . something awful odd 'appened, sah.'

'Go on.'

Delilah rubbed her jowls. 'Miss Haggie sets up ha terrible crying, sah, and the Professor tells 'er to shut 'er noise. But she says, "Can't you feel it? Can't you feel it?", and that's when I gets this 'orrible feeling. Like when Hi gets one of me black dogs, you know, sah.'

I knew what was coming.

'Then Miss Haggie points a'ead through the snow. Hi thought someone was coming to meet hus, sah, but the Prof just let out an 'orrible moan and fell to 'is knees. There was somebody there, Mr Box. But it weren't 'uman! This terrible face! And the eyes on it!'

I patted her hand. 'I know, I know.'

'What happened then?' said Flarge, keeping a wary distance from Delilah.

My servant stared into the falling snow, almost unable to bear the recollection. 'The Professor pulls out that blessed 'ankie,' she whispered, 'and waves it habout. "Hi'm 'ere!" he shouts. "Hi 'ave come!" But the thing just glares at 'im and its eyes glowed red and the Professor started screaming and . . . I don't remember no more. Hi'm sorry, sah.'

She sank into herself and began to sob uncontrollably, something I'd never seen in all our years together. Giving her a reassuring pat on the shoulder, I rose to my feet. 'I reckon Reiss-Mueller was operating on his own. He kept me alive just long enough to find out the identity of the Perfect Victim then pick-pocketed the relic from me and went in search of his destiny. He was a real expert, as he said. Crazy about the occult. And he wanted the evil power for himself. Unfortunately for him, old Nick seems to have had other ideas.'

Rubbing his near-throttled neck, Flarge came closer, gingerly retrieving the brass binoculars from Reiss-Mueller's mangled corpse. 'And the girl?' he said at last.

'From the look of these tracks, Mons's men came along and took Aggie away, leaving Delilah to freeze to death.'

'And the relic? Why the hell would they leave that?'

I shook my head. Flarge cast a longing glance at the cable above our heads. 'Well, it's a dashed hard climb for us now. Night on a bare mountain, what?'

I waved the silk under his nose. 'What you don't know is that this thing is also a kind of map. And what the late Professor and I discovered some time ago is that the location of the imprisoned brimstone-lover is located halfway up this mountain. We're almost there.'

Which was an optimistic statement, to say the least. With the exhausted Delilah slowing us down, it was terrifically hard going, the startling white of the snow coupled with the deep, deep shadows of the treacherous rocks conspiring to confuse our every step.

Trudging on regardless, the snow buffeting us in swirling eddies like miniature cyclones, we made our way up the mountain track as it began to level out.

Machine-cut chips of rock littered the drifts beneath our boots like black threads in ermine and, as I peered through the white curtain of the weather, I made out, just ahead of us, the semicircle of a tunnel entrance.

'Mons's work, you reckon?' I cried.

Flarge frowned, then advanced and began to rub with a gloved hand against the rock wall. A rusted metal sign emerged from the peppering of snow, bearing the letters *PTT*.

My new ally let out a little laugh. 'No, old boy. This is something far more powerful. Its pernicious tentacles spread across the globe!'

'What do you mean?'

'*PTT!* Postal Telegraph and Telephones! It's the Swiss Post Office! Clearly they had cause to dig into this rock long before Mons did!'

'Very handy for the bugger, I'm sure.'

'Look 'ere, sah!' called Delilah, beckoning me over.

I hauled my way through the drifts and looked down to see where Delilah had brushed away the snow, revealing the rusted tracks of a narrow-gauge railway leading into the cave. Dear me but the Swiss were funny beggars. Why the hell would they build a post-office railway inside a mountain? Nevertheless grateful for their eccentricity, I led our little party through the narrow entrance into the tunnel and it was a huge relief to be out of the howling gale. Pushing down the snow-soaked scarf from over my mouth, I took in our new surroundings.

From somewhere close by there came a repetitive throbbing beat, reminiscent of the pounding drums at the F.A.U.S.T. rally. But what drew our attention at once was the ruddy glow coming from up ahead. Gingerly, the three of us advanced until we reached a much more ragged archway, which, judging by the great piles of dusty rock that surrounded it, had only recently been excavated.

There were voices coming from within. As if the place weren't uncanny enough, it sounded for all the world like a sermon in a country church; low, monotonous grumbling followed by hushed responses. Well I knew, though, that it was some hideously bastardized version of the familiar ritual.

We listened for a time, Delilah getting her breath back, Flarge concentrating on reloading his pistol. At last, I signalled them to follow and we crept stealthily forward to spy out the unfamiliar territory.

The tunnel opened into a cathedral-like chamber, its ceiling festooned with stalactites that dripped like the venom-laden fangs of some great serpent. The place exhibited the signs of its hasty excavation, though vast black drapes had been strung from the rock walls, their surfaces beautifully worked in diabolical designs of crimson, azure and gold. At the centre of the chamber stood a big stone altar, draped in black cloth.

I swallowed hard. Agnes Daye lay sprawled nude on her belly on that altar, seemingly insensible, her arms bound behind her back. Even at that distance I could see the ugly wound in her shoulder, black against the burnt-sugar brown of her smooth flesh. Around her, wreathed in smoking incense, were scores of equally naked men and women, their faces covered by grotesquely carved animal masks. Pigs, wolves and bug-eyed insects leered out of the miasmic gloom, chanting, writhing and wildly gesticulating.

Only three faces remained uncovered: my sister Pandora, swamped by a floor-length robe of Roman purple, Olympus Mons, who stood at a sort of lectern, and a corpulent figure clothed in black, his multiple chins wobbling over the tight collar. It was Joshua Reynolds, his eyes shining with depraved joy. Once Flarge had told me his tale I'd suspected as much but here was the living proof. Who was better placed to lure Percy Flarge into his nefarious schemes than the head of the Royal Academy himself!

I thought back to that fateful meeting in the Moscow Tea Rooms. Of how he'd taunted me, dismissed me as a relic of a bygone age – whilst all the time I'd been vital to his terrible plans. He'd counted on my skills to hunt down Agnes Daye and return the relic to its rightful place. Rage boiled within me but I tried to suppress it and concentrate instead on the lectern before which Mons was standing. Upon it was stretched what I knew at once to be the remainder of the Jerusalem Prayer, patched together like an exquisite quilt. The left-hand corner was missing.

Mons was naked save for his own black robe, embroidered all over with slithering serpents, chased in silver and bronze. There was a wildly triumphant look in his searchlight eyes as he intoned his blasphemous verses. 'He comes! He that is Spoken Of! As it is written, so mote it be!' he bellowed. 'The Prayer speaks truly! All unknowing he returns the last piece to the whole!'

I was so absorbed by this performance that at first I didn't notice the cold barrel of an automatic pressing into my neck. Whirling round, I groaned at the sight of amber-shirt guards depriving Flarge of his pistol and others training their machine-guns on Delilah.

With a sharp jab in my side, I was propelled through into the incense-soaked chamber beyond.

Mons paused in his declamation, his ruddy face suffused with delight.

I smiled in clubbable fashion. 'Oh. You've started without us. And I thought I was being fashionably late.'

Mons seemed amused and rubbed his hands like a genial host. 'Very good, Mr Box. Ever so good.'

'Welcome Box!' cried Reynolds.

'Welcome brother!' giggled Pandora. 'At last you're here. And you've fulfilled your side of the bargain admirably.'

Delilah stumped to my side. 'What the 'ell do they mean, sah?' she grumbled. 'What bargain?'

Reynolds rubbed his massive belly in delight. 'What other kind is there, Box? A Devil's bargain!'

Pandora licked her carmined lips. 'Oh, poor Lucy, you *have* been naive!'

A cold wave of sickness passed over me. What had I done?

'Haven't you read your fragment of the Prayer?' cried Mons, smiling. 'It was written there the whole time.'

'Didn't I say he was getting slow?' cackled Reynolds.

I gazed around the chamber, feeling utterly hollow. '"All unknowing will he come,"' I quoted in a dull whisper.

Mons nodded feverishly. 'The Prayer has been separated into fragments all these years but the text itself decrees that the last piece must be restored by one who comes all unknowing. You, my friend, you!'

'No!' I cried. '*No!*'

'We've been leading you here all along, Box,' sneered Reynolds. 'Why'd you think we made it so damned easy for you to escape?'

'Easy!' I exclaimed. 'I could have lost your blasted relic half a dozen times. Along with my ruddy life!'

Mons shook his head. 'You were watched over all the time,' he said, troublingly.

'Watched over?' I whispered, voice cracking. 'By whom?'

Mons stroked his waxed moustache. 'By the Prince of Darkness himself. Knowing how close we had come to releasing him, he stretched out his terrible influence to ensure you came to no harm.'

As disquieting thoughts go it was up there with the best. But now I understood why that frightful apparition had sent the police off on the wrong trail back in Norfolk, why the bullet had melted into air before my face and why Professor Reiss-Mueller had been rejected by the Dark Master he so longed to serve. It was essential that I, thick-headed dolt that I was, bring back the last fragment of the Prayer without ever knowing I was being used as its hapless courier. What had the cypher said? 'Box *must* have the Prayer.'

'So you've put me through all this, *all this*,' I seethed, 'just to bring back that bloody dish-rag for you?'

'It was ours all along,' laughed Mons. 'But the ritual is clear. One of those annoying little codicils that were meant to stop us from raising the Beast. Only one all unknowing could restore the final piece.'

My mind raced back to Hubbard the Cupboard, scrabbling between the bells in that clapboard church what felt like months ago. He'd told me then and there that he was a patsy. Suddenly my mouth was bone dry. 'You . . . you planted the handkerchief on Hubbard? You meant me to find it?'

Reynolds nodded gleefully. 'Oh yes! I must say you've more than lived up to the reputation I sought so hard to debase for young Percy there.'

Flarge looked suitably miserable and shook his fist at his former boss. 'Gad! You utter swine! How could you?'

Reynolds gave an idle flick of the hand. 'You were useful, Percy, that's all. You added – what's the word? – *verisimilitude*. Box had to believe he was a wanted man so that he wouldn't suspect for a moment that, all along, we were leading him here.'

Mons took up the tale. 'We made it a fascinating journey, as full of surprise and co-incidence as any tall tale. There were even surprises for us! Like discovering that the smuggling operation I'd been running across the Atlantic was rather more important than I thought.'

I felt dazed and nauseous. It was all I could do to stay upright. 'Sal Volatile found the girl, didn't he?' I murmured. 'Hidden away on that rotten old ship of yours. But he kept it a secret. Kept it until—'

'Until Daley tortured the truth out of him,' said Mons, evenly. 'But he'd only got as far as naming the convent of St Bede before he. . .expired. I must say, it was a most hair-raising time for us. All our plans tottered on the brink of collapse. For without the Perfect Victim, the Prayer was useless.'

I looked over at poor Aggie, naked and insensate on the cold stone of that profane altar. 'And I brought her to you, didn't I?' I whispered, utterly demolished.

'Practically gift-wrapped,' tittered Reynolds. 'With a little help from Professor Reiss-Mueller. Poor sap. He thought he could leap-frog the competition. But it doesn't work like that. One must play by the rules.'

Pandora straightened up, clearly enjoying the pantomime bold-ness of her luxuriant gown. 'We've wound you up like a little clockwork mouse, dear brother. And now you've come home.'

My sister stepped forward and, after rifling my coat pockets, took the last fragment of the Prayer and handed it with great cere-mony to Olympus Mons. He smoothed out the ancient silk, placed it on the frame alongside the rest of the heathen text and, sweeping back his hair, advanced towards the altar where Aggie lay on cold stone.

'It begins at last!' he cried. 'The Devil is loose!'

23

The Sabbat of Olympus Mons

Amber-shirt thugs swooped on Flarge, Delilah and myself, rapidly binding us at the wrists and pushing us down onto our rumps, Pandora supervising.

'Don't want you to miss the show, Lucy,' she said, cheerily, tying off the knots before slipping back into the throng.

'Damn you,' I hissed.

'Too late for that,' she cried gaily, smoothing some strange and noxious brown unguent onto her chest and calves.

A shattered cross had been rammed, upside down, into the stone of the altar and close by stinking candles fizzled and flared. From their stench I reckoned them to be made from corrupted human fat.

Mons's acolytes, all of them naked save for the amber-shirts who guarded us, began to sway and rock on their heels as the filthy incense took hold, a low murmur bubbling in their upturned throats. Pandora thrashed about amongst the throng, grunting horribly, her hands held aloft in gleeful ecstasy, her bare feet scuffing over a carpet of broken Communion wafers – real this time – that had evidently been looted from some church. I saw, to my disgust, that several of the masked lunatics were busily urinating on the Host.

We could only gaze on in absolute horror as the obscene ritual was enacted before us: the most finished piece of blackguardism since Caligula ran amok. Poor Agnes lay sprawled on her belly, rump in the air, whilst Mons pushed back his cape, revealing the strongly muscled contours of his body and intoned his hideous inversion of the Mass, kissing her all over at the points where a congregation would normally have muttered the responses.

As the animalistic grunting and snuffling increased to shattering volume and Mons's hissed repudiation of Christ and the Virgin topped even that, I became aware of a piercing cry that turned my blood to ice-water.

'Oh God,' whispered Flarge. 'Not that!'

'What is it?' I cried.

I could feel Flarge sagging right by me as his head sank onto his chest. 'It's all in the rituals they told me of. The slaughter of the innocent.'

I jerked my head around. A slim naked youth of perhaps fifteen years, his head disguised by a wolf-mask, was dragged forward by two of the amber-shirts. Evidently the news that he was to be sacrificed to his Nibs had been only recently relayed. He was jabbering in terror, trying desperately to convince his captors that they must choose another. But the burly guards merely scooped him up and, with awful strength, held him upside down by his shins. His hair, ringing wet with cold sweat, flopped towards the dusty floor and the wolf-mask fell with a sharp clatter, revealing a flushed face red and contorted with fear.

'For God's sake, Mons!' I yelled. 'Think what you're doing!'

Pandora was at my side in an instant and I felt her hand crack across my cheek. 'Silence!' she shrieked. The Dark One must feed! He must *feed*!'

The amber-shirts staggered slightly under the youth's weight but still they held him firm, like a trussed chicken. Despite the terrible rapture that seemed to be consuming Mons, he spared a moment to glance aside and wink at me. I whimpered with sheer impotent fury, calling upon all the saints to help me.

For answer, Mons produced a tiny silver blade, like a fruit knife, and slipped it quickly across the youth's throat. The boy made no sound at all and the commotion in the chamber suddenly ceased. The heavy wet bubbling of arterial blood from his throat was the only noise to be heard, splashing horribly to the floor of the chamber in a great, frothing rush.

Mons stooped to catch the blood in a chalice, then, lifting it to his lips, he drank deep.

'Oh my Christ,' groaned Flarge.

Mouth befouled with the boy's blood, Mons suddenly flung the remainder in a wide arc over the curve of Agnes's smooth backside. At this, the girl began to stir and turned her face towards us three bound together. I prayed for her to remain insensible but she seemed to take in the full dread of her situation all at once and let out an awful scream.

Two more animal-masked followers leapt forward and, grasping her by the wrists, swung her over onto her back. From the blond braids of one and the flabby little body of the other, I knew them to be the amber-shirt elite who had stood with Mons on his Manhattan platform.

The 'congregation' responded to Aggie's scream and the grunting, squealing and frenzied dancing took up again, a pounding drumbeat sounded from close by.

I turned away in disgust at the dark rime of blood that clung to Mons's black moustaches. The dead body of the sacrificed youth was dropped to the rocky floor and then, with a whoop of bacchanalian delight, Mons gestured towards the corpse, inviting his acolytes to rub the foul substance onto their naked torsos.

Pandora rushed to the altar and dipped her hands into the ghastly wound on the youth's throat that gaped like an empty sleeve. She smeared blood carelessly over her breasts and face and then reached out for Mons as though seeking praise – but he pushed her aside with some violence. Appallingly, I could see that beneath his black robe, Mons had become as priapic as a goat. Pandora fell back, looking, I have to say, a little put out.

'Choose me!' she yelled. 'Why can't it be me?'

Mons glared at her, apoplectic with rage. 'Get back! Get back, you worthless drudge!'

Pandora wrang her bloodstained hands. 'I know she's the Perfect Victim, but, please, after the ritual's done. You know how I feel—'

Mons's face was growing black with fury. 'You bother me with such trivia now? At the very moment of my greatest glory? You loathsome sow, do you think I could ever, ever even spare you a solitary thought?'

Pandora looked as though she'd been cracked across the chops.

Mons shook his head and laughed. 'You were only chosen to join my side after your luckless brother was selected to be the one. He Who Comes All Unknowing. You pathetic parasite! Now get back amongst the rest of my worthless slaves and keep your mouth shut.'

Pandora literally staggered where she stood.

'Oh, crumbs,' I cried. 'Boyfriend trouble again, sis? Just like old times.'

Expecting the usual scowl, I was shocked to see the utter blankness in Pandora's face. She looked completely undone and her skin showed waxy and deathly pale beneath the streams of blood and stinking unguents that covered it.

Now Mons returned his attention to poor Aggie. He moved slowly, almost reverently towards her, his hands gory with haemoglobin, his cock twitching in anticipation of the diabolical coupling to come.

But it was not to be. I was suddenly aware of a muttering voice from close by. At first I assumed that some hellish ritual was to accompany the dread moment, but to my astonishment I saw that Pandora had moved to one side, bending over the Jerusalem Prayer on its frame, her lips moving quickly as she declaimed the ancient and forbidden text.

Mons span round, appalled. 'What are you doing? It's too early! Too early, you senseless fool!'

He threw aside the little knife he'd used on the poor boy, sending it clattering down the steps of the altar as Pandora's voice raced on, chattering through the ritual with almost supernatural speed. Mons dashed towards her, his fist raised to strike, but then stopped dead and whipped about as all the flaming torches and the beastly candles in the chamber suddenly. . .winked. . .out.

My scalp prickled and I felt as though a great weight were pressing on my chest.

'Bloody 'ell,' gasped Delilah. 'What's going hon?'

'Yes,' whispered Flarge. 'I feel it too.'

A freezing draught crept through the darkness, colder than the snowy journey to the mountain, colder than anything I had ever known.

'My God,' I hissed. 'Something's coming!'

'*He* is coming,' croaked Flarge, his voice tiny and broken in that dreadful, dark place.

And then I felt once again that curious blanket of silence, as though we were all spinning in the total vacuum of space. In the sepulchral blackness, there was suddenly a form of light, a dreary, ghastly light like something rotten and long buried that has been unwisely disturbed. In this greenish phosphorescence, I became aware that all of Mons's acolytes were silently creeping closer to the altar. Despite their ambitions, they were as terrified as us. In the shadows, though, something else was approaching. At first I took it to be more of the naked, animal-masked throng, but even in that weird luminescence I could see that the flesh was somehow *wrong*.

What I took to be several people was in fact one great lumpen thing, its pale and spindly body thrashing about as it slobbered and crawled its way towards us. It was covered all over with eyes, tiny black orbs like those on a spider, yet somewhere in that mass of disgusting tissue there was the semblance of a human mouth. And to my unutterable horror, it was *singing*.

It was some kind of bastardized plainsong, rather like a gramophone record of monks chanting that has somehow gone awry. And between gasps of this foul cacophony, the thing began to giggle.

As I looked, a second creature shuffled and crawled towards us, extruding itself from the darkness like an obscene sausage skin. This one had a vast maw that sparkled with filth and spit and waves of corruption seemed to spill from it. It was a thing of the grave, a thing of utter and profound darkness, and I shuddered to my very soul in its presence.

Something moved behind me and I yelled in terror – but it was only Flarge. 'Shh!' he hissed. 'If you value your life, Box, silence! We haven't much time!'

I thrilled with shock as I saw that the enterprising chap had managed to grasp the sacrificial knife – abandoned by Mons – between his heels and was dragging it towards him.

Delilah and I, with our backs towards him, could be of little aid but I was grateful for any distraction from the grisly apparitions. In seconds, Flarge's straining hands had grabbed the knife and we had it between our hands, sawing desperately at the ropes that bound us.

"Ow we gonna get out hof 'ere?' hissed Delilah.

'We can't escape,' said Flarge flatly. 'But there is a chance, a *chance*, we might be saved.' To my surprise, he waved the little old book he'd retrieved from Daley's pocket on the train. 'It's a dangerous business, this. None more dangerous. So there are safeguards. In *here*.'

I felt him jerk away and realized he was suddenly free. He looked wildly about but the entire wretched coven had eyes only for the filthy, squealing beasts that were undulating towards them.

With the book in one hand, Flarge got into a crouching position and grasped a small, powdery rock. In seconds, he had made a circuit of me and Delilah and I realized that he was scrawling as though with chalk on the rough floor of the cave. But it was a five-pointed star that he drew, not a circle as I'd expected. Flicking through the brittle pages of the book, he muttered under his breath and then frantically scrabbled some words and symbols that it was impossible to make out in the queer light.

'If only there were more time,' cried Flarge, hoarsely. 'It's a bad job! *Hod, Malchut, Kether, Binah, Cerburah*! A bad job. But the best I can do. You see, your sister's intervention means the invocation hasn't been properly performed. Like the cad Reynolds said, there are rules – and that might give us hope.'

He froze and I too turned to see that all of us, Mons, Pandora, the acolytes, were completely surrounded by legions of the unspeakable creatures, rolling and slobbering over one another like maggots in a fisherman's basket. The stench was so overwhelming that I gagged.

But it was not this that arrested us. For over the altar, forming in the very air, was the strange, hazy smoke that I had seen out on the *Stiffkey* and again on the Norfolk marsh. Just as before, twin points of red light suddenly blazed into life but this time the apparition rapidly assumed a terrible solidity.

The thing was gigantic. The wreaths of smoke wound round and round each other like the bindings on a mummy until massive furry haunches, greasy and bestial, emerged from the murk. As though for dramatic effect, the flaming torches and candles relumed and an awed gasp rippled through the assembly.

The great muscular legs of the creature terminated in hooves, black and smeared with filth that was even now creeping upwards in concert with the pall of strange smoke. This too began to solidify and a great human torso rose up above the legs, the skin oily with sweat, yet the stomach was covered all over in lurid green scales like those on a fish.

Now, with great rapidity, the rest of the monstrous beast took shape. Mammoth female breasts, firm, ripe and *blue*, rose from the torso, the swollen nipples dripping with black milk. At last the head was revealed, resolving itself around those pitiless red eyes in the shape of a sheep's head, vast shining horns projecting from the furrowed brow, patches of bare bone showing through amongst the long, lank human hair that spewed from its scalp.

'Oh, God!' gasped Flarge. 'He's free! Banebdjed! The Witch Lord! He comes to conjoin with the Lamb in mockery of God!'

The creature – this devil, whatever it was – began to turn its head. It was such an uncanny sight that my guts turned absolutely to water. The furious eyes blazed within its withered, skull-like face, a face covered in matted hair, fur and feathers. Immense leathery wings projected from the shoulders.

I was stupefied with terror and almost didn't notice as Delilah suddenly seized my hand as the pentagram was completed. Flarge did the same, his own palms pouring with sweat – and put his mouth right by our ears. 'If you value your souls, don't look in its eyes. We're face to face with the very Devil himself. Keep hold of each other's hands and pray. Pray as you've never prayed. And believe! *Believe!*'

I needed no urging. What I had considered lunacy only scant days ago was there before my eyes: profound, abject, undiluted evil. I strained to recall every schoolboy prayer, every catechism, but my mind was like a stone, refusing to dredge up even the slenderest memory.

Mons alone seemed not to fear the apparition. Stretching to his full height he strode towards it, cape billowing behind him, his handsome face alight with energy and triumph. As he smiled, his lip curled up over his fanglike tooth.

'Lord of the Sky! Banebdjed! I, Olympus Mons, have summoned thee back from the darkest place. I shall shatter the bonds that have laid thee low these past millennia. And in return you will grant me power! Power over these feeble scum and millions like them! This world shall be mine! Everything refashioned into my image! Nothing will live, nothing will think without my granting it leave to do so. I have made all this possible, Banebdjed. I am *your* saviour!'

Still I struggled to remember anything even vaguely holy. *Jesus' hands were kind hands*, ran a ludicrous voice in my head. *Onward Christian soldiers!* insisted another. But then something did come to me. Not a half-remembered prayer from schooldays, nor any invocation to the forces of light. It was something from that wretched silk relic. The part that Reiss-Mueller could not fathom. 'And only he who makes himself alone in the world can defeat the Beast'.

The ram-headed creature had dropped its mighty head to gaze with horrible, patient desire at the prone body of Agnes Daye: the perfect victim whose sacrifice would release it from its earthly prison. Putrid saliva coursed from its wet mouth as it reached out one vast, human hand towards her. The unholy conjunction was only moments away. Then this force of destruction, this rampant evil would be once more unleashed upon the world.

And only he who makes himself alone in the world can defeat the Beast.

I stood up within the five-pointed star. Flarge grabbed at my ankle but I shook him off.

'What are you doing?' he hissed. 'Sit down! Sit down, you fool!'

'Mr Box!' gasped Delilah.

I stepped out of the pentagram and immediately felt that awful, draining misery that I had endured before, as though every depressive thought, every wasted moment had been condensed into a liquid transfusion that now crept into my very bones.

But I fought back, struggling towards the terrible monster, my every step weighted down as though my shoes were made of oak.

'Banebdjed!' I gasped. Then, louder – 'Banebdjed, hear me!'

Mons turned in surprise then let out a peal of laughter. 'Oh, you really are persistent, Mr Box! Well, then, Lucifer. Meet LUCIFER!'

I ignored him and turned my face towards the creature, averting my eyes from its own and focusing instead on the abomination that was its body. 'Banebdjed! I don't care what this . . . specimen here says. *I* have brought you back. *I* was the one who transported the last fragment of the Jerusalem Prayer to this unholy place. *I* am the one spoken of in the forbidden texts. I brought it here, all unknowing, as the prophecy states!'

'Box! Box, what are you doing?' screamed Flarge.

Pandora jerked towards me, the tendons on her neck standing out like cords. 'Get back! Get back, you pathetic little man! This is our moment! The glory is ours!'

I didn't even look at her. 'I am the one who found the Lamb of God! I am He That Is Spoken Of! Is this not so?'

Mons shrugged. 'I cannot deny it. This man has done all these things. But I am the one who seeks your freedom! I am the one!'

'Banebdjed!' I yelled. 'Do you acknowledge that I am He That Is Spoken Of? DO YOU?'

The ram-headed abhorrence seemed to consider for what felt like hours, rancid breath streaming from its nostrils and the black, black hole of its poisonous mouth. At last, the great head inclined downwards just a fraction.

Adrenaline surged through my body. I felt a kind of thrilling victory.

'Then!' I bellowed. 'Being thus, I claim the right to send you back whence you came!'

Mons laughed again. The creature made a low, grumbling roar that ran through me like an earth tremor.

Now Pandora was chuckling. 'You fool! You blind fool! You don't even know what you're saying. Only one who makes himself all alone in the world can do that!'

I looked at her. 'And I'm not alone, am I? I have *you*!'

My hand flew to my coat and I whipped out the knife that Flarge had used to slice through our bonds. Pandora's carmine smile fell. Then I dashed forward and with one smooth action cut a new and redder smile in her throat.

24

The Charm's Wound Up

Well, we'd never got on, had we?

Hell, having already broken loose, was content to bide its time at this singular intervention. Pandora slipped to the rocky floor, her neck fountaining blood and soaking her hair, a last look of complete surprise on her cruel, pallid face.

Mons staggered backwards, his bare feet clapping on the cold stone. 'What have you done? What have you *done?*'

Then a strange primal howl began to escape from his breast, immediately silenced by the shattering and ghastly cry of the foul sheep-headed monster that towered above us all. Its great red eyes rolled in its head, and stinking black smoke began to billow from its nostrils and vast mouth, filling the chamber as though a four-alarm fire had broken out. Then the Beast's hooves began to beat an enraged tattoo on the floor like a Spanish bull venting its spleen, and the whole chamber shook with the percussion.

Behind me, Flarge was frantically intoning prayers but I found myself filled with renewed confidence. The game was up. I'd played this Devil by his own rules and bested him.

The creature's dreadful maw fell open and a hideous belching moan erupted from deep within its cavernous chest, great ropes of saliva hanging like slug-trails from its cracked and blackened lips.

Mons pushed me aside and staggered towards the abomination, his hands plucking at its rancid fur. Already it seemed to be diminishing, as though it was being propelled backwards down a long, fathomless tunnel.

'*No!*' screeched Mons. 'Come back! You must come back!'

The creature's body was unravelling, great strips of flesh and bone turning once again into the strange wispy blue smoke. One by one the dreadful crawling horrors that surrounded the creature were absorbed into it as though sucked up by a hurricane.

'You!' raged Mons, pounding up to me and pummelling at my chest with his bare fists. 'You have done this! After all these years of planning and hoping and—'

Suddenly he caught sight of the Jerusalem Prayer, still on its frame, and his face lit up as he raced towards it.

'It's not too late! Of course it's not! I shall simply summon him back again!'

Grasping the edges of the frame he bowed his head and began rapidly to intone the forbidden text.

I was on my feet at once and haring towards him but Flarge was suddenly at my side, laying a restraining hand on my arm. 'Let him finish, old boy.'

'Are you insane?' I yelled. 'I've just slit my bloody sister's throat so that he couldn't unleash that blasted monster—'

Flarge shook his head. 'The Jerusalem Prayer has already been misused once. For the same person to try again is suicide. *One must play by the rules.*'

Joshua Reynolds seemed to know this too. He raced to his master's side and tried to drag him away from the lectern. 'You mustn't!' he screeched. 'You know what will happen!'

But Mons grabbed at the silver chalice and smashed it across Reynolds's face. He crashed to his gargantuan belly, then, staggering to his feet, tottered from the chamber.

I goggled at Mons as he raced feverishly through the ritual, glancing every now and then over his shoulder, willing Banebdjed to reverse his trajectory.

'He's crazy!' yelled Flarge. 'We've got to get out!'

Suddenly a lurid light began to infuse Mons's features. He grinned, obviously confident that, great all-powerful sorcerer that he was, he alone had managed to confound the rules and resurrect the Beast once more. But the light was coming from the Prayer itself. Its edges were on fire.

Mons gasped and looked down as the strange, almost liquid flame licked across the silk. In seconds it had caught the trailing sleeves of his black cloak and was running over his hands like quick-silver.

He screamed and looked wildly around him, looking for support from his loyal acolytes who, like loyal acolytes across the ages, were running to save their skins.

'Banebdjed!' he screamed. 'Save me!'

Staggering towards the satanic creature, his arms ablaze, Mons collapsed onto his knees. Banebdjed, its ghastly ram's head twisting and writhing in agony, was vanishing fast, darkness enveloping its rancid fur and scaly flesh. Flames burst into life under Mons's jaw and his lips drew back in one last snarl. There was a great whoosh of air and orange fire exploded within his skull, belching from his open mouth and sending his eyes shooting out of their sockets. Like twin comets they flared across the cavern, explod-ing against the rock wall. Then the rest of Mons collapsed into a ball of flame that span round and round before hurtling straight into the maw of the creature, its jaws snapping shut with terrible finality.

There was a final, almost pathetic sigh and then, as if I had emerged from a dip underwater, everything sprang sharply into focus. The temperature rocketed and that curious sensation of muffled sound vanished on the instant. Naked amber-shirts were fleeing in droves from the chamber, leaving only Flarge, Delilah and me standing as the place shuddered to its very foundations.

Clearly, Banebdjed intended to take down the place with him. I raced towards the altar and scooped up Agnes in my arms.

'Lucifer!' she cried, tears streaming down her beautiful face. 'You have saved me?'

'I promised, didn't I?' I breathed. Delilah was by me in an instant, draping her own heavy coat over the poor girl.

'Let me take 'er, sir,' cried my servant. 'You and Mr Flarge concentrate on getting hus outa 'ere!'

I nodded dumbly, passing Agnes into Delilah's massive embrace. The girl managed to stand, Delilah's coat completely encasing her.

Rocks were tumbling all about and the way out was simply stuffed with screaming, desperate Satanists who'd seen their dreams turn to ashes and now cared only for themselves. We'd never get past them and would in all probability be crushed to death if we tried.

Then my eyes alighted on a wonderful sight. It was a little metal sign bearing the legend *PTT* and, right by it, the arched entrance to some form of maintenance tunnel. Blessing the Post Office in all its forms, I hared forward and popped my head inside. The tunnel was narrow and cramped but looked wholly sound.

'This way!' I yelled. 'Come on!'

Delilah and Agnes moved first and I waved them through.

Flarge paused at the entrance and I urged him on with a thump on the shoulder blades.

'What if it just leads further into the mountain?' he yelled.

'We've no choice!' I cried. 'Get moving!'

He nodded dumbly, then held out his hand. 'Look here, Box, I've got to say this. I'm sorry for everything that happened. If I could undo—'

'Buy me lunch at the Berkeley sometime, eh? Now, go!'

I pushed him in the small of the back and then crumpled to my knees as the floor shook. Enormous chunks of the cavern were coming loose now, peeling from the walls and ceiling, and the black Satanic drapes that had decorated the place billowed and were torn asunder like the sails of a doomed pirate ship.

The fang-like stalactites cracked and fell, spearing amber-shirts with deadly accuracy. There was no time to linger and I staggered through the archway into the Post Office tunnel where all was hot, oppressive darkness.

Crook-backed by the low ceiling, I stumped forward only to run headlong into the rest of the party. I felt my guts revolve as the tunnel shuddered about us, Delilah's sweaty bosom stuffed into my face and Flarge's bony elbow jammed into my side as I tried to get my bearings.

'This way!' gasped Aggie through clouds of choking dust. I groped for my cigarette lighter and flicked it into life. Rock particles glittered in the sudden yellow glow but I could see that Aggie was on the right track. The tiny tunnel snaked round to the left and the flame of the lighter suddenly sputtered as it met a cold breeze.

I could feel Aggie's hot breath against my cheek as I inched forward on my knees, clearing away rubble and then rising once more to a semi-crouching position as I moved, crablike, towards the tantalizing night beyond.

I felt queasy with bending so low, my legs cramping appallingly and the rough tunnel mortar scraping against the nape of my neck, but all at once I was through and breathing stunningly fresh air.

I turned round at once and dragged first Agnes, then Delilah, then Flarge after me.

We lay dazed for a long moment, retching and coughing and shaking our heads. Above us, the star-packed night sky was immense and wonderful.

There was a distant percussion from inside the mountain and a billowing cloud of choking smoke puffed from the tunnel exit like a dragon's last breath.

'Cor!' croaked Delilah. 'What a night!'

I got to my feet and sighed heavily. Agnes Daye bounced nimbly to my side, her lithe form all but invisible within Delilah's enormous trench-coat.

I ran my hand over her hair and smiled warmly. 'We'd better get you warm, eh? You'll not last long in the buff.'

She chewed her lip and shuddered. 'Is it really over?' she cried, plaintively.

About to reply, I took in a great lungful of the blessed Swiss air, then looked up suddenly, hearing the sound of grinding gears and metal on metal. Flarge was by me in a flash and both of us craned our necks to see the cable cars from Mons's castle stirring into life.

'Capital!' I cried. 'We hopped off when it came close to the mountain. Perhaps we can jump back on board and get a lift down!'

The carriage was blazing with light and I kept my eye on it as the four of us raced through the snow. To my surprise, the light in the car was momentarily blocked by a bulky shape and I realized the thing was occupied.

Flarge whipped out the binoculars he'd taken from Reiss-Mueller's corpse. 'Probably just one of Mons's guards fleeing the castle – hello!'

'What is it?' I cried.

Flarge slowly lowered the glasses. 'It's Joshua Reynolds,' he grinned. 'Fatty Reynolds, trying to save his worthless skin.'

I felt a surge of new purpose rush through my veins. 'I see,' I said calmly. 'Percy, do you reckon you can see these ladies safely to the village?'

'Nothing to it, old sport. Got something to attend to?'

'You might say that. You might very well say that.'

Aggie cocked her lovely head to one side and frowned. 'Lucifer?'

I bent to kiss her on the forehead and then took to my heels, racing through the powdery snow and casting rapid glances at the descending cable car. Within minutes I'd reached the rocky point where the car would come close to the mountainside. Crouching low lest my treacherous chief spot me, I watched as the metal box slid downwards on its steel wire, hovering only a foot or so above my head.

Summoning my last reserves of energy, I hurled myself upwards and grabbed hold of the bottom of the car, swinging up my legs and nestling within the metalwork. The car rocked slightly but there was otherwise no sign that I had thus stowed away. My old injury suddenly flared back into life, however, and I hissed in pain at the renewed agony in my palm.

As the cable-car trundled away from the mountainside, dizzyingly empty air opened up below me. I took a deep breath and concentrated on the matter in hand, probing with my fingers at the housing above my head and soon locating the edges of the hatch. Electric light showed through in a thin yellow rectangle. Planting both feet firmly into the recesses of the undercarriage, I pressed my hands to the hatch, counted to five and pushed upwards with all my strength.

Taken aback by how easily it shifted, I suddenly found myself looking into the car at floor level. The light was blinding after the darkness outside and the hatch clattered backwards with a noise that would've woken the dead. Reynolds, still in his absurd black costume, span round from the window and gawped down at me.

Before he could move, I put out both hands and hauled myself into the cabin, leaving the hatch wide open. 'Evening!' I cried. 'Going so soon?'

Reynolds's paunchy face was utterly ashen. 'You!' he squealed. 'How did you—? What . . . what happened back there?'

I settled back against the glass and folded my arms nonchalantly. 'Oh yes. I forgot. You didn't stay for the Main House, did you? Scuttled up to the castle, eh, and decided to take the posh way down?'

Reynolds's great pale paw flashed into his robe and pulled out an automatic. 'You'll tell me, Box, if it's the last thing you do,' he snarled. 'Which, incidentally, it will be.'

I shrugged. 'I'm content. I've done my duty. The Devil has been trapped once again and the Jerusalem Prayer destroyed.' I turned to the window and watched our swift progress down the mountain.

Reynolds chins quivered alarmingly. 'And Mons?'

'Gone to Hell.'

Passing a shaking hand across his face, Reynolds heaved a great, shuddering sigh, then seemed to recover himself. He levelled the gun at me and there was black vengeance in his hooded eyes. 'No matter,' he whispered. 'Who knows of my role in all this save you and your amusingly motley band?'

'I wouldn't underestimate any one of us.'

'No? I'm disappointed with Percy, I must admit. He showed great promise. I'm afraid the tales of one obese Domestic and a callow girl with a shade too much of the tar-brush about her won't hold much water back in Blighty.'

'What about me?'

Reynolds's face turned sour. 'You? Didn't I tell you a long time ago that it was time for you to retire?'

He cocked the automatic. I held my breath. And in the blink of an eye, stepped forward and dropped through the open hatch.

My belly lurched horribly as I met empty air but I struck out at once, grabbing hold of the undercarriage of the cable-car and swinging myself back into my previous position. Reynolds's pistol appeared through the open hatch like a rat out of a drainpipe, his hand twisting uncomfortably round as he loosed off a random shot.

The bullet sparked off the metal right by me and I ducked as it whistled past my cheek. I caught sight of Reynolds's eye as he pressed one flabby cheek to the floor and then poked out his hand once again, determined to get a clear shot at me.

The fat man's exposed eye swivelled in my direction and the corner of it creased into a smile as he spotted me, skulking amongst the metalwork. 'I've got you, Box, you interfering bastard!' he screamed, blasting off another bullet.

I dodged out of the way but the shot was true, searing a neat hole through the flapping tail of my leather coat. I wasted no time, swaying from metal strut to metal strut so that I was on the other side of the hatch – behind Reynolds – and out of his firing line.

His plump hand scrabbled about the rim of the open hatch as he tried to reorientate himself but I moved like lightning, grasping his thick wrist and trying desperately to wrestle the gun from his grip. But he was a tenacious bugger, and try as I might I couldn't get him to relinquish it. Twisting round his wrist, I yelled as the pistol spoke again and a bullet smashed through the floor of the car above my head.

Without warning, the whole vehicle lurched and there was a curious, tortured whipping sound from somewhere above. I looked down and saw, to my intense relief, that the station was now only a hundred or so feet below us. If I could only hang on and avoid getting shot, I'd be able to drop off into the snowdrift. The strange lashing sound came again and the car suddenly dropped fully two feet. I fell forward from my place of safety and found myself hanging onto Reynolds' wrist for grim death. The fat man tried desperately to shake me off and he dropped the automatic. It fell like a stone and I grabbed at Reynold's arm, trying to haul myself up.

'Let go!' he gasped.

'No thanks!' I cried.

The car rocked again and I realized with horror that Reynolds's last shot, the one that had penetrated the car, must've struck the steel wheels that attached the car to the cable above! If they sheared away now, the gondola would be literally hanging by a thread! My own grip on my boss's sweaty arm was fast loosening and I scrabbled frantically at his sleeve, trying to get a purchase on the thick black fabric. Reynolds howled in pain and fought back with the tenacity of a tiger, wriggling his arm back through the hatch and evidently attempting to slip out of his costume to free his put-upon limb.

Then, with the cable station only twenty feet below us, the car gave a great lurch and Reynolds himself fell halfway through the hatch. I clutched at his collar to stop myself from falling and he cried out in frustration and terror. The mechanism above us was disintegrating fast and the air was alive with a metallic splintering sound.

I locked my arms around Reynold's great thick neck, and blow me if he didn't try to bite me! I glanced below again and suddenly knew I was safe. The car dropped one last time. Above us, the steel wheels fell apart and suddenly the car was falling free. With a delighted laugh, I kissed Reynolds on the forehead and let go, falling only ten feet or so and rolling expertly into the snowdrifts.

I looked up as the cable car plummeted towards earth, Reynolds jutting from the hatchway like a cork in a bottle. Shrieking, he tried to force out his massive body from its confinement but it was too late. Like a yo-yo snapped from its string, the cable car went smashing

'I fell forward and found myself hanging onto
Reynolds' wrist for grim death'

into its station, shearing the corpulent chief of the Royal Academy neatly in two.

As the car came to rest amidst the tangled machinery it burst into flame and I averted my face, taking solace in the freezing snow in which I lay half buried.

I walked slowly back towards Lit-de-Diable, the cable-car terminus blossoming into flame far behind me, but the roar of the explosion was almost blotted out by the sweet pattering of snowflakes. Down here, snow blanketed every wooden gable, every glowing gas lamp.

As I neared the inn, the door flew open and Delilah, Flarge and Agnes emerged.

'Good to see you, sah!' cried Delilah. 'Hi trust everything's been sorted out to your satisfaction?'

'Rather,' I cried as Aggie slammed into me and threw her arms about my neck. 'Have you got us all beds for the night, Percy?'

Flarge grinned hugely. 'Naturally. No flies on me, old thing. Could I buy you that dinner now, do you think?'

I thought of warm food and wine and a downy bed and sweet Agnes Daye and suddenly I was the happiest of men. I kissed the girl full on the mouth and then whistled at the rather fetching Swiss peasant costume of gingham dress and tight blouse that she seemed to have acquired.

'Glad you've changed, my dear. You'd've frightened the yodellers!'

She gave a glum look and plucked at the pretty frock. 'That was shaming. I must have looked indecent.'

'Nun's training kicking in again, eh?' I shrugged. 'Well, it was nothing I hadn't seen before.'

She batted me playfully on the arm. 'Brute. You are a beast and I cannot think why I like you.'

'Well,' I said, putting my arm around her shivering shoulders and leading her towards the warmth of the inn, 'better the devil you know, eh?'